coming
attractions

Also by Robin Jones Gunn

Katie Weldon Series

Peculiar Treasures

On a Whim

Coming Attractions

Finally and Forever

Christy Miller Series

Sierra Jensen Series

Christy and Todd: The College Years

www.robinjonesgunn.com

katie weldon series

coming attractions

BOOK THREE

ROBIN JONES GUNN

ZONDERVAN.com/
AUTHORTRACKER
follow your favorite authors

ZONDERVAN

Coming Attractions
Copyright © 2009 by Robin's Nest Productions, Inc.

This title is also available as a Zondervan ebook.
Visit www.zondervan.com/ebooks.

This title is also available in a Zondervan audio edition.
Visit www.zondervan.fm.

Requests for information should be addressed to:

Zondervan, *Grand Rapids, Michigan 49530*

Library of Congress Cataloging-in-Publication Data

Gunn, Robin Jones, 1955-.
    Coming attractions / Robin Jones Gunn.
       p. cm. — Katie Weldon series; bk. 3)
      ISBN 978-0-310-27658-6 (pbk.)
    1. College students — Fiction. 2. Self-actualization (Psychology) — Fiction. I. Title.
    PS3557.U4866C66 2009
    813'.54 — dc22
                                         2009010832

Published in association with the Books & Such Literary Agency, 52 Mission Circle, Suite 122, PMB 170, Santa Rosa, California 95407-5370. www.booksandsuch.biz

Printed in the United States of America

---

12 13 14 15 16 17 /DCI/ 25 24 23 22 21 20 19 18 17 16 15 14 13 12 11 10 9 8 7 6

For my wonderful daughter-in-law, Kelly Joy. You bring a touch of calm wherever you go. I am so grateful for the way God brought you to our son and knit your hearts together. You are a gift to all of us.

K atie checked the time on her phone and pulled her sweatshirt's hood over her dancing red hair. Upper campus at Rancho Corona University could be surprisingly cold this time of year. Especially when the winds came up.

"Come on, Rick. Where are you? So much for your romantic idea of meeting up here at nine. It's 9:15, and I'm freezing."

Tapping out a third text message to her tall, dark, and tardy boyfriend, Katie hit Send and looked around. Another couple had made themselves cuddly and comfortable on the bench where Rick had told her to meet him. She stood to the side, under the row of shivering palm trees. Even their decorative strings of white twinkle lights seemed to tremble with the chill.

Katie coughed. Her throat was hurting more than it had at dinner in the cafeteria, when she had loaded her tray with soup, applesauce, and two glasses of orange juice.

I can't do this. Rick, you'll just have to come to my dorm if you want to see me tonight. It's too cold out here.

Starting back down the path to lower campus, Katie texted Rick again as she walked. It wasn't like Rick to leave her waiting, and even more unlike him not to respond to her messages. He was organized and efficient and . . .

Her cell phone rang.

"Hey, don't be mad." Rick's voice came across loudly. She could tell he was on speakerphone, which meant he was in his new car. "I left my phone at the café and had to go back for it. I'm on the road now. Sorry I'm late, Katie. I can be there in a half hour."

Katie ignored the apology. She had heard a few too many of those lately. Three months ago Rick and his brother were presented with an opportunity to open not one but two new cafés. Ever since then, Rick had been "on the road."

"Let's just reschedule, Rick. I'm—"

"No, we can't reschedule. It's Valentine's Day!"

"Oh, really?" She would have expanded her sarcastic remark, but her head was pounding. How could a tickle in her throat escalate so quickly to feeling as if she were swallowing razor blades?

His voice softened. "I have something for you."

"I already received the flowers. They're beautiful. Thanks, Rick. You really don't have to give me anything else." Katie was feeling a familiar awkwardness over the gift-giving imbalance that had existed in their relationship since they officially started dating last summer. Rick enjoyed giving. So did Katie. The problem was that she could rarely come up with gift-type expressions of affection the way Rick could. She felt forever behind in the gift-giving department.

"I want to give the present to you tonight. Come on, Katie. Don't be mad at me. I'm really trying here."

"I'm not mad. Honest. I don't feel well. It was too cold and windy on upper campus, so I'm heading back to my room. Besides, another couple was on our bench."

"That's not a problem. Are you back at the dorm yet? I'll meet you there. We can go get something to eat."

Even though Katie knew better than to argue with Rick when he had his mind set on something, she switched her phone to the other ear and said, "I'm really not hungry. I think I have the flu."

"Listen, I can be there in fifteen minutes. Twenty at the most. Take some cold pills and drink some orange juice. I'll come up to

Crown Hall and give you a call when I drive into the parking lot. We'll decide what to do then."

Katie hung up, already knowing what she would want to do when he called later. It was the same thing she wanted to do right now: curl up in a ball under a warm blanket and sleep off this creeping crud.

Over half the girls on her floor had been hit with this year's variety of the flu. Just days ago Katie had bragged about how her prevention tactic had succeeded this year. She had spent the past three weeks drinking loads of herbal tea and downing lots of vitamin C. Her immune system was fortified against the attack.

Or so she thought.

The way she felt now was quickly surpassing anything a cup of tea could fix. It bugged her that Rick couldn't just let her be sick in peace.

As she entered Crown Hall, she avoided looking at any of the Valentine's Day couples seated in the lobby and made her way to Nicole's room. Her friend Nicole was the other resident assistant who shared with Katie the responsibility of overseeing the welfare of the fifty-four students on their floor. Katie knew she was going to need someone to cover on-duty hours for her as this virus ran its course.

Knocking on Nicole's half-closed door, Katie pushed it open and announced, "Guess what? I got it."

"You did? Oh, Katie, let me see!" Nicole jumped up and dashed toward her.

"What are you doing?" Katie pulled away. "I'm telling you I have the flu. I don't think you want to get close to me."

"Oh!" Caught off guard, Nicole froze in place. She nervously flipped her dark, silky hair behind her ears as her smooth complexion took on a rosy hue.

"What's wrong?"

"Nothing." Nicole returned to her bed on the other side of the room. "I just ... Hey, I'm sorry to hear you're not feeling well."

"Not half as sorry as I am. How long did you have this bug?"

"Almost two weeks."

"I can't be sick that long."

"Hopefully it won't be that long for you."

"Yeah, hopefully. Can you cover the front desk for me tomorrow at 2:30?"

"Sure." Nicole was sitting perfectly still, trying to blink away the deer-in-the-headlights look that had overtaken her earlier.

"You sure you're okay?"

"Me? Yes, I'm good. I hope you feel better."

Katie gave a weak nod and exited. Her room at the end of the hall felt miles away.

Even though it was open-dorm night, the steady lineup of closed doors seemed to indicate that the majority of the women in Crown Hall were out that evening. Either that or they were holed up watching romantic movies with their roommates and telling each other that next year Valentine's Day would be different for them both. They would have somewhere to go and someone wonderful to go there with.

Or many of them could still be fending off this flu bug.

Katie paused at The Kissing Wall across from her door. The wall had been decorated at the start of the school year with a sweet variety of photos of innocent kisses. Along with the photos were verses and poems celebrating that ageless expression that brings fanciful hope to the heart of every young woman — a kiss.

Katie unlocked her door and thought of how, for so many years, she had hoped and dreamed of having a relationship with a guy who would bring her flowers and give her kisses on Valentine's Day. Now she had exactly what she wished for. But it wasn't exactly what she thought it would be.

Things with Rick were fine. Better than fine. Things were good. They had been good for months. At Christmastime Rick and Katie agreed to let their relationship bob along through this final semester of Katie's senior year. Once she graduated, they both would be in a better place to figure out the all-important question of "what's next?" For now, they agreed they were content with their status of "happily almost after."

Katie flopped onto her unmade bed and let out a self-sympathiz-ing moan. A pestering thought floated in her foggy brain. *What was Nicole so skittish about?*

Pulling her cell phone from her sweatshirt's pocket, she stayed flat on her back and called Nicole. "So what do you know that I don't know?"

"What do I know about what?" Nicole's voice went up high at the end of her response.

Katie noted the inflection. "Why did you jump up when I came into your room?"

The other end of the phone went silent.

"Nicole, come on. You said, 'Let me see.' See what? What was I supposed to have?"

"Katie, I thought you and Rick had gone out to dinner tonight and—"

"No, I didn't see him at all today."

"You didn't?"

"No."

"But it's Valentine's Day."

"Oh, really? I hadn't noticed." Katie coughed.

"You sound awful."

"Don't change the subject, Nicole. You know something. I know you do."

Over the past two months Nicole had spent time with Rick's mom, working on designing the cafés' interiors. As a result, Nicole often knew more about what was going on with Rick than Katie did.

"Nicole, just tell me. Come on."

"Oh, Katie, I feel terrible!"

"You feel terrible? I'm the one who's sick here."

"I can't say anything. I really can't. I'm sorry."

A pause lingered between them before Katie's eyes widened and she lifted her head. "Tell me it's not a ring. Seriously, Nicole. Tell me Rick did not go out and buy me a ring." The cough started up again.

"Katie, I ..."

"An engagement ring?" Katie weakly propped herself up on one arm. "Did he go and buy me an engagement ring? You have to tell me, Nicole. Did he?"

Silence.

Katie flopped back on the bed. "He bought me a ring, didn't he? I can't believe it. Why would he do that?"

"Katie, it's not ... you just ... oh, this is frustrating!"

"Tell me about it."

"Just wait until you see Rick. Everything will make sense then."

"Yeah, I could do that. Or you could tell me everything you know right now and spare me the suspense. You know how I hate surprises. Just tell me, Nicole. We can keep it as our little secret."

Even before Nicole answered, Katie knew her friend would never agree to such an alliance. Nicole was too pure of heart and too well trained in the ways of integrity. It bugged Katie, though, to realize that Nicole did have an alliance going in all this. Nicole shared a secret with Rick and his mom, which was something Katie couldn't say she had ever experienced.

"Truly, Katie, you'll be glad I didn't say anything. Just wait. Everything will make sense when you see Rick."

If Katie hadn't been feeling so awful, she would have pressed the conversation until she could squeeze at least a few clues out of Nicole. Instead, she gave up and hung up. Staring at the ceiling, she coughed again.

Rick Doyle, you were not *planning to propose to me on Valentine's Day. I mean, seriously, Rick. Valentine's Day? What happened to us waiting until I graduate before we decide what's next? And what if I don't like the ring you picked out? Did you ever think of that? You probably bought some huge diamond, and I don't want—*

Her cell phone rang. She thought the ring tone was the one she assigned to Nicole, so she answered with, "Changed your mind, did you? Talk quick and make it good because I'm dying here."

"Did you get it?" a male voice asked.

She held out the phone and saw by the ID that it was Rick's roommate, Eli. Katie had forgotten she changed his ring tone as well. She'd have to change it again. It was too close to Nicole's.

"Did you get it?" Eli repeated.

"Get what?" she replied flippantly. "The ring? Are you in on this too? Nicole wouldn't give me any details, so go ahead. Spill your guts. I promise I'll act surprised."

"I have no idea what you're talking about. I'm calling to see if you got the email from my dad with the Kenya update."

One of the things Katie appreciated about Eli was that little fazed him. His brushing right over her ring comments was typical of his steadfast temperament. If he did know details, he certainly wouldn't squeak a peep to Katie or anyone else if Rick had told him not to.

Over the past few months, Katie and Eli had been working on a fund-raiser for clean water in Africa. Eli's dad headed up the headquarters in Nairobi and kept Katie in the loop on how the funds were being distributed. During the correspondence among the three of them, Katie had come to appreciate Eli's straightforward approach. He was a lot like Rick in that respect. Except with Eli Katie didn't sense the same sort of aggressiveness that was stitched into the fiber of Rick's temperament.

"I haven't checked my email since this morning. I'm sick, Eli. I have the flu."

"What have you taken for it?"

"Nothing. Well, tea and extra vitamin C for a month, but I guess that wasn't enough."

"Is your throat sore?"

"Yeah."

"Fever?"

"Yes, Dr. Eli. I have all the usual symptoms. I need to get some sleep. Do I have to answer the email tonight, or can it wait until tomorrow?"

"You don't need to respond. It was good news. My dad was able to make the final arrangements for the wells in Sudan. We're not going to need to raise the extra funds. The drilling can begin next week."

"That is good news."

"I'll let you get some sleep."

"Yeah, sleep is good. My head feels like a bowling ball."

"Take care of yourself, Katie."

"I will." She closed her phone and closed her eyes.

Good ol' Eli. Nine months ago, when she first saw him at her best friend's wedding reception, Katie thought he was unusual and dubbed him "Goatee Guy." His intense stare unnerved her. Then Eli moved into Rick's apartment, and now she considered him one of her closest friends. She was going to miss him when he moved back to Kenya after graduation.

Eli grew up in Africa, where his parents were missionaries. In some ways Katie guessed he had never quite moved all of his heart to California when he came to Rancho Corona to finish up college. Part of him seemed always to be somewhere else. Off on safari, perhaps.

Katie pressed her open hand to her throat and tried to feel if it was swollen. She rolled onto her side in an effort to find a more comfortable position. Changing into pajamas would help with the comfort part, but she didn't want to get up.

I hate being sick.

Her phone rang again. This time it was Rick. In a soothing voice, he tried to coax her out to the parking lot to meet him so they could get something to eat. "I'll be on campus in five minutes, Katie. We'll go someplace that serves soup. Chicken soup. How would that be?"

"Rick, seriously, I ... am ... sick. Really."

"Then I'll come in to see you. It's open dorm tonight, right?"

"Rick, you'll be exposing yourself to someone who is a walking flu hive, buzzing with live, viral flu bees."

He laughed. "You can't be too sick if you're still funny."

"I'm not funny, Rick. I'm coughing, and I'm sneezing and ... well, I'm not sneezing yet, but I feel like sneezing."

"Katie, honey ..."

"Honey?"

Rick had never called her "honey" before. At least not that she could remember. Was that his attempt to play off her comment on the flu hive?

He ignored her challenge on the term of endearment and pressed forward. "Listen, I don't care if you're sick. I want to see you anyway. I have something I want to give you, and I'm determined to give it to you tonight."

"Well, I have something I could give you, and I'm determined *not* to give it to you tonight. It's called two weeks out of commission, Rick. This is the worst possible time for you to —"

She almost said "to propose," but he interrupted. His voice was loud and firm. "Katie, I'm coming to see you. I'll be there in four minutes. Five at the most. Why don't you gargle or take some cough syrup or something? I'm coming to your room, so open a window and let all the bee germs out. Or whatever you called them. Viral bees. Whatever. I'm almost there now."

He hung up. Katie stared at her cell phone.

Open a window? Gargle? Did he really just say those things to me?

She couldn't move. Her fifty-pound head felt as if it had sunk permanently into her Little Mermaid pillowcase.

Rick, what are you doing? If you walk in here and ask me to marry you, you'll ruin everything.

Katie had maneuvered through a variety of life challenges, but this dilemma had her baffled. If Rick stepped into her dorm room, got down on one knee, and held out a jeweler's box, what would she say? What would her truest, from-her-heart answer to him be?

She didn't know.

Since junior high Katie had dreamed of being with Rick. When he actually asked her out nearly a year and a half ago, Katie dared to believe her dream had come true. All she had ever wanted was to be Rick Doyle's girlfriend. Now that that dream had been fulfilled, marrying Rick was the next dream.

Only at this moment, with her head pounding, Katie didn't feel ready for that dream. They were supposed to wait until she finished college. That's what they had agreed. All she had left were twelve weeks of classes. Twelve jam-packed weeks, then her mind would be free to think about what was next and when and how and where she and Rick could get married.

She wasn't ready to think about any of that now. Last year she watched her roommate and best friend, Christy, navigate her final semester after she became engaged, and Katie knew she didn't want to put that sort of pressure on herself. Not with her demanding position as a resident assistant. Not with her class load this final semester. And especially not with this horrible, reality-bending flu pressing her down with unrelenting force.

A knock sounded at her door.

"Go away! This is the yellow fever ward. You enter, you die."

Rick, or whoever it was, disregarded her warning, opened the door slowly, and made quiet rustling noises.

Katie opened her eyes and turned her head toward the door. "Eli?"

He held up a paper bag. "I bought you some stuff for your cold. I'll leave it here on your dresser."

"No, bring it here." She held out her hand weakly, like a fallen elfin princess.

Eli didn't hesitate. He walked across the room and pulled the bottle of medicine from the bag. "Have you taken this before? You just open your mouth, point it at your throat, and spray three or four times."

Katie took the bottle from him and dutifully followed his instructions. "Mmm. Wild cherry." She gave herself another squirt. "Thanks, Eli."

He pulled a box of cold tablets from the bag. "With these, I think you're supposed to take just one." He scanned the back of the box while opening the end. "Yeah, one every four hours. And don't operate heavy machinery."

"I'll keep that in mind." Katie took the pill from Eli and swallowed it, using two more squirts of the spray syrup instead of water.

"Here." Eli pulled the final item from the bag. A uniquely shaped bottle of drinking water.

"Hey, my favorite! How did you know I like New Zealand glacier water?"

"That's all I've ever seen you buy at the gas station where Joseph works. I bought two bottles. Where do you want me to put the other one?"

"On my desk next to the flowers. You might have to move them. They're a bit much, don't you think? I keep telling Rick he overdoes it with the flowers. A single poppy. That's what I tell him. Just a single poppy is all I need. Maybe you can talk some sense into him."

Eli didn't comment. He turned toward Katie, and she smiled at him.

His wild, naturally curly brown hair had been growing out for the past few months and made him look more like the adventuresome guy Katie had discovered he was. Earlier in the year he had kept his hair short, his conversations with her shorter, and in general, seemed short. Short and strange in an out-of-place sort of way.

As Katie got to know Eli, she realized the only thing short about him was his name. Even that was longer than he let the general public in on. Elisha James Lorenzo grew up on the mission field in Africa and kept a library of untold stories hidden inconspicuously under his unassuming demeanor. Stories about prowling lions, hand-carved Masai spears, and dances around tribal fires. He wore a drab gray uniform most of the time, as he was now. His campus security job meant he spent his working hours driving a beat-up golf cart around the mesa on which Rancho Corona was built. Eli took the off hours no one else wanted.

If Katie had one regret about the past few months, it was that her consistent efforts to get Eli and Nicole interested in each other had failed. Katie couldn't understand why. She thought Nicole was wonderful and amazing. She thought Eli was fantastic. Why didn't the two of them see in each other what she saw in them?

"I'm going to go." Eli stepped over to Katie's bed, closed his eyes, and lifted both his arms to the ceiling.

"What are you doing? Reenacting a scene from *The Lion King*?"

"Hush. I'm praying for you."

"Praying for me? Okay, sure, as long as this isn't like in the movies where they give the dying patient last rites."

He didn't respond. Instead, with his palms open to the heavens, reaching up like a child, he spoke in a calm, steady voice, asking God to heal Katie, to comfort her, and to give her body the strength she needed.

Katie was so caught off guard by Eli's actions that she didn't close her eyes. Instead, she watched his face, feeling her rattled spirit calming as he prayed. It seemed as if he felt every word before he spoke it. He wasn't just repeating a bunch of phrases. He was really talking to his heavenly Father, and what he was saying sounded just the way it would if one friend were asking a highly honored friend for a special favor.

Katie's throat tightened. Not because of the swelling from the virus. This tightening came from swallowing tears before they made it all the way to her eyes. She couldn't remember the last time she had prayed with that kind of closeness to God. She knew what it was like to feel an intimate sort of connection with Christ, but not until this moment had she realized how far from that closeness she had drifted over the past weeks and months. Here she was, a senior at a Christian college; yet if she had to rate her relationship with the Lord right now on a scale of one to ten, she would have to give it a two. Maybe a two and a half.

On the heels of Eli's "amen," Katie added her "thank you" in a calm voice.

Eli gave a humble sort of nod and started to leave, but Katie reached out her hand. Not princess-style but as a friend reaching to clasp the hand of another friend. Eli paused and then awkwardly took her hand and gave it a conciliatory squeeze. She had never realized what rough, carpenter sort of hands he had.

"Hey," Katie said, still holding onto his hand, "you have no idea how much I needed that. And I don't mean just the wild cherry juice. When you prayed, I — "

Before Katie could finish her sentence, her half-closed door burst all the way open, and in strode Rick with another bountiful bouquet of red roses, announcing, "Your valentine is here at last."

Eli quickly let go of Katie's hand.

"Eli? What are you doing here?"

"I brought Katie some stuff for her cold. I have to get back on duty. I'll see you guys later." Eli exited swiftly.

Rick leaned back and looked down the hall, watching Eli walk away. Turning back to Katie, Rick said, "What was all that about?"

"Like he said, he brought me some stuff, and I was thanking him."

"Thanking him for the cold pills?"

"Yeah, and also thanking him for praying for me. As he was praying, I realized how I've been — "

"That's why he was holding your hand? He was praying for you?"

Katie swallowed, and her throat felt raw again. She reached for the spray bottle and gave her mouth another squirt while taking the easy way out and answering Rick with only a nod.

Rick was already onto other things, striding over to her desk. "You have another vase, don't you? These need some water."

"There's one on the top shelf of my closet, but can't you just add the roses to the other bouquet?"

Rick reached up to the top shelf with ease and stuck the roses in the vase. Carrying them to the desk, he picked up the bottle of water Eli had left there and unscrewed the cap.

"No!" Katie squawked, and her voice cracked.

"What's wrong?"

"Not that water. That's my New Zealand water."

Rick looked at her as if she were speaking another language.

Katie's hand went to her throat. It hurt to talk. "Rick, do not use that water. I mean it."

"Fine. I'll be right back."

He removed the roses and strode out of the room with the empty vase in hand.

Katie closed her eyes, and put her hand over her forehead. Her eardrums pounded. She thought about how she liked Eli's "valentine" to her a whole lot more than she liked Rick's bold gesture of another bouquet, not that anyone was asking her to compare.

She was grateful her boyfriend cared enough to come bearing more flowers. She knew, thanks to a conversation she had with Christy, that was how Rick expressed his affection. Katie had learned to "take it and be thankful" instead of trying to change Rick and his ways of expressing himself. This was how Rick did things. If she loved Rick, and she did, then she needed to love the things he did for her as well as the way he did them.

Katie felt a single, uninvited tear tiptoe over the edge of her right eye and slide down her cheek. She couldn't bear feeling the way she did right now. She wanted Eli to come back and pray for her. Only this time she wanted him to pray longer and more intently so she could close her eyes and somehow get her heart back into that same sort of close-to-God rhythm she had heard in Eli's voice.

Rick returned just then with the vase filled with water. He pushed the roses into the vase. "Nicole said to let her know if you needed anything."

"Okay. Thanks. And thanks for the flowers."

"You're welcome." Rick pulled out the chair from the desk and sat down across from her.

Katie offered him a weak smile. She could only imagine how rumpled she looked. Rick looked good. He always looked good. His chocolate brown eyes were set on her.

"How are you feeling?"

"Like I have the flu. I really don't want to give it to you, Rick."

"I know. But, Katie, I really want to give something to you."

Without further warning, Rick pulled a small jewelry box from the pocket of his leather jacket.

Katie propped herself up on her elbow, feeling woozy but ready to protest.

"Actually," Rick said, withdrawing the box, "I should explain something first."

"Yeah, like explain why we aren't waiting until I graduate before we do this? And why couldn't you just let me be sick and get it over with? I mean, who cares if it's stupid Valentine's Day? This is a really, really bad way to propose."

Rick leaned back in the chair, looking stunned. "Propose? You thought I was about to propose?"

Katie didn't move. She didn't blink. Had she read all the clues wrong?

In a small voice she said, "Yes."

Rising from the chair, Rick marched to the door. For a moment, Katie thought he was going to walk out, just like that, without any explanation of what was going on. He turned and came back to her bedside, his face red.

"Why do you do that, Katie? Why? I've never understood that about you. You blurt things out at the worst possible moments. You know you do that, right? Everything is going along great, and then you just blurt out something uncalled for and the whole thing is ..." Rick kicked at the leg of the chair—not hard enough to topple it, but enough to make the chair wobble and to make Katie wobble emotionally.

"I'm sorry. I just ... I don't know. I thought ..."

"You thought I was going to propose. Why did you think that?"

Katie coughed again. She looked away and covered her mouth.

"You know what? Let's drop it. You're not feeling well. It's late." Rick rubbed the back of his neck and said in a lower voice, "You were right. We should have rescheduled."

Katie swallowed again and felt as if she were downing nails. She didn't say anything.

"I'm going to go. We can get together another time."

"No, stay." Katie pulled together all the strength she had left and tried to smile. "You rushed to get here. Stay and talk to me for a little while. Let's start over. Tell me about the café. How's everything coming?"

Rick shuffled his feet and tossed out a few lines about how the electrician had to rewire the kitchen area at the café in Redlands. As he warmed to the topic, he returned to the chair, and Katie tried to get comfortable. She felt chilled and pulled her covers up to her chin as Rick talked.

Rick reached over and smoothed out the corner of the crumpled comforter. In an awkward way he seemed to be tucking her in.

"I'm really sorry you're so sick, Katie. I don't think I've ever seen you this sick. I thought you might spring back after you got to your room. It is cold out tonight. I apologize again for making you wait on upper campus."

"It's okay."

"Do you want me to get you anything? I can make you some tea."

Even though tea sounded good to her at the moment, she said, "No, that's okay."

"You sure? I feel like I should do something."

"Okay. I'll have some tea, then. My hot pot is on the floor over there by those books. I have some tea in the box next to it. I have no idea where any of my mugs are."

As Katie watched, Rick navigated his way around her piles of messes and projects and mounds of dirty clothes to plug in the hot pot and prepare a cup of tea for her. Somehow, the visual was poignant to her. This was her life. This was how fragmented and disorganized and embarrassingly scattered her life was at the moment.

And there was Rick. Determined Rick, navigating his way around, finding how to accomplish his goals without being thrown off track, in spite of all the obstacles.

She had to give the man an A for effort. Nothing had been easy or convenient in their relationship over the past few months. Yet somehow, mostly thanks to Rick, they had managed to carve out time for each other and move forward as a couple. Katie had convinced herself this was good preparation for the two of them, if they did end up marrying. This was how they would live. Rick ever the man on a straightforward mission; Katie ever a woman on a less straightforward mission but on a mission nonetheless. Rick was a straight line. She was a wavy line. If they could keep being themselves and keep finding ways to weave their lives and schedules together, Katie had great hope for them as a couple.

By the time Rick located a cleanish mug and managed to steep the tea, Katie was finding it nearly impossible to keep her eyes open. The cold tablet was taking effect.

"Here you go. Sit up, Katie, so you can drink this."

She took a sip and burned her tongue. "It needs to cool."

Rick took the mug from her and set it on the edge of her desk. "You're almost asleep, aren't you?"

"Yes."

"Okay. Well, I should go then. I'll call you tomorrow." He leaned over and barely touched the side of her temple with a peck of a kiss. "Happy Valentine's Day."

"Happy Valentine's Day to you too." Katie watched as he crossed the room and opened the door. Her eyelids felt ridiculously heavy.

"Rick?"

He paused.

"Thanks for coming, and I'm sorry I blurted out what I did earlier."

"Don't worry about it."

Katie could hear him drawing in a deep breath.

"We can talk about all this later," he added.

Katie didn't have the energy to say another word. She felt as if she couldn't remember what had really happened that evening and what she had imagined in her cotton-stuffed head.

_3_

"How long did you have it?" Christy, Katie's best friend, was seated across from her at the Dove's Nest Café. The table they shared was a familiar one. It was here, in this first café that Rick and his brother opened almost a year and a half ago, that Christy's husband, Todd, proposed to her. It was also here, while Christy, Todd, and the gang were seated at this same table, that Rick emerged from the back kitchen and surprised them all since none of them knew he was working there as the manager. From that night on, Rick and Katie had been together.

When Rick offered Katie a job at the Dove's Nest, she took it and worked as many hours as she could, not only perfecting her skills at making turkey, bacon, and avocado wraps, but also perfecting her relationship with Rick. Christy worked in the adjacent bookstore, the Ark. This was one of those rare afternoons when Katie managed to find enough time to meet up with Christy on her lunch break.

"I had the flu the standard two weeks, like everyone else," Katie said. "Although I only stayed in bed four or five days. I'm sure I was still contagious when I went back to class, but, seriously, I can't miss anything during these next ten weeks. I'm on a crazy crash course, headed for commencement, and no flu bug is going to stop me. Besides, I'm certain everyone on campus had the flu long before I did. As always, I was a late bloomer. Isn't that what your aunt called me one time?"

Christy shrugged. "I don't know what she called you. I make it a practice to let go of all Aunt Marti's little jabs as soon as I can. Who cares what she said about you, anyway? I want to hear what Rick said. What happened after he left your room that night?"

"Nothing. I've only seen him once since Valentine's Day. We call and text every day, but he hasn't brought it up, and neither have I."

"So, if he said he wasn't planning to propose, what was he going to give you? And why could he only give it to you on Valentine's Day?"

"I have no idea." Katie leaned closer and lowered her voice just in case any of the nearby diners could hear their conversation. Too many people in this café and bookstore space knew Rick and his family. She wanted to keep this private.

"I've thought about it a lot since that night—that fevered, awkward night—and I'm ready to say yes to him, whatever sort of proposal scenario he comes up with."

Christy raised her eyebrows. "Really?" Her distinct blue green eyes expressed the questions Katie knew Christy wanted to ask.

"Yes. I love him. I know I do. I think we could deal with all the challenges that seem to come with our relationship. We've been working things out for a year and a half now. I think we can get ourselves in sync much easier after I graduate and after he opens the cafés."

Christy didn't agree or disagree. She gazed at Katie and quietly nibbled her Tuscan salad. Then she held her fork midway between her plate and her closed lips, a skewered mandarin orange awaiting her full attention.

"What? You don't think we're ready?"

Christy swallowed the bite in her mouth before putting down her fork. "I don't know."

"You don't know what?"

"I don't know how to respond to questions about you and Rick. I haven't seen him in months, even though we live in the same apartment complex. I haven't seen the two of you together since the Christmas party, and that was a crazy night. I'm not the one to offer validation of your relationship."

"I'm not looking for validation." Katie frowned, irritated that her best friend wasn't jumping in and expressing excitement. When Christy was only an inch away from engagement, Katie felt certain she had been a bundle of support and enthusiasm. At least she thought so. It now seemed so long ago. Had it only been a year?

Christy leaned forward and lowered her voice, looking Katie in the eye. "All I'm saying is that marriage is hard. Harder than I thought it would be. Especially when both of you are working all the time and can't see each other long enough to finish a conversation. If there's any way you guys could be a little more established financially, that would help too. That's all I'm saying. If you can wait a little while, then wait."

"We're doing okay financially."

Christy's expression made her disagreement clear. "Katie, you don't even have a car."

"I know, but I'm going to buy one. I've been waiting."

"Waiting for what? Money for the down payment? I don't mean to be so negative, but that's the same thing Todd and I said over a year ago, and here we are, still sharing one car. It's so expensive, especially with the insurance."

"I have the money."

Christy looked at Katie as if she didn't believe her.

"I have the money," Katie repeated. "I've been meaning to tell you. There just never was a good time, and, to be honest, I'm not sure this is the right time. But here it is. My great-aunt passed away and left me some money. I have it set aside in a savings account."

With a tilt of her head, Christy's nutmeg brown hair fell to the side. "Your great-aunt passed away? I don't remember hearing you say anything about her. When did she pass away?"

"Last year some time. Spring, I think. I don't remember. The whole thing is strange, but then, welcome to my life. She wanted her money to go to anyone in her extended family who was attending college, and believe it or not, I'm the only one the lawyer could track down."

"Katie, that's incredible! I'm sorry to hear about your great-aunt, though."

"I know. I never met her, so that's what makes this even more odd."

"I can't believe you didn't tell me any of this."

"I meant to. I got the money last fall and intended to put some of it toward a car right away, but my schedule was busy, and ever since Baby Hummer coughed her last gasket, I've developed the habit of asking people for rides. It turned out to be a good way for me to have time set aside with them. I put the money away and kept borrowing cars or getting rides."

Christy leaned back. "You never stop surprising me. I have this feeling you and I will be ninety years old, sitting in rocking chairs, not a single tooth left in our mouths, and you'll pop out with some significant little fact I've never known about you."

Katie took another bite of her Canadian bacon and pineapple pizza, wondering how much she should tell Christy about the inheritance. The details were more surprising than she was letting on. Katie's resident director, Julia, was the only one who knew that Katie secretly used part of the money to start the fund-raiser for clean water for Africa.

Katie also had used some of the money to bless one of the international students at the university. His name was Joseph, and he was a friend of Eli's. Joseph's wife and daughter were living in their village in Ghana, West Africa, while Joseph completed his studies in California. Katie changed all that by arranging for them to join Joseph at Rancho Corona and live with him in the married-student apartments.

Christy leaned forward. "What about your tuition? I mean, I agree that transportation is essential, and since you've been given this money, a car would be a great thing to spend the inheritance on. But did you consider putting some of it toward your school bill so you don't end up with a lot of debt when you graduate?"

Katie chose her words carefully. She had already paid off her tuition and was going to graduate debt free. She also anonymously paid off Eli's tuition. She knew she wanted to help out another student, and Eli seemed like a good candidate since he was working his way through college just like Katie. Student services took care of the details, and Eli never mentioned receiving the funds, nor did Katie hint at it. Giving in secret filled up a part of Katie she hadn't even known was empty.

To clarify her financial situation with Christy all she said was, "I have my school bill figured out. Buying a car is at the top of my list."

"Mine too," Christy said wistfully.

Katie put her straw up to her lips in an effort to keep her mouth busy so she wouldn't blurt out anything.

Katie's original plan was to take Christy with her car shopping and, as a huge surprise, buy two cars. One for her and one for Christy. She hadn't priced any used cars yet, but she felt confident she could stretch what she had budgeted for a car to buy two used ones instead of one new vehicle.

Sitting across from Christy, Katie had a feeling it would be too much of a strain on their friendship if Katie gave her a car. Christy was used to receiving expensive items from her wealthy aunt and uncle, but Katie had watched how the weight of those gifts had affected Christy's relationship with her aunt. Not that the gift of a used car would necessarily damage Christy and Katie's relationship, but she realized now how awkward it would be. People would find out that Katie had received a chunk of money. Way more money than she ever had let on, but, still, it would be clear that she inherited enough money to buy two cars. That in and of itself was extraordinary enough to start people asking questions. Rick still didn't know anything about the money. How would all that settle with him?

She hadn't realized how complicated this might be.

"Are you okay?" Christy waved her hand in front of Katie. "You got awful quiet."

"Sorry. My brain just took a little walk. It's back now. What were we talking about?"

"You were saying you wanted to buy a car."

"Yes, I do. Do you want to go with me?"

"Sure. Do you know when Rick is available?"

"Rick? Why?"

"I thought you would want to include him in the process. It's a pretty big investment. I mean, if you guys are close to getting engaged, collaborating on a decision like a car would seem like a normal thing to do."

"I could ask him. I don't know, though. Last December, when he was looking for a new car, I only went with him on the first car-hunting trip. Within the first three minutes, I realized he and his dad saw the experience as a father-son outing. After that I didn't invite myself on any jaunts. He really likes the car he ended up with, which is good, considering how many hours he spends living in it now. I miss his Mustang, though."

"He still has it, doesn't he?"

"Yes. He parked it in his parents' garage. He doesn't plan to drive it anymore, though. He told me I could borrow it anytime I wanted, but I didn't ever feel that was right. I was more comfortable borrowing Eli's or Nicole's car. Although, I have to say, that Mustang has a lot of memories connected to it. I loved that car. It was such a classic. Such a symbol of who Rick was in high school, you know?"

Christy smiled.

"Yeah, you know. I know you know." Plopping down her drink, Katie said, "Oh, Christy, the roads you and I have traveled together, my friend."

"And the many more we have yet to travel ... in your new car!"

"I'm planning to buy a used car."

"Still, it will be new to you." Christy checked the time on her cell phone. "I have to get back to work. Let me know when you want to go car hunting, and I'll go with you. Oh, and Tracy asked me if I would consider babysitting for them. If you have time, do you want to come with me?"

"I could be persuaded."

"I'll take care of Daniel. You can use the time to study. I thought it would be fun for us to drive to Carlsbad together and maybe go for a walk on the beach afterward."

"That sounds so perfect right now. Especially since the weather is warming up. I would love to go with you. Let me know the details, and I'll check my on-duty hours. I owe Nicole a boatload of hours since she covered for me while I was sick. It's a good thing she's such a generous woman."

Christy rose, gave Katie a quick hug, and returned to the book-store side of the building.

Katie took the opportunity to check her cell phone directory. To her surprise, she still had Aunt Marti's number on her phone. It had been there ever since the frenzied days of planning Christy's wedding a year ago.

Returning to the parking lot, Katie slipped into the driver's seat of Nicole's car and closed the door. She pressed the button for Aunt Marti's cell phone and waited for her to answer. When her voicemail came on, Katie hung up. She didn't want to leave a message. As a matter of fact, she didn't really want to talk to Aunt Marti. Christy's uncle Bob was the one she wanted to talk to.

Katie found Uncle Bob's number on her phone, pressed the button, and cleared her throat. Christy's easygoing uncle answered on the second ring. The first thing Katie asked was if Aunt Marti was nearby.

"Nope. She's at lunch with some friends at the club. Do you want her number?"

"No, I wanted to talk to you."

"Sure. What's up?"

"I need your help on something that might be a little complicated."

"You got it. What can I do?"

Katie loved Uncle Bob almost as much as she was sure Christy loved him. The man was so good-natured and caring. She felt certain she could trust him and rolled through her less-than-fully-formed plan to buy Christy and Todd a car.

"Let me get this straight," Uncle Bob said. "You want to give me money to buy a new car for Christy and Todd but let them think the money came from me."

"Yes. But it's a used car not a new car."

"Right. A used car."

"Can you help me do that?"

"Actually, no. I can't."

That wasn't the answer Katie expected. "Why not?"

"I can help you find a good used car. That part isn't a problem. But I can't let them think the money came from me."

"Why not?"

Uncle Bob laughed. "That would be dishonest."

Katie frowned. For a moment she wished she had tried going through Aunt Marti with this plan. Katie felt certain Aunt Marti wouldn't have a problem hiding, changing, or embellishing the truth. As a matter of fact, Aunt Marti was gifted in such matters.

"I'm not asking you to lie. I just don't want them to know the money came from me."

"And why not? They would appreciate knowing the truth. Tell Christy and Todd your aunt left you some money, and you want to use it to buy them a second car. That's clean and honest. No mysteries to try to keep covered."

"I was going to do that, but then I thought it might get too complicated when other people find out I have that much money. Right now only two people know I received an inheritance. Christy is one of those people, but she doesn't know much."

"Katie, listen, it's no one's business how much money you have or what you decide to do with it. Remember that."

Katie thought she heard Uncle Bob's voice intensify on that last statement. When it came to money and choosing how to spend it, Bob was a bit of an authority. If he was saying she should be forthright and not plot a cover-up, she knew she should listen to him.

"How about if we do this: You think about how you want to handle the information with Christy and Todd. I'll look around for a car. I'll keep you updated, and you keep me updated."

"Okay. But there is one more thing."

"Shoot."

"Can you look around for two good used cars?"

"Two?"

"Yeah, I need one. My car died last fall. I've been putting off the inevitable purchase for too long."

"How have you been getting around?"

"I have generous friends. One of them, Nicole, arranged to include me on her insurance. We've been sharing her car for the past few months. It's worked out great, but it really is time for me to buy my own car."

"I can help you with that. No problemo."

"Thank you. I'll keep checking in with you, as you said."

Right before they hung up, Uncle Bob tenderly concluded their conversation. "You make me proud, Katie, you know that? You make me proud."

Katie choked up. She never expected him to say such a thing. Those were words a young woman should hear from her father, but Katie couldn't remember ever hearing them from her dad. Hearing them from Uncle Bob meant almost as much to her.

Almost.

A s soon as Katie hung up, she drove to the gas station to fill Nicole's car. Driving back up the hill to the Rancho Corona campus, Katie mentally tried to organize her mounds of must-dos for the remainder of that day. She was on front-desk duty that afternoon for three hours and hoped the shift was uneventful because she planned to work on a big project due next week that she hadn't started. She also had a mandatory staff meeting at seven. Katie had no idea when she was going to find time to write her already-overdue paper for her intercultural studies class. She also was behind on turning in three summaries from reading assignments that were due while she was sick.

"I'm never going to finish it all."

As a diversion, she put her phone on speaker and called Rick. "Hey. Guess who misses you and can't wait to see you this weekend?"

"Hey, yourself. Guess what?"

"No, I'm not going to guess. First you have to guess who misses you and can't wait to see you."

"Katie."

She couldn't tell if he was speaking her name as the answer or with an edge of frustration. No matter. She kept playing along with her own game.

"That is correct. Now it's your turn. What do you want me to guess?"

"We got clearance on the Redlands café. Opening day is set for April 27." He sounded elated, but Katie was pretty sure he had told her that information before.

"Cool."

"More than cool. This is going to change everything. We got in on this location at just the right time. How about if I pick you up early on Saturday morning and we come out here for the day?"

Katie hesitated. That wasn't exactly her idea of what their long-awaited date would hold. "I may have to bring some schoolwork with me."

"Not a problem. Everything's wired. Bring your laptop. The espresso machine should be installed by Friday afternoon, so I'll make you some of the good stuff while you study. It's really shaping up, Katie. Nicole did a great job on her selection of colors. Did she tell you she was able to use the interior design plans for one of her finals? She got an A."

"I knew she was trying to get credit for all the work she did with your mom. That's great. So are you in town tonight? Do you want to come by? I'm on duty at the front desk from four to seven. We could have dinner after that. Oh, wait; I think I have a staff meeting then."

"I can't come anyway, Katie. Too much is going on here right now. I miss you. Things have been way too crazy for way too long."

"I know. We're almost to the end of this particular finish line."

"I know," Rick said. "April 27 is just around the corner."

"May 16 is just around the corner too."

"What's May 16?"

She couldn't tell if Rick was deadpanning to tease her.

"Let me see, May 16 ... May 16 ... Now what was it? Something is happening May 16. Oh, that's right! Katie Weldon is graduating from college on May 16."

"Did you think I forgot?"

"I think the way your life is right now you need to be reminded. Often. This is a nonnegotiable, by the way. You have to be there, Rick. It's man-da-tor-y. Got it? Mandatory."

"Katie, relax. I get it. Don't worry. I plan to be there."

She knew she would have felt more comforted if his word choice had been "I *will* be there," but she needed to back off. More than once she had told Rick that he, Todd, and Christy were going to be her stand-in—and only—family there that day. He knew how important that was to her.

Rick had assured her he would get his parents to come and possibly even his brother, Josh, who was as caught up as Rick in the opening of the new cafés. Katie had good reason to be leery of Rick's demanding schedule. As a backup, she thought maybe she would invite Bob and Marti. Why not? Uncle Bob had just said he was proud of her. He could come watch her accept her diploma and be proud of her on May 16 too, couldn't he?

Two weeks passed before Katie managed to find time to call Uncle Bob to check on the car project as well as to give him a heads-up on the graduation date. Katie knew Marti's social calendar would require early notice on any event that required significant effort. And with Aunt Marti, pretty much everything involved more effort on her part than was perhaps necessary.

During those two weeks, Katie felt like a hamster on an exercise wheel, running, running, but getting nowhere. She made it to all her classes, two staff meetings, and even fulfilled her scheduled RA duties. That was more than she had managed to pull off in the past month. On average she was sleeping less than five hours each night, but she couldn't seem to catch up on all the work she had to do.

After Katie's last afternoon class on Friday, she headed to Crown Hall for her two-hour front-desk duty. The minute she was off, she planned to dash to the shower and change into whatever clean anything she could find in the compost pile of clothing in her room. She and Rick had finally managed to schedule a real date, and, if all went well, she would be ready at exactly 6:30, when he was to pick her up.

Julia, Katie's resident director, was waiting for her when Katie entered the office space on the lobby level of Crown Hall. She took

Katie aside and asked, "Do you have any time open tomorrow morning?"

"Tomorrow?"

"Around eight. Does that work for you? You still haven't turned in your February summary forms. I know you were sick. We can work on it together. It should only take an hour."

Katie didn't see how she could fit another hour into her schedule. She knew she had to. Maybe trying to go out to dinner tonight with Rick was a bad idea. She had way too much work to do this weekend.

What am I thinking? I haven't seen Rick in ages. Of course I have to see him tonight.

"Would later in the week be all right with you?"

"Sure. Email me your best open times and we'll figure something out."

Settling into her chair at the desk, Katie pulled out her laptop and immediately went to work on some research she needed for her final project in her class on modern Asian culture. When she had switched to humanities as her major at the start of her senior year, she didn't have a strong sense of what she would end up doing with that major. But it was a much better fit than botany had been. With humanities, she liked the variety of classes that connected with her interest in people, communication, and cultures.

Yet Katie knew, if she were to be completely honest, she was more interested in actually graduating than in what degree she was graduating with. She wouldn't admit that to anyone, but her goal had been simply to finish college. What she majored in was only icing on the cake. If she could manage to keep on track for this last sprint to the finish line, then anything could happen.

Katie's imagination gave way to the image of being draped in an elegant white wedding dress, holding a simple, single California poppy as her bouquet. She saw herself walking down the aisle, her face gleaming, her steps slow and sure. In her waking daydream she saw her wedding take place outside, on upper campus, just like Christy and Todd's wedding last May. The weather was perfect. The guests were all beaming.

She looked down and was delighted to see she was barefoot under that exquisite wedding gown. That explained her perfect balance and unhurried steps. She was happy. In her most natural habitat.

Katie imagined music playing. Guitars. No, not guitars. Violins. Yes, violins. Many violins with one cello. And butterflies. Hundreds of dainty, flittering, golden butterflies circled her as she took tiny steps forward.

She imagined lifting her eyes toward the altar where, under the flower-laced arch, a minister stood smiling, holding a Bible in front of him with both hands. Now was the moment. She would turn and look upon the face of her beloved. By his expression as he gazed on her, she would know that he was smitten with her bridal beauty. Slowly casting her daydreaming glance to the right, Katie drew in a sweet breath and—

"Yo!"

The rough voice snapped her back to the present. A middle-aged, overweight maintenance guy in a frayed Dodgers baseball cap stood by the window.

"Yeah, we got a call for a broken window."

"What?"

"A broken window," he repeated.

"Okay. Um, did anyone tell you the room number?"

"I dunno. They said to check in at the lobby."

Katie flipped through the papers on the desk and found a work order in Nicole's handwriting. "Here it is. It's on the first floor. I'll go with you."

Katie put out the sign that read, "Back in a few," and they walked to room 118 without speaking. Katie knocked three times on the door. When no one answered, she knocked again and called out that she was a resident assistant and that she was going to open the door and enter. Using the master key, Katie opened the door and was stunned at the sight that greeted her.

The room was a disaster zone. Clothes, books, shoes, blankets, and empty pizza boxes were gathered in huddles as if planning their next move. The window on the left was shattered. Shards of broken glass were sprinkled over the bed, the desk, and the crumpled clothing. In the center of the floor was a large rock. Katie knew it was best to leave the evidence right where it was.

The repairman said, "Looks like someone ransacked the place. I'll double-check the measurements and come back with the glass."

As he pulled out his tape measure, Katie stood to the side, her thoughts on the women who lived in this room. They might not know what had happened. Maybe their room had been broken into. Or maybe one of them caused the break. Either way, Katie was glad this didn't happen on her floor. She had too much to do and wouldn't appreciate logging a report on a mess like this.

The other thought that stayed with Katie as she looked around the room was how she would feel if the rock had come through her window and she had to let someone into her room. As bad as this room was, Katie knew hers was worse. And no one had ransacked it. She alone was responsible for the mess. She was never there, so all the piles of disorganization had only grown in their petrifying state. If anyone saw how she had been living, she would be horrified.

As Katie returned to the lobby with the repairman, she determined that she would do whatever it took to catch up on her laundry and clean her room this weekend.

Back in the front office, Katie returned to her research and kept on task for almost half an hour before Nicole came by and stopped to talk. Nicole had all the details of the broken window and filled Katie in.

"The guys that reported it said it was supposed to be a friendly tap on the window to see if anyone was there. They said they made a 'poor choice in the size of the pebble.'"

"It was no pebble, I'll tell you that. And I'll tell you something else you'll be glad to hear, Miss Super Tidy Pageant Princess."

"Don't call me that," Nicole said with a hint of a frown on her flawless skin.

"Okay. Sorry. Here's the point. I saw how messy room 118 was, and it motivated me at the heart level — you know what I mean? Right here. I felt it."

"Felt what?"

"The need to clean my room."

"Really?"

"Yes, really. I think you're the only one on campus who knows how truly frightening my room has become. I may need a shovel and a Dumpster, but I'm determined to clear the toxic waste this weekend."

"Good for you." Nicole looked at her watch. "Do you want a head start on it?"

"Why? What are you suggesting?"

"I could take your last hour shift. I have a lot of work to do. Might as well do it here. You said it's been pretty quiet. That way you would be able to jump into the cleanup project."

"Yeah, jump in before I change my mind or get distracted, right?"

Nicole smiled her sweet smile. "Offer stands. What do you want to do?"

"I'll take it. You're so nice to me."

"I know."

Nicole stood next to the desk as Katie leaned over to unplug her laptop cord. Hidden under the desk, Katie didn't see the person who walked up to the window.

Nicole greeted whoever it was with an extra cheery, "Hey! Hi! How are you? Good to see you."

"You too. How you been? You look great, by the way."

Katie recognized the deep voice. Her heart did a little tap dance. *He's early!*

She popped her head up.

"Katie?" Rick looked surprised. "What are you doing down there?"

"Unplugging my laptop. What are doing out there?"

"Trying to surprise you. I knew you were on duty, so I thought I would come by early. I have a few calls to make, but I thought I would hang out with you until you're off the clock."

"Really?" Katie felt a flustered sort of happiness. She actually had been looking forward to cleaning up her room before her haystacks of clothes became combustible. She also had intended to take a shower and greet Rick nice and fresh. Not frumped and frazzled yet again.

"I was just telling Katie I would cover for her at the front desk," Nicole said.

"That's great. Thanks, Nicki." Rick gave Nicole a big smile.

Katie repeated Rick's choice of a nickname. "Nicki?"

Rick was notorious for coming up with tag names for people. Sadly, all his attempts to give Katie a nickname had failed. This was the first time she had heard him use the cutsey "Nicki" to refer to Nicole.

"It fits, don't you think?" Rick turned his smile back in Katie's direction.

Nicole jumped in with a further explanation. "Rick's dad called me that a few weeks ago. I told Rick I liked it because my dad called me Nicki when I was little. Hardly anyone calls me that anymore."

"Nicki." Katie tried out the sound of the new name.

Nicole laughed. "Your expression says it all, Katie. I can tell how you feel about it. Don't worry. You don't have to call me Nicki."

"Good. Nicole fits you better, I think." She gathered up her things. "Rick, do you mind waiting for me for, like, ten minutes?"

"After all the times you've waited for me? Course not. Do you need to go change?" He seemed to be taking in her crumpled outfit, including her not-so-fresh T-shirt and her favorite pair of sandals with the frayed leather strap.

"Yes, I need to change. Definitely. In more ways than just my date-night-worthy apparel. But for the moment, that's the only change I'm going to work on. Do you mind waiting for me? Really?"

She was outside the office now, standing in front of him. Rick looked so good. He always looked good. He smelled good too.

His smile softened as he looked down on Katie. "I'll be waiting right here for you. As long as it takes. I'm not going anywhere without you."

Oh, Rick, you are still the king of smooth talk.

His tender words to Katie catapulted her down the hall, to her room, into the shower, and out in record time. She wished she had something cute, new, and nice and fresh waiting in her closet for her to slip into. She wanted to look good for Rick. She wanted him to melt a little every time he saw her, the way she melted a little every time she saw him.

Her choices were limited though. Jeans or jeans. A white blouse that needed to be ironed or a black V-neck sweater. The sweater won the selection challenge, even though it was a warm afternoon. She pushed up the sleeves, then lifted the sweater and squirted her stomach with a spritz of kiwi-coconut-lime body spray just in case she did perspire to death. At least she would smell slightly fruity in the meltdown.

Smoothing her sweater back into place, Katie noticed a string hanging from the side. She gave the wayward strand a tug, and a half-inch hole appeared.

"Oh, brother! You've got to be kidding me."

She pulled off the sweater to examine the damage, and the yarn continued to unravel. Frustrated, she grabbed her phone and called Nicole.

"I'm desperate. Please tell me I can borrow anything in your closet."

"Of course you can. Help yourself to the shoes and jewelry too. Whatever you want."

"You are a peach. And a lifesaver. Thanks, Nicole. Tell Rick I'm almost ready."

"I will. Don't rush. He's catching me up on all the details with the café."

Katie rushed anyway. She used the master key to gain entrance into Nicole's room and skimmed through the beautiful, clean, hung-up assortment of tops in Nicole's orderly closet. After trying on two different tops, she decided on the first one.

Right before dashing back to her room, Katie spotted a pair of stylish black shoes. Nicole had said to borrow shoes as well. Katie tried them on and thought they looked great with her jeans. Viewing herself from several angles in Nicole's full-length mirror, Katie thought it was about the cutest combo she had put together all semester. She definitely needed to go clothes shopping with Nicole as personal consultant.

With the shoes in her hand, Katie hurried back to her room and finished getting ready. Her hair didn't need too much tweaking. She shook it twice and let the silky red strands land in their usual happy-go-lucky tumble. Makeup would be a nice touch. She untwisted the top of her mascara tube and thought, *When was the last time I opened this?*

Her eyes fell on a green stone necklace that had been curled up on the corner of her dresser top for as long as the mascara had been sitting beside it twisted shut. Rick gave her the necklace months ago. She wasn't exactly sure why. He said he saw it when he was in Arizona and the color reminded him of her eyes. *Green, yet changing in the light.* Or something like that. Katie had never been one to wear much jewelry. Tonight, though, she was glad she noticed the necklace. Rick would like that she wore it.

Katie slipped on the black heels and took one last look in the mirror before dashing down the hall. That's when she realized going fast in Nicole's shoes was a challenge. A lady didn't dash in such heels. She had to take it slow. No matter. Rick said he wasn't going anywhere. He said he would be waiting for her.

5

Making her grand entrance into Crown Hall's lobby, Katie wasn't surprised to see that Rick was on his cell phone and had stretched out on one of the couches. He spent a lot of time on his phone. His head was turned the other way, so he didn't notice her arrival.

Katie casually seated herself on the sofa's arm at the opposite end and waited for him to notice.

Rick turned toward her, and when he did, it happened.

Katie got the look she had longed to receive from Rick—the crinkles-in-the-corners-of-the-eyes look that made his lips turn up in a smile and made it clear that he saw—really saw—her.

Katie wanted to mark this moment. She had waited for this since junior high. She was pretty sure Rick Doyle at long last realized he was in love with her. It finally, truly had happened. She saw it in his eyes. She saw it in his expression. Never again would she question if his heart was turned toward her.

It was. She knew.

Rick immediately ended the call, closed his phone, and took a long look at Katie. All he said was, "Hi."

Katie loved that "hi" was the only word to come out of his mouth.

She responded with an equally small, "Hi."

Rick took her hand in his. "You look gorgeous."

"Thanks. It's Nicole's top. Did she tell you I called a little while ago in desperation?"

"No. Hey, come here." He made room for her beside him on the couch. Katie slid in, under his waiting arm. He wrapped both arms around her and drew her close.

"I've missed you."

"Not as much as I've missed you."

Rick kissed the tip of her nose. She cuddled up next to him, not comfortable with the thought of his kissing her a lot here in the dorm lobby. Not that she didn't want him to kiss her. A lot. But she had the feeling that people were watching, and her and Rick's expressions of affection were a private thing.

"So where do you want to go to eat?" Katie hoped to steer the conversation down another path for now.

Rick kissed her again, this time on the side of her head. He leaned his head down and with his free hand, tilted Katie's chin up toward him so he could kiss her on the lips. She eagerly received his kiss, but still had the funny feeling that other students might be watching them.

Rick kissed her one more time on the lips. This time with firm intention. He pulled away slightly and whispered, "Did I tell you how much I've missed you?"

"Yeah, you did." Katie was surprised that she felt a bit agitated by his persistent attention. Hadn't they already gone over that they had missed each other? Why was he so set on being cuddly and kissy now? Did her spiffed-up appearance affect him that much?

Rick's arm remained around Katie's shoulder. He pulled her closer. "I've missed holding you like this. I've missed being with you. You smell really good." He kissed her again.

Now Katie definitely was uncomfortable. She wasn't used to Rick's responding to her like this and pressing forward with his expressions of affection. Katie knew that Rick was a "lover-boy," just as she knew he was a smooth talker. Their relationship, for the most part, in the past long months had been more on the playful, cuddly side. They had held off on even kissing each other until after they had been dating officially for almost a year. They had never had a make-out session, but Katie suspected that was where they would be heading if they were alone right now.

She received another kiss from him before pulling back and giving him a smile instead of a kiss. "Hey."

"Hey," he echoed.

"We should decide what we're going to do tonight. Do you know where you want to eat?"

"Anywhere. You pick."

The next few hours were a continuation of the Katie-Rick teeter-totter relationship tipping in Katie's direction. That too wasn't normal.

Katie went with the power suddenly given to her, as if she were the one with the remote control and no one was complaining about her choices. That never happened.

She chose where they went to dinner—a not-so-high-class Italian restaurant—and where they went next for dessert—a chain ice-cream shop—and what music they listened to in Rick's car as they headed back to Rancho. All evening Katie kept the conversation running with details of what had been happening in the dorm and in her classes. Usually Rick was the one with all the news on his cafés. Tonight he kept saying, "What else has been happening?" and "You have no idea how cute you look when you talk fast like that."

For Katie, all the focused attention felt wonderful in an alternate-universe sort of way. This just wasn't the way things usually were with Rick.

Is this what it feels like for Rick to be truly in love with me?

Katie felt a strange nervousness at the thought. Convincing Rick to decide he was crazy about her had been a goal for almost half her life. But what happens when such a long-term goal is achieved?

At Katie's suggestion, Rick drove to upper campus. He parked his new car and told Katie to wait. She stayed in the passenger's seat while Rick hustled around and opened her door, offering his hand as she exited. The black heels she had borrowed from Nicole made her footing wobbly on the gravel.

"I have new sympathy for Cinderella. I can see how she lost her shoe." Katie reached for Rick's arm as she tried to steady her steps. "Actually, Cinderella isn't alone on the shoe loss thing. I stumbled out of my shoe in this parking lot last May at Todd and Christy's wedding, remember?"

"No. When did you lose your shoe?" Rick wrapped his arm around her, steadying her steps.

"When I was running after the limo. Right after I found out about the prank you and Doug played on Christy and Todd."

"Oh, right."

Katie knew Rick didn't really remember. Now that she thought about it, Eli was the one who had kept an eye on her that evening. He was the one who picked up the wreath of flowers she had been wearing as a bridesmaid. The one who said she had lost her halo. Then he proceeded to hang the mangled wreath on the rearview mirror of his beat-up Toyota. He said it reminded him to pray.

Rick and Katie headed for one of the benches along the walkway under the palm trees. As soon as they sat down, Rick kissed her.

Katie pulled back and looked at him before he could draw her close again for another kiss. "What's going on? You're, like, off-the-chart nice and ultra-affectionate this evening."

Rick smiled the same heart-happy grin he had given her earlier when she entered Crown Hall's lobby.

"I have something I've been waiting to give you." Rick pulled from his pocket a small jewelry box.

Katie held her breath.

Is this it? Now? No! I'm not ready. I thought I was, but I'm not. Please, Rick! No! Not yet!

Rick didn't drop to his knee. He remained seated on the bench next to Katie and handed her the jewelry box. Once the box was in her hand, she realized it was too large for a ring. And too flat.

"What's this?"

"Open it and see."

Katie opened the box. The only light around them came from the strings of white twinkle lights wrapped around the palm trees. She was pretty sure the treasure in the box was a piece of jewelry, but she couldn't tell what it was.

Faintly making out the shape of what might possibly be a small medallion, she said, "Did you win a gold medal in the Olympics and not bother to tell me?"

"No, and don't ruin this by trying to be funny."

"Ruin what? I can't tell what this is."

"It's a brooch." Rick made the declaration with such finality Katie knew he thought the identity of the object should have been obvious to her. But it still wasn't.

Her confusion escalated. "A brooch? What exactly is a brooch?"

Rick removed the piece of jewelry from the box and held it up so Katie could see the way the inset stones sparkled in the faint light. The brooch looked like a round sunburst with many small stones that seemed to be winking at her.

"This belonged to my grandmother." Rick's voice had turned tender again. "She gave it to my mom. Right before Valentine's Day my mom asked if I would like to have it made into something for you."

"So this is what you were going to give me on Valentine's Day?"

"Yes. I planned to surprise you, but then I realized I couldn't have anything designed and completed in time for Valentine's Day. So I thought I would give it to you then, and you could think about what you would like to do with it. I'm giving it to you now so, once you decide, I can have it ready by graduation. It won't be a surprise, but it will be something you like, and that's more important."

"Rick, you don't have to give this to me. It was your grandmother's. It's too valuable."

"That's exactly why I want you to have it." He put the brooch back on the cotton in the box and placed the box in Katie's hand. "This is important to me. To us. I've wanted to give you a piece of jewelry ever since we became a couple. It's just that with money being so tight from opening the cafés, I couldn't put aside enough for anything of value. When my mom gave me this, it meant a lot to me. That's why I was so eager to see you on Valentine's Day. This brooch meant I had something to work with, you know? I could use this to make a piece of jewelry for you, and you would be able to wear something more than that simple necklace I gave you."

"I like this necklace." Katie touched the green stone on the end of the chain.

"I wanted to give you something more." Rick reached over and fingered the ends of her hair. "Something that expresses the importance of our relationship. We've done everything right, Katie. This is working. Our relationship, I mean. We're good together. I want you to have something you can wear all the time that symbolizes our success."

A smile clung to Katie's closed lips. She knew what Rick meant, but his word choice struck her as funny. The guy's heart was definitely in the right place. She just never expected Rick Doyle to present her with an antique brooch and say he wanted it to symbolize the success of their relationship.

"What?" Rick leaned closer, trying to read the meaning of her mirthful expression.

"This is really, really sweet, Rick. It is. I don't know what to say."

"Say that you're glad I'm your boyfriend and that you'll decide in the next week what you want to have made out of the brooch so I can have it finished by graduation."

"Okay. I'm glad you're my boyfriend, and I'll decide as soon as I can."

"Good. And if you need any help, Nicki might have some ideas."

Katie pulled back. She still wasn't used to hearing Nicole referred to as "Nicki."

"She's seen this, hasn't she? Did you show her the brooch?"

"No. She knew about it because my mom told her. I wanted to show it to you first."

Katie leaned over and kissed him on the cheek. "Thank you, Rick. This is really sweet of you. I'll come up with a suggestion as soon as I can. And I'm sorry about Valentine's Day and my confusion over what was going on."

"No apology needed." He kissed her before she could protest again. Pulling back and taking her hand in his, Rick said, "Do you remember what you said last Christmas?"

"You mean about your mom's eggnog? I told you I apologized to her about that. I didn't realize she was in the other room when I spit it out in the sink. I didn't think—"

"No, Katie, not about the eggnog. About us. Do you remember what you said about our relationship?"

"I'm not sure. What did I say?"

"A few days after Christmas, we were in my new car. I don't remember where we were going, but we were talking about how we would make it through this last semester. The fall months had been intense for both of us, with my working on the cafés and you with the RA position and changing your major in your senior year. Do you remember?"

"Sort of."

"I was saying how I didn't think much would change during the next few months for both of us because I'd still be busy with my business and you'd be busy with school. You said, 'Then we'll just have to learn how to live happily almost after.'"

"Oh, yeah, I do remember saying that."

"Well, this will be your happily-almost-after bracelet. Or necklace. Or whatever you want it to be." He kissed her again, and this time it seemed as if even his kiss were intended to symbolize their relationship. It was deliberate and lingering.

Katie pulled back. Rick tried to kiss her again, but she said, "We probably should head back."

"We will. In a minute." Rick wrapped both arms around Katie and murmured in her ear, "We're almost there. You know that, don't you? Only a few more weeks."

Katie definitely would have melted if Rick's whispered words to her right then had been the defining "I love you." Those were the words she was waiting to hear.

But for now, his whispered, "almost there," seemed one step away from a proposal. She drew in the warmth of his embrace and leaned her head against his chest.

Rick held her for a long moment. She could hear his heart beating and felt the warmth of his steady breaths on the top of her head. Her eyes were open, unblinking, as if she were trying to focus clearly enough to see into the future.

Katie stared into the darkness of the night around them and wondered if this was "it."

Am I going to marry this man? Am I really home? Why does it seem as if something is missing? What could be missing? This is all I ever wanted. Rick just said it. We're almost there. All our long-sought-after goals will be accomplished. I love him. I know I love him.

"Rick?"

"Hmm?"

"Do you hear music?"

"Music?" Rick paused before answering. "No."

Katie slowly closed her eyes, trying to catch the sound of violins in her imagination.

"Why? Do you?"

"No."

He rose from the bench, employed all the deeply imbedded gentlemanly manners that had always been part of what made Rick Doyle Rick Doyle, and gently pulled her to her feet. "Then why did you ask?"

Katie kept her hand ensconced in his. "No reason. I was just wondering."

Rick laughed. "I think you've watched too many romantic comedies."

"Possibly."

He gave her hand a squeeze. "This is our romance, Katie. We're writing the script. You and me, not some formula writer in Hollywood."

"Then I guess I'll have to 'stay tuned for coming attractions.'"

"Yes, you will. Be patient."

"I am."

"I know. So am I."

6

When Katie showed the brooch to Nicole early the next morning in the laundry room, she pretty much had concluded she wanted to have the stones set into a bracelet.

"What do you think?" Katie leaned against the washer where an extra-large load of her clothes was finally being washed. The two of them had gotten up for a staff breakfast at seven o'clock that Saturday morning. Katie was so energized after the meeting she had talked Nicole into helping her work on cleaning up her room. Within forty minutes the two of them had made admirable headway.

Nicole pulled one of Katie's freshly cleaned sheets from the dryer. "It's beautiful."

"Yeah, fresh sheets are the best, aren't they?" Katie drew in the slight lavender and gardenia scent that lingered from the fabric softener sheets Nicole had tossed in.

"I meant the brooch is beautiful."

"Oh. Right. Yeah, it is beautiful. I'm sure it's valuable. It's just that I would never wear it. Rick made it clear that he wants me to wear whatever I have the brooch made into. I'm not much of a jewelry person, as you know. I think a bracelet is a safe way to go. Or maybe a necklace. I don't know. I keep bouncing back and forth."

"I'm sure whatever you decide will turn out great." Nicole held out one of the corners of the top sheet, and Katie picked up the other end.

The two of them folded the sheet nice and tidy, which seemed pointless to Katie since she was just going to put it back on her bed.

"Nicole, you're supposed to have an opinion on this. Rick said I should ask what you would do with it."

"He did?"

"Yeah. So, if he had given the brooch to you, what would you do with it?"

Nicole pressed her lips together and focused on the door of the open dryer and not on Katie. "I would leave the brooch just as it is and find a unique way to wear it."

"How? In your hair?"

"Maybe." Nicole glanced at her phone and texted a message to someone who had just buzzed her.

"Can I ask you something?" Katie boosted herself up to sit on the top of the warm dryer. "Do you think Rick and I are a good match?"

Nicole's eyes flashed over at Katie while the rest of her didn't move. She seemed to be studying Katie's expression. "Why do you ask that?"

"I don't know. Sometimes I wonder if Rick and I are really meant to be together. Then other times it's like all my dreams are coming true before my eyes."

"Is that how you feel about him now? That your dream is coming true?"

"Yes, definitely. I think. I mean, yeah. Of course." Katie hopped down and paced the floor. "It's just that I've never been this close to a guy. Well, except maybe for Michael in high school, but that wasn't the same. Rick is so caring, and everything is going great. Really great. I think I'm trying to freak myself out. Listening for the violin music and all that. What is it when you don't mean to ruin something, but you end up destroying everything?"

Nicole still hadn't moved. Only her dark eyes remained fixed on Katie as she paced. "Do you mean self-sabotage?"

"Yes." Katie snapped her fingers. "That's what's happening to me. I'm contemplating self-sabotaging our relationship, aren't I? Why would I want to do that? I must be crazy."

Nicole's eyebrows crowded close together, and she returned her gaze to the screen of her cell phone. "I have to go," she said quietly. "I'll see you later."

"Yeah, see you later. Thanks again for all the help on my room and laundry and everything. You're the best, Nicole."

Nicole was already out the door as Katie called out the final line. She checked the second dryer, which had tumbled to a halt while she was pacing the laundry room. Her jeans were still damp, so she set the timer for another twenty minutes and returned with her spring-flowers-scented bed sheets to her clean room.

Her phone buzzed, and Katie was happy to see that the call was from Uncle Bob. "Hey, I was wondering when I would hear back from you."

"I think you'll be more understanding of the wait once you see what I've come up with for you in the car department. When do you think you can head up this way?"

"I don't know. Later this afternoon might work. Christy talked me into helping her babysit for Doug and Tracy. We probably could come your way afterward. I'll have to check with Christy. It's over an hour from Doug and Tracy's place in Carlsbad up to yours, right?"

"At least an hour."

"Then I think we could arrive about seven tonight. Would that be too late?"

Katie heard a voice in the background, and Bob added, "Marti says you should stay with us overnight. The weather has been great. She says ... Wait. Here, she'll tell you herself."

A moment later Katie heard Christy's aunt's high-pitched voice on the phone. "You girls need some girlfriend time. That's what I was trying to tell Robert. Come up and stay the night. The three of us girls will have all day tomorrow to spend together."

"That's really generous of you, but I don't know if—"

"I'll take both of you shopping and to lunch," Marti quickly promised. "My treat. It's been far too long since you girls let me spoil you. We're overdue for some together time."

Since when did Aunt Marti consider me one of the "girls" and treat me to a shopping trip? That's her technique with Christy. I've never been on Marti's list of favorites. What's going on?

"I'll need to call Christy to see if she can be gone that long. I have a lot of studying to do, and I need to write a paper this weekend."

"You can do that here, can't you? We've recently renovated the upstairs. Did Christy tell you? The guest room is twice the size it used to be. There's a built-in window seat and a desk where you can work. Christy and I can go shopping and bring back something for you. How would that be?"

Katie didn't know what to make of Marti's comments. All Katie knew was that if she were going to get anything done this weekend, she should stay locked in her dorm room.

"Oh, here. Robert wants to say something now."

"Call us back when you can, Katie."

"Okay. Thanks. I will." She could hear Marti's voice in the background right before Bob hung up. Marti was saying, "You're not hanging up, are you?"

Katie smiled as she placed a call to Christy. The possibility of going up to Bob and Marti's home in Newport Beach was appealing. Watching the two of them successfully relate to each other when their personalities were so different always was entertaining. Still, Katie knew that if she went, she would complete zero homework. Yet, when would she be invited up there again? It had been a year since Katie had been to Bob and Marti's home. Bob always made sure they had plenty of delicious things to eat. Katie wasn't scheduled for duty until Monday. Still, she shouldn't go.

On the other hand, she had asked Bob to help her to find a car, and that was the reason she was going in the first place. It made sense to stay overnight since it would be at least a two-and-a-half-hour drive back to school. Three hours, if the weekend traffic were heavy.

However, if she were honest with herself, she didn't need to settle on a car until the end of the school year. The best use of her time now would be to hunker down, focus on her classes, finish her papers early, work the extra hours she had accumulated when she was sick, and catch up on her meetings with Julia. Christy didn't need Katie to go with her to babysit Daniel. Whatever Bob's deal on a new car was, another deal would come along sometime. Graduation was the goal Katie needed to press toward now. She should lock herself in her room and do as much as she could with the open time in front of her.

That would be the wise, sensible, and responsible thing to do with the remainder of the weekend. And that was what she would tell Christy.

Two hours later, with their packed overnight bags in the trunk of Christy's Volvo, Katie and Christy motored down the hill away from Rancho Corona University.

I shouldn't be doing this. But we're on our way, and I'm not going to change my mind. Once I decide to do something, I follow through. Even if it does take a lot of debating before I decide.

"So explain to me why we're going to my aunt and uncle's after babysitting for Doug and Tracy? I wasn't clear on that part from your phone conversation."

"Your aunt invited us. And like I said, I asked your uncle to keep an eye open for a car, and apparently he has found one."

Katie reached for a book in the backpack at her feet. "I'm going to turn anti-social on you now. I really need to use some of this drive time to finish my reading. If I manage to pull off everything I need to do this weekend, I'm sure to win the Multitasking Woman of the Year Award. You wouldn't want me to miss out on that now, would you?"

"No, I wouldn't stand in your way. I already know you can get everything done. You're amazing that way. You accomplish your goals, whatever they are. No one is challenging you on that."

Christy hesitated and then added, "Please don't be offended, but for one last time, I just want to be the gentle voice in the back of your head that gives you permission."

"Permission for what?"

"You can change your mind if you want to."

Katie didn't know why Christy's evenly spoken words seemed to sink so deep inside of her. Maybe because Christy was one of the few people Katie didn't feel she had to prove herself to. Christy knew more about her than anyone. Way more than Rick knew about her. And Christy had always accepted Katie for who she was, what she was, and where she was during any particular stretch of life. Christy was the cream and sugar in Katie's cup of tea. She was everything a best friend should be.

And she was giving Katie the freedom to change her mind. To admit she was making a poor choice. To turn around and go back to the dorm.

"No, this is what I want to do," Katie said. "You drive. I'll read. You babysit. I'll write my paper. You drive to Bob and Marti's. I'll sleep in their cushy guest bed and eat their gourmet food. It'll all work out."

A smile settled on Christy's face.

"Why are you smirking?"

"I'm not smirking. I'm remembering. Remembering what I was going through a year ago when I was in your place, trying to finish my final semester and plan a wedding on top of everything."

"Well, I'm not planning a wedding. I can't even plan a bracelet."

"Plan a what?"

Katie's textbook went unopened as she caught Christy up on all the details about Rick and the cuddly, kissy date the night before. Katie described the brooch, the symbol of their happily-almost-after relationship and then slipped into the same sort of sure-unsure banter she had begun with Nicole that morning in the laundry room.

"It sounds as if I'm self-sabotaging, doesn't it? Why would I do that?"

"Your emotions are on a tilt-a-whirl," Christy said.

"I thought you would say my emotions are on a roller coaster."

"No. Roller coasters go up and down. You're in your final semester of college and deep in a serious relationship. I would say your emotions are on a tilt-a-whirl. You know, those carnival rides where you spin and fly around in a big circle and go up and down all at once."

"I know what a tilt-a-whirl is."

"So give yourself lots of grace, just like you gave me last year. Have you forgotten how impossible I was to live with?"

"I don't remember your being impossible to live with."

"Well, I remember." Christy reached over, and with one hand on the steering wheel, she gave Katie a comforting pat. "Don't try to push yourself too hard. Rick isn't pushing you. Just let things spin through all their cycles and come to their natural conclusion."

"Now you sound like Eli."

"I do?"

"Yeah, I was talking to him a few weeks ago about where I was going to live after I graduate, and he said I should go to Africa."

Christy laughed.

"I think he was half-serious. He said I should experience a whole circle of life before I got married, and he thought I would experience it if I went some place like Africa."

"He didn't really say 'circle of life,' did he?"

"I thought that's what he said. Or did I get that from *The Lion King*? My African references are overlapping. Must be that tilt-a-whirl effect you were talking about. Eli says my mind is full of wavy lines that wiggle all over the place, and when they intersect with another wavy line, I never know where one line stopped and the other started."

"Eli said that, did he?"

Katie nodded. "He's an observant guy."

"Yes, he is."

Katie opened her book and made an effort to find where she had left off reading earlier that week. It seemed as if one of her wavy lines had intersected another wavy line, and now her thoughts were off in faraway lands where giraffes galloped and lions crouched.

"Do you think I should go to Kenya?"

Christy looked at her and then back to the road. "When? Why?"

"I think I have a little crush on the idea of going to Africa."

Christy laughed.

"I think I just figured something out." Katie straightened her posture and nodded slowly. "I don't want to miss out on an adventure, do I? That's what it is, isn't it? I'm questioning my feelings for Rick because I'm afraid I might miss something if he and I move ahead and become engaged anytime soon. That must be why I keep feeling hesitant. I know what life will be like with him. Rick is a straight line up against all my wobbly lines. He sets a goal and goes after it."

"So do you."

"I know, but I love having the freedom to decide on a new goal every fifteen minutes. Rick picks one goal, and that's it for months. Years."

"That's a great leadership quality."

Katie nodded. "Yes, but we're still young. There's a lot of world out there to see. Don't you remember how great it was a few summers ago when you, Todd, and I traveled around Europe?"

A dreamy expression came over Christy's face. "I think about that trip a lot. Things were so simple then. I know I fretted and complained while we were traveling, but now I think it was one of the best things Todd and I did together before we got married. I loved being with him, and with you, and sharing so many amazing experiences together."

Katie leaned forward eagerly. "That's exactly what I'm saying. I want to have an experience like that with Rick before we get married. Or, well, if we get married. Before we get engaged at least. I want to experience new things with him. He and I have been stuck in a rut our entire dating relationship."

Katie crossed her arms and leaned back, contented and convinced. "It's settled. Rick and I need to go to Africa."

"And exactly how do you think Rick will take to that idea?"

Katie didn't answer immediately. "I can convince him. He'll see once I explain why we need to have this sort of experience. We'll go after I graduate, after the café opens. Just for a week or two. We'll go with Eli when he goes back. It will be sort of like when we were in

Europe and Antonio traveled with us in Italy and took us to his parents' home. If we go with Eli, he will show us around. This will be the most important and defining thing Rick and I have ever done together. I wonder when we need to take our typhoid shots. Soon, I would imagine. I think Eli said we have to get yellow fever shots as well."

"Whoa, Katie! Before you get immunizations against tropical diseases, don't you think you should talk to Rick about it?"

"Like I said, I'll convince him. What better time to go than this summer?"

Christy seemed to have run out of arguments. Katie took advantage of her silence to follow a wonderfully long, wavy line in her mind that contained bountiful information on Africa, Kenya, and the clean water project Eli's dad was involved in. After working on the clean water fund-raiser so closely with Eli, Katie knew a whole lot more about Africa than she had realized. She told Christy about the way the funds were making it possible for heavy drilling equipment to be taken into remote villages where people were dying from lack of clean water. New wells were being dug. Entire villages were becoming healthy after years of losing people to dysentery and disease.

"Eli said that the verse about offering a cup of cold water in Jesus' name is happening, literally, because of these wells, and children who were close to death now are becoming healthy. Schools are starting up, and crops are growing in areas that had become arid. It's a whole other world over there, Christy. So much needs to be done to help. Can you imagine how great it would be if Rick and I could go after I graduate and spend a month there just to help out?"

"So now it's up from a week to a month?"

"Or the whole summer. I think it would be incredible. The best thing we ever did. We can always settle down in suburbia, and he can always open another café. But this! A chance to go to Africa — this would be golden."

Christy didn't reply.

Katie's imagination swirled with possibilities. She felt happier than she had in a long time. "We can do this. It won't be that hard to pull it together. I should text Eli to find out what day he's leaving. The three of us could take the same flight."

"Katie, are you sure you want to do that without first giving Rick a chance to weigh in with his opinion?"

"I'm not telling Eli we're actually going; I'm just gathering information." Her thumbs had completed the text and were about to hit Send.

With a glance over at Christy, she said, "What's with the scowl? Do you think I'm moving too fast?"

"I think you hopped on a pretty wavy line, and it's taking you way off in a crazy new direction."

"Yeah, but why not?" Katie put down her phone. "I want to do this, Chris. Is there something wrong with me that I'd rather go to an African village after I graduate than go shopping for engagement rings and a wedding dress?"

"No, there's nothing wrong with you, Katie. Nothing at all."

"But you think I should slow down. Take it one step at a time."

"One step at a time is always a good way to go."

"Fine." Katie deleted the text message to Eli. "I'll talk to Rick first. And now I suppose you're going to tell me I should probably pray about all this."

"That's always a good way to go too."

Katie turned her focus back to her textbook while Christy drove. She knew she should pray but she wasn't quite ready to talk to God about all this. Not yet.

K atie faux studied for the rest of the drive to Carlsbad and the charming beach cottage where Doug and Tracy lived. The distance had given Katie time to roll out several of her wavy lines of thought and place them in nice straight rows. At least for the time being they appeared to be nice straight thoughts. When her thoughts were stretched out like this, they seemed dormant. Asleep. Unable to wiggle around in her imagination.

Katie felt as if all the zing had gone out of her. It was all too much to think about at the moment.

Doug met them at the door and wrapped his arms around Christy and then Katie, welcoming them with a warm, bolstering hug. Katie had forgotten how wonderful it felt to be on the receiving end of a Doug hug. She felt a smile rising inside her spirit as she entered Doug and Tracy's home. This cottage contained vivid memories of the night Christy and Todd became engaged. That was when Katie and Rick reconnected, talking all night and working side by side the next morning to make omelets for everyone. The happy feelings of the beginning moments of falling in love were floating in the air as Katie looked around and remembered sitting on the couch with Rick, exchanging smiles and feeling the first sprouts after a long winter of hidden hopes.

Note to self: You might be crazy for thinking about going to Africa. What you have with Rick is all you ever wanted. Remember?

Tracy stepped into the living room, her heart-shaped face glowing. "It's so good to see both of you! Thanks for doing this."

Baby Daniel was in her arms, shyly tucking his chin and cuddling up to Tracy.

"He's huge!" Katie blurted out. "How old is he now?"

"Almost nine months. Can you believe it? When was the last time you saw him?"

"I don't remember, but he was tiny," Katie said. "He slept most of the time."

"Those days are over," Doug said. "He's on the go all the time, aren't you, Danny boy?"

Blond-haired Daniel turned and looked at Katie and then bashfully curled back up to his mama.

"I was trying to get him down for a nap," Tracy said. "But I think he knows something is going on."

Christy put out her hands and smiled. In a soft voice she said, "Will you let me hold you? Come here."

It took a few minutes, but Daniel decided to warm up to Christy and let her take him from Tracy's arms.

"You have a way with kids," Katie said playfully.

"She does," Doug agreed. "Last time she and Todd were here, Daniel wanted her to hold him the whole time. Hey, we'd better slide out while we can. All the info is on the kitchen counter. We expect to be back around four."

"That's great," Christy said. "Have fun. We'll be fine here."

Christy walked into the kitchen with Daniel in her arms and went over to the sink while Doug and Tracy slipped out the front door. Katie watched as Christy pointed to a few small items in the windowsill above the sink and talked to Daniel in a low voice.

"You really are a natural with kids," Katie said.

"I learned a lot the year I worked at the orphanage in Switzerland. Little ones just want to feel safe. Isn't that right, Daniel? You remember me, don't you? Oh, you are so cute. Do you know how cute you are? You definitely have your mama's eyes."

"While the two of you have your little goo-goo fest, I'll retrieve my backpack from the car and write my paper." Katie strode out the front door, accidentally letting the screen door slam behind her. She cringed. A second later she heard Daniel wail.

Uh-oh. Not good.

The next three hours turned into the most challenging study time Katie could remember. She later conceded that she should have given up and just helped Christy keep Daniel entertained. He didn't nap, as the note from Tracy said might happen. He would be happy and interested in a toy one moment, then he would try to crawl over to where Katie had her laptop plugged into the wall. When Christy stopped him, he wailed.

"I had no idea kids could be so exhausting," Katie declared when Doug and Tracy returned. "How do you keep up with him? I mean, he's adorable, but you have to watch him every minute. He kept Christy going the whole time."

"I didn't mind a bit," Christy said. "He was perfect. Weren't you, Danny boy?"

Tracy gave Christy a hug. "You'll make a great mom. Both of you will."

Katie couldn't see herself as a mother. Not anytime soon, at least. She wondered if Todd and Christy were thinking of starting a family. It had been awhile since she had talked to Christy about any of the more personal details of her marriage to Todd. He was working as a youth pastor at their church and seemed to be busy all the time. Katie couldn't remember the last time she had seen him.

She would have to get an update from Christy once they were back on the road to Bob and Marti's house in Newport Beach.

Instead of leaving right away, they lingered awhile, talking with Doug and Tracy, who had used their time away to go house hunting. Their little cottage was too small now that Daniel was growing and Doug was working part-time from home on consulting projects for the financial investment business a relative had connected him with.

"Any leads on a house?" Christy asked.

"No," Tracy said. "We have a better idea of where we don't want to live and what's out there that we can afford. It doesn't look like we'll be moving anytime soon. We'll just have to be more creative with the space we have here."

"Rick was smart to grab both those café properties when he did," Doug said. "He gave me an update a few weeks ago, and I have to say, that was a smart business move. He and his brother look to make some good money."

"That's what he tells me," Katie said.

"You know, I was thinking the other day about when Rick, Todd, and I all shared an apartment back in our UC San Diego days. How long ago was that? Five years? No, it has to be at least six. Anyway, it's pretty awesome how everything has turned out, isn't it?"

Katie smiled. Not only had she forgotten the all-encompassing, warm, and affirming way Doug gave hugs, but she also had forgotten that *awesome* was his favorite word.

"Yeah, and speaking of awesome, who would have ever guessed that I would be the one to end up with Rick?"

"Not me!" Doug spouted. "You're the last one I would have ever ..."

Tracy shot him a look that caused him to backpedal.

"I mean, who would have ever guessed you guys would be the last of us to marry? You're the catch of the bunch, Katie. Rick is one blessed man ... I mean, that is, if the two of you are getting closer to ... to announcing any particular ..."

"Doug, you can stop anytime you want," Katie said.

"Good. I couldn't manage to bring up the nose on that one, could I? Crash and burn."

Katie smiled. She liked Doug. She always had. When it came to crash-and-burn comments, in the past, Katie was often the one heading the conversation into a nosedive, and Doug was the one offering her a parachute. It felt kind of nice, actually, to be the one handing out the crash-landing gear.

"On an unrelated topic," Tracy said, reaching for a small toy truck and handing it to Daniel, "what did the church board decide about Todd's position? Are they going to keep it as a full-time job?"

"What's this?" Katie asked.

"I didn't tell you yet, but Todd found out last week the church is cutting back on staff, and he's the last one they hired. They might cut his hours and ask him to go part-time. But they haven't asked yet."

"Part-time? How in the world could Todd do all that he does part-time? If anything, they should hire an assistant youth worker to help him out."

Christy shrugged. "They're going through a rough time at the church right now. So far, Todd still is employed. We'll see what happens though."

Katie had no idea anything out of the ordinary had been going on at the church. But then, she only came and went on Sunday mornings, and even then it wasn't every Sunday. That was one pattern from this past semester she planned to change once she finished school.

As a matter of fact, she remembered a conversation she had had with Todd several months ago. She had told him once summer arrived, she could volunteer to go on outings with the youth group as well as help out on Sundays and at events.

I guess I won't be much help to Todd if I go to Africa this summer. If he has to scale back to part-time, then he's going to need more help than ever.

Doug, Christy, and Tracy kept chatting, but Katie's attention flitted out of the conversation. She wondered if the same fluttering-flock-of-butterflies feeling she had when she first thought about going to Africa would be there if she helped with Todd's youth group. Was the anticipation of being free from school and studies what propelled her toward the rush of making new plans?

There's one thing I know for sure right now. My judgment on just about any given topic can't be trusted.

Katie confessed her feelings of uncertainty to Christy as they drove on Interstate 5 to Newport Beach. "It's the stress, isn't it? I think

I need to take a stress-reducing vitamin. Could you pull into the first drugstore you see? Maybe I need more calcium too. My fingernails haven't grown beyond their nub stage all semester. Milk has lots of calcium, right? Pull off on the next exit, will you?"

"What do you want? Vitamins or milk?"

"I was thinking more along the lines of a milkshake. I'm paying. When was the last time you had a thick, fat, happy, vanilla milkshake?"

"Chocolate," Christy corrected her. "If I'm going to drink that many calories, it's definitely going to be chocolate. And you're right. It's been far too long. Let's find a place that serves milkshakes before we get to my aunt and uncle's and Aunt Marti puts me on a soybean diet for the rest of our stay."

"Aunt Marti wouldn't do that!"

Christy laughed. "You don't know my aunt. The first summer I stayed with them I came down for breakfast one morning, and Uncle Bob was making waffles."

"Ooh, waffles. I'm so hungry right now." Katie crossed her arms across her middle.

Even though Tracy had said to help themselves to anything they wanted to eat, both Christy and Katie felt a little funny about raiding the sparsely filled refrigerator.

"So my uncle served me a hot waffle, complete with butter melting in every little square and just the right amount of warm maple syrup."

"Stop! You're torturing me!"

"That's exactly how I felt when my aunt walked into the kitchen and shrieked. Mind you, I was only fifteen and weighed at least ten pounds less than I do now. I was ready to take my first delicious bite, but my aunt Martha—"

"Ooh, I love it when you call her Martha! This is going to be good!"

"My aunt Martha comes marching into the kitchen, snatches the fork from my eager little hand, and whirls up something horribly nasty but decidedly nutritious in the blender. She tells me that's what a young lady should drink for breakfast if she wants shiny hair and clear skin, or whatever."

"Did you drink it?"

A playful grin edged up Christy's face. "No. I poured it down the drain — in front of my uncle, no less. I felt like the most rebellious teenager alive! Then I ate as much of the waffle as I could stuff into my face."

Katie laughed. "I don't think I ever heard that story. That's classic."

"Yes, it is. I'm glad we're going up there tonight. I need to feel young again."

"And maybe a little rebellious?"

Christy gave a mock expression of shock. "Rebellious? Oh, yes, please! What should we do? Leave our wet towels on the bathroom floor? Put our feet up on the coffee table? No, I've got it. We'll make waffles tonight for dinner. With syrup and whipped cream on top."

"You are in a snarky mood! No waffle making for me, though. Not after the cooking disaster I had at your apartment last fall with the microwave popcorn."

"I almost forgot about that." Christy put on the blinker, preparing to turn the car into a fast-food restaurant. "I bet they have shakes here. What do you think?"

"I think we're going to treat ourselves to large milkshakes for dinner. And french fries. We can dip the fries in our shakes."

Christy pulled the car up to the drive-through menu and waited for the attendant's voice to come over the loudspeaker. "We'll take two chocolate shakes and one large fry."

"No, make one of those vanilla," Katie piped in. "One vanilla shake and one chocolate. And make it two large fries."

"Will that be all?"

"Yes."

"Oh, look, chili-cheese dogs!" Katie was eyeing the rest of the menu. "And onion rings. I'm really hungry now."

"I'll have your total at the window," the attendant said.

They drove up and soon were handed two bulging bags of food. The attendant told them the amount, and it was much more than they expected.

"I think there's a mistake," Christy said. "We must have someone else's food. We ordered one large vanilla shake, one large chocolate shake, and two large french fries."

The attendant checked the order. "Right, and you also ordered two chilidogs and an onion ring."

"No, we didn't really order those," Katie said. "I was only saying, 'Oh, look, they have chilidogs and onion rings.' I wasn't ordering two chilidogs and an onion ring. Do you see what happened? I was merely commenting that you have them on your menu in case I would want to order them."

The attendant looked so confused that Katie said, "Never mind. Here, I'll pay. We'll take it all." She handed over more than was owed. "Keep the change. And have a nice day."

"Thank you!" The young woman looked grateful.

Christy drove off and said, "What are we going to do with all this food?"

Katie reached into the bag and pulled out a french fry. "Guess we'll have to eat it. Do you want me to put your straw in your shake for you?"

"Yes, thanks." Christy slipped her hand into the bag and pulled out a few fries. "They're hot. Nothing like a good hot french fry."

The two friends snacked all the way to Newport Beach. Even though they were ravenous when they left Carlsbad, both of them felt uncomfortably full by the time Christy wedged her Volvo into the narrow parking area near Bob and Marti's beach house.

"I feel like letting out a huge burp right now." Katie put her hand up to her mouth.

"Don't you dare! You have to mind your manners here, Katie. You know that, don't you?"

"Yes, of course I know that. What if we go in first, say our hellos, and then come back for the overnight bags? Then I can belch in private."

"Good idea."

They walked the familiar front walkway up to Bob and Marti's door. Christy knocked politely. A demure ruffle of a burp escaped from Katie's closed lips.

"Katie!" Christy whispered.

"Hey, I had my lips closed. You should be glad for that."

"Well, keep your lips closed so no more surprises leak out."

Just then the door opened with a jerk. Both Katie and Christy opened their mouths and nearly in unison drew in a gasp of surprise. The off-guard gasps were followed by unladylike hiccups.

Standing in front of them were two surprises.

8

T odd!"
      "Rick!"

"What in the world—hic—are you guys doing here?" Katie spouted between hiccups.

Rick and Todd looked pretty pleased with their surprise.

"Surprising you both," Todd said.

"It worked," Christy said with another hiccup. "Now you have to scare us so these hiccups will—hic—go away."

"Seriously, though." Katie pressed her cheek against Rick's chest and received his big hug while Christy and Todd gave each other a hello kiss laced with a hiccup.

"What's with the hiccups? What have you two been doing?" Rick asked.

"Just eating."

Todd lowered his voice. "Your aunt isn't going to like that. She made dinner reservations, and apparently you're late."

"Late?" Christy and Katie looked at each other and hiccupped again, followed by shared laughter.

"We didn't know we were supposed to be here at a certain time," Christy said.

"Christy, darling, is that you?" Aunt Marti's shrill voice called from the living room.

Rick put his finger up to his lips and gave Katie a warm grin. "She has plans. It seems best we just go along with them."

"By any chance would the two of you be part of her plan?" Katie asked.

"She called and asked if we could come up and surprise you."

"Why?" Christy asked. "What is she up to?"

"I have no idea. Come on in, and we'll find out."

"I need to get my bag out of the—hic—out of the car," Christy said.

"I'll get it for you," Rick offered.

"I'll go with you," Katie said. She and Rick walked hand in hand a few feet away from the front door before Katie felt an overwhelming need to burp. She put her hand over her mouth and tried to silence the culprit.

Rick turned and looked at her as the muffled belch rumbled behind her closed lips. "Are you okay?"

Katie nodded but didn't dare open her mouth quite yet. She felt much better. Her hiccups were gone as well.

The first thing Rick commented on when they opened the door to the car was the unmistakable scent of fast food. "What were you two eating?"

"Chilidogs and milkshakes. And onion rings and fries. But the chilidogs and onion rings weren't our idea."

"What?"

"Nothing. Never mind. The bags are in the trunk. So how did you manage to get away and come here? I'm stunned."

"Are you glad I came?"

"Yes, of course. Very glad. I thought I was going to spend my time here working on projects for school, but this is much better. It's going to be lots more fun being with you."

"And shopping for a car," Rick added.

"Oh, Uncle Bob told you?"

"Marti did." Rick closed the trunk, picked up both overnight bags and stood in front of Katie with a not-so-happy look on his face. "Why didn't you tell me, Katie?"

"Tell you what?"

"That you were ready to buy a car."

"I knew you were busy. I called Uncle Bob awhile ago and asked him if he could help me."

"I'm not so busy that I can't be there for you at times like this. I want to help you with important decisions. You know that, don't you?"

"Christy said I should have told you. I just got so busy, and to be honest, I didn't think you would mind."

"It's not that I mind. I mean, it's your car and your money. But I just don't understand."

"Don't understand what?"

"First of all, where did you find the money to buy a car, and second, why didn't you tell me?"

"Tell you about the money or about buying a car?"

"Both."

"Well, I ... I, um ..."

Rick looked impatient, standing there holding both bags.

"Can we go inside, and then I'll tell you the whole story? It's kind of long."

Rick's expression made it clear he didn't like that idea. Katie knew it would be impossible to talk with Rick privately once they were inside with Aunt Marti running the show.

"Okay, I'll just tell you. Actually, it's not that complicated. I've probably made it more complicated than it really is." Katie shifted her weight to her other foot. "I had a great-aunt who passed away, and she left me some money. I decided to use some of it to buy a new car. Well, actually, a used car. But it will be new to me."

Rick tilted his head and scrutinized Katie. Even when he was edgy, he looked handsome. His dark hair was longer than usual and hung across his forehead in a tussled sort of way that made him look as if he were ready for adventure, even though Katie knew his idea of adventure were meetings with a banker, a realtor, and a contractor all on the same afternoon.

Rick's next question came out slowly. "When?"

"When am I going to buy the car? Tomorrow, if everything works out."

"No, Katie. When did your great-aunt pass away?"

"I don't know. Almost a year ago, I think. I never met her. I didn't know about the money until my mom forwarded me the letter from the lawyer. That was last fall sometime."

"You never told me this."

"Well, a lot was going on at the time. You know Julia, my resident director? She helped me figure everything out. As a matter of fact, Rick, do you remember that day last fall when you and Josh were at the bank working on a business loan, and I was there with Julia?"

"I remember."

"That was the day I received the money and put it in the bank."

"And you didn't tell me until now? Why?"

"It was a lot of … it was … I don't know. It just seemed easier not to make a big deal of it."

Rick put down the bags and placed his hands on his hips. Katie didn't like this stance on Rick. She never had. This was his I'm-going-to-act-like-your-boss-now stance. She had never responded well at moments like this when she worked for him at the Dove's Nest Café.

"Katie, exactly how much money did your aunt leave you?"

"She was my great-aunt, actually."

"Please don't do that. Don't try to avoid the topic. Just tell me. I think I have a right to know when my girlfriend inherits a substantial sum of money. I would tell you if I had inherited money. How much was it?"

"I don't want to tell you." Katie felt defiant and irritated by Rick's approach.

"You don't want to tell me? Why?"

"It was a lot. Can we just leave it at that?"

"What's 'a lot'? Are you talking about ten thousand dollars? Twenty? Thirty?"

Katie kept her lips pressed together as Rick kept going up the scale. When he hit one hundred thousand dollars and her expression still hadn't flinched, Rick threw his arms up and turned away from her.

Spinning back around he shouted, "Katie, you have to be kidding me! You inherited more than one hundred thousand dollars?"

"I'm not saying."

"Your lips might not be saying, but your face is telling me everything." Rick paused, analyzing her more closely. "It was more than a hundred thousand, wasn't it? Was it more than two hundred thousand?"

When Katie still didn't flinch, Rick put both hands on top of his head and bellowed, "I can't believe this!"

Katie's heart was pounding with anger at Rick for pressing her when she had made it clear she didn't want to talk about this now.

"You're telling me you were sitting on more than what Josh and I needed for our start-up funds for the cafés, but you never told me. You never offered to make us a business loan so we wouldn't have to sell our souls to the bank at high interest. Why do you think I've been trying so hard to make a financial success of these cafés? Are you not seeing the importance of what we need for our future together, Katie? I can't believe this. I can't believe you kept this from me!"

A dozen comeback lines were on the edge of her fired-up spirit, but surprisingly Katie kept them all inside. For once in her life she held back. She knew she could ruin everything if she shot out the wrong response to Rick.

Instead of white-hot words flowing from her mouth, steaming silver tears flowed from her eyes.

Rick looked at her in the dimmed light from the streetlights and changed his expression. He went from Furious Rick to Neutral Rick. Katie knew he had rarely seen her cry. She just wasn't big on sobbing, especially around him. Now the tears were flowing so quickly that her vision turned blurry. A gasp caught in her throat, and she parted her lips just enough to let the wobbling, desperate sound escape.

"I don't get it," Rick said quietly. "What happened to our relationship, Katie? We were doing everything right. When did you stop trusting me? What else haven't you told me? What am I supposed to do with all this?" His voice rose. "Especially when you won't even tell me now. Why won't you tell me the amount? What have I ever done during the past year and a half that would make you withhold something as significant as this? Why don't you trust me?"

"I do trust you!" Katie choked out. "All I'm asking is that you trust me and not badger me to tell you!"

"If you trusted me, this wouldn't be an issue. We wouldn't be having this argument. Especially not now, when everyone inside is waiting for us, and we're supposed to be having a great time together. I can't believe this, Katie. All you had to do was tell me."

"Fine!" She knew she had flipped an internal switch and was running on raw response. Even though she had told herself she would never reveal to anyone the amount she had received, she spat it out in front of Rick and then grabbed her overnight bag and marched toward the house.

Rick hustled after her and grabbed her by the arm. The expression on his face was one of mixed delight and awe, shadowed by the still-present fury.

"That's why I never told you," Katie said in a lowered voice. "That look, right there. I never wanted you to look at me like that."

"Look at you like what?"

"Like I'm a big, juicy pork chop, and you haven't eaten in a week."

Rick pulled back. He loosened his grasp of Katie's arm. "Don't put that on me, Katie. I'm not like that."

"I don't want anyone to know, Rick. I mean it. No one! It's none of their business. If I ever find out that you told anyone—"

"Katie, honey, relax." He tried to hug her, but she pulled back and stayed rigid. All her tears were gone. Her jaw was set. She wanted to scream and stomp off to be alone long enough to calm down. This was the worst feeling in the world.

"I won't tell anyone. You have my word on that. But, Katie, you have to know that I'm not just anyone. It's me. Your boyfriend. Soon to be your fiancé."

Katie felt her face involuntarily flinch when he said "fiancé." It was the first time he had used the term outright.

"I'm not just anybody," he repeated.

Katie gave a slight nod. Something inside her softened just a little. Silently she admitted she should have told Rick. Even if she didn't want to disclose the amount, she could have been the one who controlled the information rather than ignoring the topic, putting herself at risk for the sort of revelation that had just occurred. She could have handled the whole thing better. Rick was her boyfriend and, according to him, soon to be fiancé. She should have told him.

"I'm sorry," she whispered.

Rick's strong arms were around her in an instant. "Me too. I didn't mean to blow up like that."

"It's okay. I shouldn't have kept this from you. You're my boyfriend."

Rick pulled back and repeated, "Yes, I am. I'm your boyfriend." A warm, affectionate look for her started in his eyes and moved to his mouth where a smile curled his lips as he added, "But not for long." Then he kissed her.

Katie didn't enjoy the kiss. She wasn't ready to kiss and make up. She would have preferred waiting until her emotions had receded and her heart had gone back to pounding at a less anxious rate.

Rick kissed her a second time, but she barely responded.

"Here, let me take the luggage for you. I'll go back to the car and get the other one."

"I'm going inside," Katie said.

"I'll meet you in there. And Katie? Let's put all this aside for the moment, okay? We can talk more later. I don't want anything to ruin our time together."

She nodded, but in her convulsing stomach she already felt that things were ruined.

As soon as she stepped inside the house, Christy met her with a concerned look on her face. "Everything okay?"

Katie was pretty sure Christy had glimpsed through the window by the front door what was going on outside.

With a nod, she said, "I need to use the restroom."

She stayed in the downstairs restroom longer than necessary. She knew the others were waiting for her. Aunt Marti would be flustered because of her undisclosed dinner plans. Rick would be weird. He always was weird when he went into his Neutral Rick mode. She liked it better when Rick was furious or flirty or joking around. The controlled, mild temperament he had been developing wasn't present in his life when she had such a killer crush on him back in junior high and high school. She liked knowing where she stood with him. Even during the long stretch when Katie was the school mascot and Rick never gave her the time of day, at least she knew what he thought of her.

The only feeling that Katie didn't mind experiencing in her encounter with Rick was the heart-melting sense of anticipation that came when Rick said "fiancé." He was serious about her, about them, about their future. Of course he would want to know about the money and to be called on as she made decisions on what to do with the inheritance.

"I've been thinking as an individual," she whispered to her reflection in the bathroom mirror. "If Rick and I are going to get married, I need to think in terms of 'us.'"

A tap sounded on the door. It was too soft a tap to be Aunt Marti. Had to be Christy.

"Katie, are you sure you're okay?"

Katie opened the door and offered her best friend a fully recovered smile. "My stomach ..."

"Mine too," Christy whispered. "Is everything okay with Rick?"

"Yeah, we're fine."

"My aunt changed the reservation. It's in twenty minutes. She's determined that all of us go to dinner at a particular Italian restaurant.

I told her you and I already ate. Uncle Bob suggested we order some pizzas and eat here. But you know my aunt; she won't hear of it."

"That's fine. I'm good to go. Do you need to get in here?"

"I do. Tell everyone I'll be ready in a minute."

Katie drew in a fresh breath and strolled calmly through the tastefully decorated house, making her way to the living room, where she knew everyone would be gathered. "Sorry for holding up the party." She faced Aunt Marti and gave her a half-curtsy, as if she were royalty. This wasn't at all in Katie's nature, but she had been around Christy's aunt enough to know that if she didn't put on the royal act, things could go bad quickly. After what had just happened with Rick, she was determined not to be the one to sabotage the evening.

Marti, a petite, dark-haired woman in her fifties, gave Katie a look of pardon. Marti was dressed in an outfit much nicer than the rest of them, but that was how it usually was with her. Her hair, makeup, and nails all were presented in top form.

Uncle Bob rose from the leather couch and gave Katie a side hug. "Great to have you back here, Katie. Rick went ahead and put your suitcase up in the guest room in case you need anything out of it."

Katie had avoided eye contact with Rick when she first entered the room. She glanced at him now, and he offered her a steady, affirming grin. He seemed unaffected by the upset they had gone through ten minutes ago.

Katie, however, still felt deeply affected. More affected than she wanted to admit to anyone, especially to herself.

9

O nce all six of them were seated in the amber-lit restaurant, Marti clicked into her typical high-style form. The restaurant owner came over to the table and greeted Bob and Marti by name. Marti introduced the "young people" around the table and treated the gathering as if it were her birthday and all her grown children had come home to see her.

Both Katie and Christy ordered small dinner salads. Rick and Todd made up for the women's slight orders and went all out. Katie could hardly look at Todd's full plate of lasagna or watch Uncle Bob use the edge of his fork to cut into his eggplant parmesan.

During most of the dinner, Marti peppered Rick with questions about the cafés. He opened up with even more details than Katie knew about. Then came the clincher question. It sprang from Marti along with a wry grin just as Bob was paying the bill.

"So you haven't given any specifics about the news we're all waiting to hear." Marti looked at Katie and then back at Rick. "Have the two of you set a date yet? Fall weddings are always so lovely. Late fall. After all that wretched heat from the Santa Ana winds subsides. Early November, perhaps. That would give you seven months of planning. Almost eight. Christy and Todd only gave me six months to help plan their wedding."

Since Bob and Marti had no children of their own, they had been vitally involved in Christy's life. It now appeared that Marti expected to have the same sort of influence over Rick and Katie's future.

Katie spoke up. "We're not there yet, Marti."

Marti blinked at Katie's evenly spoken comment and turned her head toward Rick, as if he would give a different answer than Katie had.

"We're still in the happily-almost-after stage." Rick turned to Katie and gave her a wink.

"The happily-almost-after stage?" Marti repeated. "What is that supposed to mean?"

"It means they're taking their time and figuring things out on their own." Bob's tone emphasized the words *on their own*.

Undaunted, Marti turned to Katie. "You do know, don't you, Katie dear, that when the time does come, Robert and I want you to call on us for anything? Anything at all. We hope both of you will think of us as your own aunt and uncle. We would love to be involved in your plans."

"Thank you, Marti, Bob." Rick gave each of them a nod. "That means a lot to us."

When no one else at the table responded to Rick's comment, he added, "Doesn't it, Katie?"

Even though Katie didn't feel particularly warm and fuzzy about the way any of this was going, she did appreciate the support. "Yes. Your support means a lot."

She then reminded Bob and Marti about her hope that they would come to her college graduation. Possibly the decoy topic of her graduation would divert Marti from Rick and Katie's yet unannounced engagement and unplanned wedding date.

Bob gave Katie a smile and answered, "We'll be there for you, Katie. I have your graduation on the calendar already."

"Be sure to add April 27 to your calendar," Rick said. "That's the date the Redlands café' opens."

Marti seemed less than enthusiastic about committing to the opening of Rick's café. She rose from her chair, indicating it was time to leave. "I thought you young people might enjoy going for a short walk. Does that appeal to everyone?"

No one protested. They all seemed to know it didn't really matter if the idea appealed to them. Marti was at the helm.

Rick took Katie's hand as the group strolled through the open-air shopping plaza where the Italian restaurant was located. Southern California was shamelessly showing off her mild climate, the way a gleeful three-year-old shows off her new party dress with a twirl. The air was warm and calm.

Katie caught a whiff of the star jasmine that grew liberally in the open areas throughout the plaza. "What a beautiful night."

Rick slowed down and pulled Katie close. He kissed her.

"What was that for?"

Rick gave her a playfully exaggerated look. "On a night like this, do I need a reason?"

"I suppose not." She gave his hand a squeeze, and they kept walking.

Even with the sweet kiss, the fragrant air, and the beautiful night, Katie didn't feel quite right. Her emotions were on the surface like a rash that she should know better than to scratch.

In the back of her mind, her original plan to work hard on her paper in a quiet corner of Bob and Marti's guest room rankled. Instead, they were on a guided tour for the evening, and she was pretty sure tomorrow would hold more of the same.

"You know, maybe this was a bad idea," Katie muttered.

"What was a bad idea?"

"My coming here for the weekend. I have so much to do. You do too. Maybe I should have stayed in the dorm, locked in my room all weekend. I'm too far behind on everything. I don't know what I was thinking when I agreed to come here overnight."

"Hey." Rick stopped walking and tilted her chin up with his free hand. "What happened to the Katie who is always saying things like, 'go with it' and 'live in the moment'? What happened to the Katie who does everything on a whim?"

"I'll tell you what happened to her. She started her final semester of college."

"And she is almost done with her final semester of college."

"Almost. But I have so much to do."

"Relax, Katie. When was the last time you and I had a chance just to be together and enjoy some down time?"

"I don't know. A long time. Christmas, maybe?"

"Even then we were on the go. Listen, it wasn't easy for me to take all this time off so I could be with you."

"I know. Thanks, Rick."

Katie gave his hand a squeeze, and they picked up their pace to catch up with the others. She still couldn't shake the reality that, even though she knew leaving campus for the weekend was a bad choice, she had chosen to do it anyway.

One thing she did know for certain. She was the only one who could take responsibility for her choices. For a brief moment, she wondered what other poor choices she might have made lately.

"You know, it's probably a good thing I haven't decided what to do with your grandmother's brooch yet."

"Why do you say that?"

"I don't think I've been making good decisions lately. I think it's all the stress. Do you feel that way too? It never seems to let up."

"I know. That's how my life is right now too. Nonstop. But it's all for good reasons. Things will change soon enough."

"I'll believe it when I see it."

Rick drew her closer in a side hug. "Whatever you do, Katie, don't go hormonal on me, okay?"

She pulled back and gave him a searching gaze. She couldn't tell from his expression if his comment was serious or if he was trying to give her a hard time. She chose to go with the belief that he was teasing her and quipped, "And you promise me you won't go macho and know-it-all. Especially when it comes to picking out cars tomorrow."

They were at the parking lot. Todd and Christy decided to ride with Bob and Marti, leaving Rick and Katie alone in Rick's car. Rick drove out of the covered parking structure and nonchalantly said, "So aside from buying a new car tomorrow, what are you thinking about doing with the money?"

"A used car."

Rick glanced at her. "Why not buy a new one?"

"I want to get a used one. Not very old. Low miles and all that. It's a better route to go economically."

"Okay."

When Katie didn't respond to his first question, he once again asked, "Anything else you're thinking about buying?"

"No."

"Oh, come on Katie, let's not do this."

"Do what?"

"This game with the short answers and roadblocks. This isn't the way you and I communicate. Talk to me. I want to know what you're thinking about the inheritance."

She let out a long, low breath. "I'm not ready to discuss all this, Rick."

"Why not?" The irritation in his voice escalated.

"I'm just not. I need to think things through some more."

"I know you need to think it through. That's exactly what I'm saying. You have a lot of big decisions to make." Rick's tone softened. "All I'm saying is that I want to be the one who helps you think through everything, that's all. Is it wrong for me to want that in our relationship?"

"I don't know. Probably not."

He waited until the traffic light changed before asking his next question. "Can you see any particular reason this is difficult for you to talk about with me? I mean, do you see me as not being on your side or as being out of line in any way?"

"No."

"Then what is it? What's bothering you? Why can't we talk about this?"

Katie gave him the first answer that came to mind. "I think you're not going to like my choices."

Rick let out an odd sort of snorting laugh that wasn't typical of him. "Why wouldn't I like your choices?"

"You just wouldn't." Katie knew that if Rick found out she had already spent more than half the money on things like tuition scholarships and the clean water for Africa campaign that she and Eli had worked on, he would flip out. Also, a large amount went out earlier that year when she paid her taxes.

With all her heart, she wished she hadn't told him the amount of the inheritance. "The way I see it, Rick, if you and I are going to truly relax and enjoy being together tonight and tomorrow, then I'm telling you, you have to drop the inheritance topic. Just drop it. I promise I'll talk with you about everything when my mind is clear. Right now, it's not a good idea for me to talk about it."

From the way his profile changed as his jaw set forward in frustration, Katie knew Rick didn't like her declaration. His face flinched slightly, and then he said in a flat voice, "If that's the way you want it to be."

Katie leaned back and stared out the front windshield. She told her shoulders to relax.

Neither of them spoke the rest of the short drive to Bob and Marti's. When they got out of the car, Christy and Todd were laughing about something and looking as if they had all shared a lighthearted trip.

"We have cheesecake," Bob said to them as Rick and Katie entered the house with everyone else. "Either of you ready for some dessert?"

"Sure," Rick said. "Do you need any help in the kitchen?"

"Not necessarily. Although you're pretty comfortable in the kitchen, if I remember correctly."

"He's a great cook," Katie said. "As a matter of fact, you should have Rick make omelets for everyone in the morning. That is, if you don't mind turning your stove over to a genius."

Rick gave Katie a confused look, as if he couldn't tell if she were praising him or mocking him. She realized she was overdoing it. The fast-flung compliment was overcompensation for the thin line of tension that still lay between them like a tightrope. All evening neither of them had managed to walk all the way across that communication tightrope without slipping off and falling into the safety net below. That safety net was the longevity of their relationship. They had bounced back from arguments and tense conversations plenty of times. Katie believed they could do so yet again.

Unfortunately, that never happened. For the next two hours, everything Rick or Katie said was misinterpreted not only by each other but also by Marti. By the time Katie found her way upstairs to the newly remodeled guest room, she felt like crying.

That wasn't her style at all.

The sleeping arrangements were a little odd. Marti insisted that Christy and Katie take the upstairs guest room while Todd was assigned the sofa in the family room and Rick was relegated to a blow-up mattress on the living room floor. It was as if they were back in high school.

"You and Todd should be sleeping together in this bed," Katie said once she and Christy were under the fresh sheets of the guest bed. "I'd be more comfortable on the air mattress than Rick. Todd should be here, Rick should be on the sofa in the family room, and I should be on the air mattress."

Instead of answering Katie's objection, Christy said, "Hey, listen, whatever you and Rick are going through right now, I know it must be frustrating and confusing, but I think it will all work out, Katie. You don't have to tell me what it is, but I know things are bumpy for you guys. I've been praying for you both all evening."

Katie didn't respond. She stared at the ceiling in the darkened room and listened to the faint but steady roll of the ocean waves as the ageless melody of the sea floated through the half- open bedroom window. Even though Katie knew she could tell Christy anything and that her best friend would stay up with her all night if necessary to talk through all Katie's feelings, Katie didn't want to talk.

Again, that wasn't her style. She didn't know what was going on with her.

"Thanks, Chris," she whispered after a pause that brought no peace. "Sleep well."

"You too, my peculiar treasure friend."

Christy's words sailed across the surface of Katie's confused heart like a well-aimed pebble. Each place the sentiment touched produced a small, expanding circle, pushing Katie into a flustered state. Now nothing inside her felt settled.

Within a few minutes, Katie could tell by Christy's easy breathing that she had fallen asleep. During their year as college roommates, Katie had come to know the sound of Christy's sleeping. She also knew how deeply Christy could go in her sleep pattern once she dove into dreamland.

As exhausted as she was, Katie lay awake, her eyes fixed on the faint shadows across the room caused by the dim nightlight in the adjoining bathroom. Instead of the waves' sound lulling her to sleep, it seemed to have the opposite effect. With each curl and unfurl, Katie prayed.

What is it, God?

Are you trying to tell me something?

What?

Is all this unsettledness just normal emotions, hormones, or whatever? Or am I losing it? I'm about to go berserk, aren't I?

I hate feeling so unsettled like this. What's my problem?

Christy stirred in her sleep and turned toward Katie. Christy reached over, and her hand fell on Katie's arm. She snuggled closer, leaning her head into Katie's shoulder.

"Hey, I'm not Todd," Katie murmured.

Christy didn't retract. She continued her even-paced breathing with her cheek gently resting against Katie's shoulder and her hand on Katie's forearm.

You and Todd sleep together.

The thought had an odd effect on Katie. Of course she knew that Christy and Todd slept together. That intimacy between them as husband and wife was an obvious part of what had changed after they married.

However, this close, cuddly sort of connection between them every night was something Katie never thought much about. What would it be like to go to bed each night and have the man you love be right there beside you, breathing peacefully and welcoming you into his arms?

Katie could see Christy and Todd sleeping like this every night. Close, cozy, and invisibly knit together forever at the heart.

As soon as that thought came to her, Katie felt her throat tighten. As if a clear and steady light suddenly had turned on inside her head, she could see, really see, what the problem was with her emotions and, more deeply, with her spirit. This wasn't hormonal. This was true at the gut level.

The old, on-a-whim Katie was back. She knew what was wrong. She knew what she needed to do.

And she knew she needed to do it now.

10

Rick?" Katie knelt down to where her sleeping boyfriend lay on his side on the air mattress. She placed her hand on his shoulder and gently shook him. "Rick, wake up."

He stirred and slurred his words as he said, "What's wrong?"

"I need to talk to you."

Rick rolled over and drew in a deep breath. "Katie?"

"Yeah, it's me. I need to talk to you."

"Now?"

"Yes. I need to talk to you now."

"What time is it?"

"I don't know. Can we go into the kitchen?"

"The kitchen? Why?" He propped himself up on his elbow and blinked at her in the dimly lit room. "What is it, Katie? What's the problem?"

"Us."

"What?"

"Please get up. Let's go talk in the kitchen. Please."

By all the grunts and heavy exhaling Rick did, Katie was aware that he wasn't happy about her midnight 911.

"Can't this wait until morning?" He followed her to the kitchen.

"No, I don't think it can. I'm sorry to be so dramatic and wake you up and everything, but I couldn't wait. I figured it out, and I knew I had to talk to you right away."

They stepped into the kitchen, and Katie flipped on the light switch. The brightness momentarily blinded both of them. She slid over to the stools tucked under the counter and sat down. Rick lowered himself onto the stool next to her. His hair was sticking up funny on the side he had been sleeping on, and his face was scrunched up in an unpleasant expression.

"What is it, Katie? Is it the money?"

She was surprised that the inheritance was the first topic his mind had gone to. But then again, she wasn't surprised.

"No, it's not the money. It's us. Our relationship."

"What about our relationship?"

"We're not knit together at the heart, Rick." Her voice came out cracked and full of all the clarifying pain she had felt when the revelation came to her a few moments ago.

"What in the world are you talking about?"

"You and me—us—it's not a good idea anymore. We're not meant for each other. We need to see things as they are and call it a day. Or a year. Or actually more like half my life. It's what it was, and now it's over."

She felt her throat tightening. This was more difficult to say than she expected. But then, this wasn't something she planned or ever expected to say.

An angry shadow fell across Rick's face. "Katie, what are you doing?"

"I'm ... I'm breaking us up."

"No, you're not," he snapped.

"Yes, I am! I'm breaking up with you, Rick Doyle."

"No, you're not." He shook his head and growled, "We aren't breaking up, Katie. It's not going to happen."

"Yes, it is going to happen. It's happening now. I'm breaking us up because I just figured it out. You and I have gone as far as our hearts can carry us. This is it. We're not knit together at the heart, and I don't think we ever will be."

Rick rose and stood over Katie with his hands on his hips. "This is insane. You're insane. Do you know what you're doing? You're ruining this weekend. Completely ruining everything. It's the stress, isn't it?"

"No, it's not the stress."

"I think it is. Why else would you do this? I think you're letting the stress of school get to you. It's just school. You're never even going to use the stuff you're writing papers on now. All you have to do is make it through these last few weeks without doing anything stupid, and then you're going to graduate and—"

"Yeah, and then what?"

"You're going to come work for me."

Katie pulled back, stunned. "What? Work for you?"

She had thought he was going to say, "After you graduate, we're going to get engaged" or "We're going to plan our life together." His answer confirmed everything Katie's gut had told her upstairs in the darkened guestroom.

"I'm not going to work for you, Rick. I'm not going back to the café."

"Why not?"

"That's not what I want to do."

He towered over her, scowling and blinking. "Since when did you decide that?"

"Since always. We never talked about my working for you. You made that up. I never said I wanted to do that."

"But you did last summer."

"That was then. This is now."

"Okay, fine. Don't come work at the café. But if you don't work for me, what do you want to do?"

Katie set her jaw firmly. "I want to go to Africa."

Rick stared at her as if he suddenly had no idea who this woman in front of him was.

"Actually, I wanted both of us to go to Africa."

"What are you talking about? I would never go to Africa. Never. Not for any reason. You've heard Eli talk about Africa. Why would you want to go there?"

Katie held out her hands palms up and said, "This is exactly what I'm talking about. It's obvious. We're not knit together at the heart, Rick. Don't you see?"

He folded his arms across his chest, keeping both hands in fists. "I … you … you know what? I think both of us should go back to sleep and start fresh in the morning. This is a nightmare. You're acting out a nightmare, Katie. That's what this is. Some sort of stress-induced, hormone-overloaded nightmare. It's insane. You're insane."

"No, I'm not."

Rick raised his voice and his height. "We are not breaking up, Katie."

Katie kept her gaze fixed on him and stated firmly and evenly, "Yes, we are."

"No, we're not!"

She rose and stood with her shoulders back and her chin up as she gave him a look that expressed her determination. "I am breaking up with you, right here, right now. This has nothing to do with my hormones. This is in my heart, and I will not change my mind. Tomorrow morning we will still be broken up. And I know that once you get over being furious with me, you'll see this is right. This is true. This is as far as we go, Rick."

Rick didn't budge. He stared at her with vivid anger. Neutral Rick didn't return as was usually the case when they argued. Instead, Katie was looking at the true Rick. He was furious, and he should be. She liked him better this way, true to his emotions. She knew that she was being a thousand percent true to her heart and her emotions. This was right.

Rick marched past Katie and exited the kitchen, leaving her alone at the counter with all the lights on. She lowered herself onto the kitchen stool and sat for a long time, letting the reality of what had just happened roll over her. Her heart was pounding, and her hands were shaking. Her bare feet felt tingly from the cold floor.

Katie stared at the clock on the microwave. The green digital numbers clicked to 1:11.

A painful wince caught in her throat. A parade of memories came to her of the times she had spent with Rick in kitchens. Doug and Tracy's kitchen was where they first had started their flirt-fest that led to this long relationship. The kitchen of the Dove's Nest Café had been the location of many moments for them—mostly good ones. And in Rick's apartment kitchen Katie had challenged him to express his feelings for her and demonstrate them outwardly by kissing her.

She and Rick had shared a lot of life together. Had she done the right thing by breaking up with him? She thought so, but at the same time she realized that the way she had handled the unveiling of her decision hadn't been fair to him. He hadn't seen this coming. She could have waited. They could have done this differently. But if she had waited, she had a feeling she would have talked herself out of it.

Katie's sensitivity to how Rick was feeling right then came over her with heart-pounding intensity. She loved him. She knew she did. She never wanted to hurt him.

"I'm sorry, Rick." Her whisper was far too soft to reach his ears, but her small words were nonetheless sincere.

What have I done?

With urgency rising up inside her to try to smooth things out, Katie paced the floor. *What if I go into the living room and apologize? I'll tell him I still think we should break up, but I realize I didn't handle it well, and I'm sorry I hurt him. And, by the way, Rick, I still love you, even though I know we're not supposed to be together anymore.*

No, I can't do that.

Katie chewed on the cuticle of her thumbnail, trying in vain to think of a way to take the sting out of all this. But the only way she could think of to make things better was to go into the other room and retract everything. If she apologized profusely, she knew Rick would forgive her and take her back. He would wrap his arms around her, and the calming sensation of his closeness, his touch, his deep voice would make her feel happy.

But for how long?

A tear rolled down her cheek.

This really is the end. It's over between us. It really is.

A chorus of soft tears rose from the depths of Katie's heart and cascaded down her face in mournful unison. With them came the painful, certain affirmation that this was right. Everything she had said to Rick was true. This was as far as they could go. Her delivery of that truth may have been less than compassionate. But she knew she couldn't do anything to change the circumstances—short of an elaborate apology and passionate plea for reconciliation. And she knew she couldn't do that.

Her relationship with Rick Doyle was over.

Turning off the kitchen light, Katie returned to the guestroom as quietly as possible and crawled back into bed. The tug of war continued. She tried once more to work out a scenario in which she could go downstairs and wake Rick again. Could they talk this through? Would he see that she was right? Would he agree to be good friends on the spot and stick around tomorrow to help her shop for cars?

No, this wasn't the time for that conversation.

A shiver ran up her legs as she rubbed her cold feet together, trying to warm them. Sleep seemed the only right answer to anything at this point.

Katie could feel herself letting go. In time to Christy's even breathing, Katie released everything—Rick, their relationship, her future, all her strained emotions. She felt her weary spirit sinking into the rest that had eluded her for far too long.

Under the covering of blessed sleep, Katie let go.

When she awoke, she knew by the amount of sunlight streaming into the room that the morning was half spent. Christy's side of the bed was vacant, and the house was quiet. Katie lay in the stillness without moving.

Her mind systematically reviewed the drama she had initiated in the middle of the night.

I broke up with Rick.

A tightness constricted her throat, and a queasy feeling rolled around in her stomach. But her heart felt oddly settled.

Did I do the right thing, Father? I did, didn't I? I shouldn't change my mind, should I?

The strange, fixed sense of peace remained.

"This is weird. This is so way weird. I shouldn't feel this calm, should I? Unless that's you, God. Is it? Is this what I'm supposed to feel right now?" Katie sat up and looked around the empty room. For some reason, God felt close.

She wondered if Rick felt any of these same feelings. Had he come to the same conclusions during the night? Had he told the others yet? How would the rest of this day roll out? Would Rick still want to be involved in helping her to shop for a car, or would he just want to be on his way back to the café?

Katie knew she had messed up the whole weekend, just as Rick had said. She also knew she couldn't have gone through today faking that everything was great in their relationship. No, not after the defining realization that had come in the middle of the night. None of what she had done was smooth or particularly considerate of Rick, but she somehow knew it was right.

Pressing her feet to the floor, Katie went through a pace of quick steps to shower, dress, and head downstairs.

The house was quiet. No one was in the living room. The air mattress Rick had slept on was put away. The Sunday morning paper and two coffee mugs rested on the coffee table.

Katie made her way to the kitchen and found Marti at the kitchen sink, rinsing off a cluster of red grapes.

"Hi."

Marti spun around. In one swift motion she turned off the water, put the grapes on the counter, and dried her hands with a towel.

"Well, at last! You certainly had an extravagant sleep."

Katie brushed off the twinge of guilt that seemed to ride Marti's comment and asked, "Where is everyone?"

Marti looked at Katie as if the answer should be obvious to her. "Rick left sometime in the middle of the night. I found a note from him on the coffee table, apologizing for the inconvenience. We assumed it must have been an emergency with the café. What a disappointment that he had to leave and ruin this time for the two of you. He really needed to be here to help you to decide on your new car."

Katie felt her jaw clench and a wave of sadness tighten her stomach.

"Of course, Bob, Todd, and Christy went to church." Her tone gave away how much she disapproved of that particular choice. "Christy said she tried to wake you, but you wouldn't budge."

Katie nodded.

"I believe our guestroom is the quietest room in the house. Now that we've redecorated it, it is quite an oasis, isn't it? Did I show you what we did with our bedroom? I don't think you were in the house last night when I took Christy and Todd upstairs to show them. Come with me. I'll show it to you now."

In a crazy little way, Katie was glad she was with Aunt Marti. She hadn't considered the possibility of Rick's leaving in the middle of the night, but she didn't blame him. She knew she would have done the same thing if she were in his position. Katie also was relieved that no one knew the real reason for Rick's departure. It was better that way.

Typical Rick Doyle. Manners over mayhem every time. His mother trained him well. I feel like I should call him. What would I say? No, don't call yet. It's better to wait. I shouldn't call him. We both need space and time so that this can sink in.

Katie followed Marti upstairs to view the redecorated master suite. Marti chattered the whole way, but Katie tuned her out in favor of giving space for all her morning-after thoughts and feelings.

If no one knows that I broke up with Rick in the middle of the night, I wonder if I can keep a poker face the rest of the day. I have a car to buy, a paper to write, and a long drive back to school. It would be fantastic if I could press forward on all this without getting tangled up in my emotions. I did the right thing by breaking up with Rick. I know I did.

Didn't I?

Oh, this is going to be more difficult than I realized. I didn't think this through, did I?

I should call him. No. Well, maybe later. On the way home.

Katie entered the master bedroom, which was decorated in an elaborate Mediterranean style with sheer, flowing curtains billowing in the late-morning breeze. "It's beautiful, Marti."

Marti continued the tour, going on in great detail while Katie made appropriate ooh and ahh sounds. Inwardly, Katie was in another place. A place of wiggly lines. And in that place, she was trying to put together a plan for how the next few days needed to line up.

She knew Rick and she would end up having a long conversation before the week was over. He was a master of exit interviews for people who had worked at the Dove's Nest. He was good about closure and liked checking off unfinished tasks from his continual lists. While Katie certainly wasn't a task, she was a big part of his life and had been for a long time. They would need time for an extensive conversation. Katie wanted a few more days to organize her wiggly lines before that conversation.

Marti invited Katie to join her on the newly expanded deck that extended from the master suite through French doors. Two elaborate lounge chairs with extra-thick, padded blue cushions awaited them.

"This is one of my favorite spots in the house." Marti stretched out on one of the loungers. A canvas umbrella in a fixed stand between the loungers provided shade. Just over the railing of the deck was an expansive view of Newport Beach. The caramel-colored sand stretched wide and far in both directions, dotted only by strategically placed lifeguard stations and weekend beachgoers. Beyond the sand, the gray blue ocean spread out like a wrinkled blanket all the way to the horizon. Overhead, the late morning sun tossed out its golden rays up and down the beach for free.

"It's beautiful here," Katie said.

"Yes, it is, isn't it? I keep telling Robert we should move, but then a day like this shows up, and I find myself quite content here on my balcony." She extended her arm in a sweeping gesture of the beach and ocean before them. Katie thought Marti looked as if she might start singing an aria from an opera.

"I think I'll go for a walk," Katie said before Marti had a chance to continue. "When do you think Bob and the others will be back?"

Marti checked her watch. "An hour. Maybe less. I made reservations for us for lunch."

"Of course you did."

Katie realized the thought had popped out of her mouth. With a sheepish grin, she quickly added, "You're always good about taking care of us that way. I'll be back in less than an hour."

With a slightly wounded tone, Marti said, "Take your phone. I'll have Robert call you when they get back."

Katie left before her mouth got her into any more trouble with Marti.

What is with my timing? I don't want to be insensitive to other people. Just because I think something, I don't have to spout it. I have to work on that.

Grabbing her phone as well as her sunglasses, she took off for the beach. With her sandals in one hand and her cell phone in the other, she wedged her bare feet deep into the cool sand.

Some good times had taken place at this beach. Katie knew that Christy had lots more memories around the fire pits and along the shore than she did, but her memories were golden nonetheless. Doug had tried to convince her once that a shark was after her in the water. Antonio had fun teasing her the day they were here. She and Christy had walked and talked along the water's edge one evening at sunset and shared their dreams for the future with each other. As long as Katie could remember, Rick had been that hint of a dream in the back of her mind. He was always her "what if" guy. And now the "what if" had become a "what was."

Katie stared out across the expanse of greenish blue and blinked back the misty cloud of tears that surfaced without an invitation. She wished Christy were with her now. Her forever friend would help her to make sense of everything she was feeling.

Settling in the sand, Katie drew in a deep breath and turned to her true Forever Friend. The one who promised he would never leave her or disown her.

"At least you and I are knit together at the heart, aren't we, God? Yeah, we are. You and me, Lord. So go ahead and tell me: Am I a train wreck, or am I on the right track? Have I made too big of a mess of everything? Is Rick going to be okay? Is this just how life is? Tangled and messy? Nothing for me has ever seemed clear or clear-cut. Is it normal for someone who is sincerely trying to follow you with all her heart to end up in such a mess all the time?"

Just then her cell phone vibrated. She assumed Bob was calling to say they were back. Katie regretted that her heart-to-heart conversation with God was being cut short.

Without looking at the caller ID, she answered with, "I'm on my way back to the house right now."

Eli's voice responded. "Katie, are you okay?"

"Oh, Eli. Hi. I thought you were someone else. Yeah, I'm okay. I don't know if Rick is, though. What did he tell you? I'm sure he's still pretty upset. I wish I'd been more—"

"Katie," Eli interrupted her, "I'm not following you."

"You talked to Rick, right?"

"No, not since Thursday afternoon."

"Oh." She switched the phone to her other ear. "Wait, then why did you ask if I was okay?"

"I left you a couple of messages on your phone and texted you. Did you get the messages?"

"No. I didn't look. What were the messages?"

"I, um, I thought something was wrong. That something had happened."

"When?"

"Last night. I sensed a really strong prompting to pray for you."

"You did?"

"Yeah. I prayed for a while and then—"

"Eli, when were you praying for me? What time last night?"

"It was sometime between midnight and one. My heart felt really heavy for you."

Katie was a little creeped out and a little in awe at the same time.

"Katie? Are you still there?"

"Yeah. I just can't believe God woke you up to pray for me in the middle of the night."

"So are you okay?"

Katie drew in a deep breath of the brisk ocean air before speaking the words aloud to anyone for the first time. "I ... I broke up with Rick."

11

Five days after Katie told Eli she had broken up with Rick, she was standing next to Eli in Crown Hall's parking lot. They stood practically shoulder-to-shoulder, examining her new-used car. Eli's campus security golf cart was a few yards away. He had clicked off the engine and hopped out when he saw Katie leaving her car.

"So are you going to name this one 'Baby Hummer 2'?" Eli asked.

"No, there was only one Baby Hummer." Katie ran her thumb over a white scratch on the door of the Subaru Outback. The deep green car had the rectangular shape of a small SUV. "This one looks more like a Baby Land Rover."

"We had a Land Rover when I was little."

"What did you call it?"

Eli shot Katie a wry grin. "Same thing we called all the vehicles in the compound. 'Car.' That way all we had to do when we wanted to go somewhere was call, 'Here, Car. Come, Car.' Whichever one happened to miraculously be working at the time would come running."

"Cute," Katie said. She smirked at Eli and took one more walk around her new car. "I could call her 'Mini Rover' or 'Red Rover.' Except she's green."

"Green Rover?" Eli suggested.

Katie thought another moment, and the name came to her. "Clover! She's not green like a Rover; she's green like clover. Clover the mini-Rover. I like it. What do you think?"

"I think you are the only person I know who names her car."

Katie turned her attention on Eli. Now that his curly brown hair was growing out, it gave him a free-as-the-wind and wild-as-the-ocean look. It was a good look on him.

Katie was about to tell him how great his hair looked, but then she suddenly felt awkward. This was the first time she had talked to Eli since their phone call on the beach, and she knew she had opened up far too much to him in that call.

She knew at the time she would have been better off talking over her deeply personal feelings with Christy. But at the moment, when she needed a friend, Eli was the one who was there for her as she sat alone on the beach. He listened to everything she spilled out, and then he said he was going to be praying for her and for Rick.

"So has Rick said anything to you yet?" Katie asked.

"No. We've been together at the apartment a couple of times, but he didn't bring it up, nor did I. I think it would be good if you told him that you and I have talked about your breakup. I don't want him to feel caught off guard."

"Yeah, you're right. I'll tell him the next time we talk. He sent me flowers yesterday. This is a lot harder than I thought it would be."

"Are you still certain you made the right decision?"

"Yes." Katie nodded and looked down at the keys in her hand. "I know it was the right decision. The timing and my wording really stunk, but, yeah, I still know that Rick and I went as far as our hearts would take us. I know that."

"You need to talk to him."

"I know."

Eli stood beside her, not saying anything. She again noticed the L-shaped scar on the side of his neck. She had always wondered if Eli had surgery on his throat or if the scar was from something odd like falling on a toy fire truck as a child.

"You know what's been really strange?" Katie asked. "After I talked to you when I was on the beach, I decided I didn't want to say anything to anyone until Rick and I had a chance to talk things through some more, and I haven't talked about it with anyone."

"You didn't tell Todd and Christy?"

"No. There wasn't time. Marti rushed us off to a big Sunday brunch at the yacht club, and then Todd went back to the beach house to surf. Marti and Christy went shopping. It ended up that just Uncle Bob and I looked at cars, which worked out fine because I only bought one."

Eli grinned. "You only bought one? How many cars were you planning to buy?"

Katie realized she had almost said too much. Her plan of surprising Christy and Todd by buying them a car was dismantled while she shopped with Uncle Bob. Christy's steady, calm uncle convinced Katie to concentrate on her own need for a car and to wait until after graduation before following through on her idea to bless Christy and Todd with a car.

Answering Eli honestly but letting the sarcasm shine through, Katie said, "Oh, I thought I would start with two cars as long as I had my checkbook out. I mean, what better way to drown my sorrows after a big breakup than to buy a couple of cars?"

Instead of laughing at her joke, Eli reached over and touched the curve of her face along her jaw line. The brief, tender touch caused Katie's heart to stir unexpectedly.

"It's going to be okay, Katie. You're going to be okay. Rick is going to be okay."

"I know," she said softly. She could feel her face turning rosy.

"You need to open yourself up to other possibilities." His gaze was fixed on her in a way that hinted at affection.

When Katie first met Eli, she had quickly realized that one of his distinguishing traits was the way he stared at people curiously without realizing how unnerving and rude it came across. This gaze wasn't like his old way of staring. This was a compassionate look from the heart of a caring friend.

Katie tried to conceal her self-conscious feelings by talking fast. "If by other possibilities you mean having a look around for a new boyfriend, you can stop right there. I can tell you now that isn't going to happen. I'm done with relationships for a while. A long while. You don't know me, but I'm famous for my declarations of giving up on guys. This time, though, I mean it."

"I know you, Katie," Eli replied in a low but firm voice.

"No, you don't. Not in this area. I always come out of tailspin crushes and say I'm going to focus on the Lord and get my heart right with him. But this time I actually feel as if my heart is right with God. So, if by any chance you were trying to say that I should be open to other possibilities because you're thinking of asking me out on a charity date to cheer me up, don't bother, because I wouldn't go with you."

"I actually meant being open to other possibilities about what you'll do after you graduate."

"Oh."

"But thanks for the subtle hint on your feelings about ever going out with me." Eli gave her another one of his wry grins and climbed back into the security cart.

"Don't take what I just said too personally."

"I rarely do." He drove off, and she watched him turn the corner.

Eli Lorenzo, you are one unique piece of God's creative efforts in the world of men, I'll give you that.

Katie headed into Crown Hall, trying to sort out what Eli had been communicating under the surface just then. Was it possible he was interested in her? Why would he be?

What was the phrase Rick used last summer? Rick said Eli thought I was memorable. Was that it? No, not memorable. Unforgettable. Yeah, that was it. Eli told Rick I was unforgettable. Why?

She thought back to the many conversations she and Eli had shared since last fall, when she went out to the desert with him one night to watch a meteor shower. They had worked shoulder-to-shoulder for weeks on the clean water fund-raiser. Katie had learned a lot about Eli and his childhood in Africa. The guy had been nothing but a friend to her. At least, that's how she saw him, once she got past her initial awkwardness over being around him. A good friend who made no secret that he prayed for her. The praying, she was sure, was a habit he must have developed as a missionary kid.

Taking the elevator to the third floor, Katie made her way to Julia's apartment. She easily put thoughts of Eli aside. She had lots to settle with Julia and a bunch of past-due paperwork to turn in. This was the first chance she'd had to connect with her after continually stalling on setting up a meeting time.

The door to Julia's apartment was open a few inches. Katie took that as a sign to go on in until she heard voices from inside. Hanging back, she intended to listen just long enough to determine if the conversation was personal.

She recognized the voice as Nicole's and felt confident that whatever she was telling Julia, Nicole would end up telling Katie.

Katie was about to enter when she realized Nicole was crying. Katie hesitated, realizing she might be interrupting something.

"It's not her at all," Nicole said. "It's me. She doesn't know how I feel or how horrible these past few months have been every time I'm around him. I've worked hard to hold back my feelings. I really have tried to die to myself, like you told me, but it's killing me. I know it's wrong, but I can't get rid of these feelings for Rick."

Katie froze. *Rick! Feelings for Rick!*

"I would never want to do anything that would hurt Katie. She's one of my closest friends."

Katie's feet felt glued to the floor.

"Have you tried being around Rick less?" Julia asked.

"Yes. But then he shows up here to see Katie and ..."

"Has Rick given you any indication that he might be interested in you? Does he flirt with you or come on to you in any way?"

Katie could barely breathe.

"No, Rick doesn't flirt with me. He's nice to me, but I don't think it's much different than the way he's nice to other people."

"Do you think all the interest is on your side, then?"

"Yes, I'm sure of it. The interest is all on my side. I wish I could make it go away. Rick loves Katie. That's obvious. I don't know why I can't get that through my head and just move on."

"Because your heart is engaged in this. You've opened your heart to the possibility of love, and therefore your heart isn't taking orders from your head on this one."

Katie knew she should leave, but she couldn't make herself move.

"Do I need to close down my heart then? Is that it? I feel foolish for letting these feelings go on for so long. I've really tried not to feel what I feel, but it isn't going away."

"You don't have to understand what's going on, Nicole, but you do have to confront it, and that's why I'm glad you're telling me all this."

"Tell me what to do."

Katie could hear Nicole crying. Part of her wanted to dash into the room and scoop up Nicole and say, "He's available, Nicole! He's all yours! You can pursue Rick now. I'm no longer in the picture."

But another part of her wanted to march in there and stand in front of her friend, shaking her fist and yelling, "How dare you let your heart get all mushed up over my boyfriend when you knew we were serious about each other!"

Katie felt sick to her stomach. The last thing she wanted to do now was to have her evaluation meeting with Julia. She knew she couldn't be found standing there in the hallway listening to them.

With quick, airy steps, Katie turned around and made her way back to the elevator. She pushed the button for the ground floor and exited into the lobby, where a number of students had congregated on the couches.

Talitha, one of the other RAs, called to her from the open window at the front office. Katie turned and slowed her pace just long enough to point toward the door and say, "I gotta run."

"These came for you," Talitha called back, pointing to a bouquet of mixed yellow and blue flowers.

Katie leaned her head back and let out a groan. *Rick, enough with the flowers! I'm not your girlfriend anymore!*

She waved her hand at Talitha as if to say, "Just keep 'em."

Hurrying to the parking lot and to the warm and comforting solace of her car, Katie climbed in, shut the door, and pulled out her cell phone.

After thinking through her options, she at last sent a text to Julia, apologizing for being late and asking if they could meet another time.

Drumming her finger on the steering wheel, Katie tried to think how she would respond the next time she saw Nicole. *How could Nicole carry these feelings for Rick and still be so nice to my face?*

As Katie dissected the past few months, she saw Nicole's behavior around her and Rick in a different light. Instead of gaining evidence to convict her friend of being two-faced, Katie realized that Nicole had been herself all the way through. She really had repressed her feelings for Rick.

It made Katie wonder: Did Rick have repressed feelings for Nicole?

The two of them were such a better fit than Rick and Katie ever had been. Nicole deserved Rick, and he certainly was worthy of Nicole.

Why didn't I see all this before? Nicole really kept her feelings under control. But then, that's Nicole.

Katie was having a hard time maintaining her original burst of fury at Nicole's confession. Nicole had done nothing inappropriate. At least nothing Katie knew of. Nicole hadn't tried to turn Rick's attention toward her.

Katie's cell phone buzzed. Julia's returned text message read, "COME NOW."

Puffing out her cheeks as she exhaled deeply, Katie muttered, "This isn't going to be good."

Before she could text back a message, another text came through. It was from Rick.

"CAN WE TALK?"

Katie answered Rick first. "SURE. WHEN?"

"NOW. I'M ON UPPER CAMPUS."

She paused, prayed, and then swallowed a mouthful of emotion before responding to Rick and then to Julia.

To Rick her answer was, "SURE. MEET YOU AT THE BENCH."

To Julia she texted, "SORRY. ON MY WAY TO IMPORTANT MEETING. TOMORROW OKAY?"

Then she turned off her phone, put the key in the ignition, and drove to the upper campus parking lot. Whatever happened next, Katie had a feeling she would remember it for the rest of her life.

12

T he gravel parking lot on upper campus held only eight cars when Katie parked and strode up the walkway. She was glad not many other people were around. It meant Rick and she could have this conversation privately. She had bumbled so much the previous weekend; this time their communication had to be clear. In her estimation, they both had to come to the same conclusion.

Rick was waiting, seated on the bench. He didn't look toward Katie as she approached.

This was "their" bench, a place where the two of them had sat and cuddled on many occasions. She thought of how they had sat there and watched the sun set behind Catalina Island. They kissed as the sky blazed a vivid shade of burnt orange. Rick said he was proud of them. Proud of their relationship.

This afternoon the sky was thick with smog and haze. On a day like this, it took a lot of imagination to believe the vast Pacific Ocean could be viewed from this perch on top of the high mesa. Katie's spirit felt the same thickness and haze. She couldn't imagine that any relationship with Rick would be left after this conversation.

Taking a seat on the bench, Katie stared out at the soupy, smoggy vista, waiting for Rick to speak first.

"Tell me something," Rick said.

Katie looked over at his staunch profile.

"I have gone over every inch of our relationship, and I don't understand why you said the things you did Saturday night." He turned to her. His eyes were red.

Has Rick been crying?

She thought she had done all her crying, but as soon as she looked in his eyes, a second season of tears assembled.

"We've done everything right, Katie."

"I know."

It killed her to see him like this. Something inside her screamed, *Just slide over! Go to him. Let him put his arm around you. You can make everything go back to the way it was. You don't have to feel this pain.*

Rick shifted his position and his line of questioning. "I have to ask, as much as I don't want to know. You have to tell me, Katie. Is there someone else?"

"No! Rick, no!"

"Was it the money, then?"

Katie blinked. "The money? What do you mean?"

"Were you mad at me Saturday for pressing you about the inheritance money?"

"No, the inheritance has nothing to do with any of this. It never has. That's separate."

"Then help me to understand, Katie. I don't get what's going on. Especially when you're sitting here, looking at me like that."

"Like what?" Her words came out choked.

"Like you're feeling as torn up about all this as I am."

Katie's second season of tears released with monsoon effects. She knew she had to tell him the truth. "It's because I love you, Rick. I love you."

His expression melted, and he reached for her hand. Katie didn't pull away. Rick drew her cold hand to his lips. He kissed her knuckles and then lowered her hand but kept holding it tight.

"I know we can make this work, Katie. We've followed all the rules. I've made a huge investment in our relationship. This isn't the time to pull out. You must understand that. You obviously feel the same way."

"Rick, just because I love you doesn't mean …"

His jaw clenched. Tears tumbled from the corners of his chocolate brown eyes. His voice was barely a whisper. "We can make this work."

Slowly pulling back, Katie tried with all her might to keep speaking what she knew to be true. "Rick, listen. You have to listen to me. Making something work or making a huge investment, as you say, isn't the same as being knit together at the heart."

"But you just said you love me. I know you love me, Katie."

Katie regretted her words. They were true, but at this moment that particular truth wasn't setting her free. She let go of Rick's hand and exhaled as if a connection between them had been released.

Feeling a little stronger, she said, "Our relationship as a dating couple went as far as it could go, Rick. If you're honest with yourself, I know you'll agree."

He drew in a deep breath. "I do agree with you, Katie."

She felt a wash of relief coming over her. Finally! Acceptance.

Rick sat up straighter. He seemed more in tune with what Katie was saying and not as torn up.

"You know" — Rick cleared his throat — "this isn't exactly how I thought this part of our relationship would go."

"I know. Me either."

"But you're right. We couldn't go on the way we were."

Katie nodded and hoped Rick would turn into his gallant self now. He needed to put a final seal on their relationship with his usual strength and confidence. She didn't want to lose everything they had shared. Not the friendship. Not the memories. Not all the great times. She wanted them to move on from there.

"I can't say I liked the way things went down Saturday," Rick said.

"I know. I'm sorry I was so blunt and in-your-face in the middle of the night."

"That's okay. You were being honest. That's you, Katie. That's how you do things. I accept that in you. I thought I was taking things at the right pace for us, but maybe I should have brought us to this point sooner."

"It doesn't matter now." Katie felt relieved they could talk about their relationship objectively.

"You're right. It doesn't matter now. What matters is what happens next."

"I agree."

Rick gave her a look filled with all the wild vigor he had displayed on the football field when they were in high school. His chin was set and firm. With a narrowing of his gaze, he slid off the bench and went down on one knee.

"Katie, I love you."

She froze.

What? Now? Now you tell me this? Rick, what are you doing?

Rick reached into the pocket of his jacket and pulled out a ring box. He opened it and in firm, even words said, "This also was my grandmother's. I need to have it sized for you, but I was waiting until—"

Katie sprang to her feet and yelled, "Rick, no. No!"

He looked lost and confused, stuck there on one knee with a diamond solitaire in his hand. "Katie, I haven't asked you yet."

"Then don't. Please!"

With her heart pounding, Katie grabbed Rick by the hand and pulled him to a standing position. "Listen, you have to hear what I'm saying. We broke up! You and I are still broken up."

Rick frowned. "I thought you were trying to motivate me."

"Trying to motivate you?"

"I thought you were upset because Marti asked if we had set a date."

"No!"

"Then you weren't using the breakup as a threat to get me to propose?"

"I can't believe you just asked me that. No! I wasn't threatening you. I would never do that. What I said Saturday night wasn't a false ultimatum. I've never tried to force you to say you love me. I would never press you into a corner so that you thought the only option was to propose. Don't you know I'm not like that?"

He pulled back. His jaw clenched. "I don't know what you're like anymore, Katie. I really don't. The way you've been acting makes no sense to me. You're all over the place. How am I supposed to understand what's going on with you?"

"This is what I've been trying to tell you! You and I aren't good together anymore. Not for the long term. We're at odds. Our communication skills are awful. Our life goals are in opposition to each other. Our hearts might be in the right place, but we're definitely not headed in the same direction. Can't you see that?"

The more straightforward she tried to be, the more firmly Rick's jaw became set. Katie knew he must feel humiliated as well as frustrated out of his skin. Nothing was going to enable her to smooth this over.

For a fleeting moment, Katie considered tossing in the wild card and telling Rick how Nicole felt about him. But that wouldn't help right now. And it would betray Nicole's confidences in Julia. A confidence that Katie wasn't intended to hear.

For once in her life, Katie kept her mouth shut. Her heart was pounding and her adrenaline was pulsing, but her lips weren't moving.

Rick drew back his shoulders. The lines across his forehead were tight. His mouth was a short, thin line. Katie knew that look. Rick was furious.

"You know what? I'm done with this. All of it. You and I are through, Katie. It's obvious we're not headed in the same direction."

Katie's jaw dropped. She wanted to pop back with, "Hello! What do you think I've been trying to tell you?"

Instead, she let the words of finality come from Rick's lips so he could take ownership of them. She noticed he had tucked the ring box back into his jacket pocket as if the treasure never had been revealed.

"It really burns me that we had to end this way, Katie. You have no idea how ..."

He seemed to bite his final words in half and swallow them, fiery and whole, instead of spitting them out at Katie.

"We're done." With brusque motions, Rick pressed past her and made his exit.

"Rick, wait!"

He kept walking, brisk and determined.

"Rick!"

He didn't slow for a moment.

Katie refused to run after him. She felt a fury rising in her that he would be the one to march off and mark their relationship with this final memory. Instead of calling to him a third time, Katie let him go. This was Rick. The real Rick. She had been saying she wanted him to be his true self and not the stifled Rick who had lost all his fire. If he wanted to make a grand exit, let him.

Sinking back to the bench and staring out at the soupy bowl of smog in the valley below, Katie tried to decide what to do.

This is awful. As right as it is, it's awful.

Rubbing her forehead, she frowned. Her anger over Rick's exit had flared and burned off quickly. All she wanted now was to be near a friend. A true, forever friend.

Christy.

It took Katie awhile to get to the Ark Bookstore where Christy worked. The early evening traffic was heavy, and one of the main traffic lights wasn't functioning.

Just to make sure Christy was at work, Katie called the Ark. To her surprise, Rick's mom answered the phone. The Doyles owned the café and bookstore, but Rick's mom no longer managed the bookstore.

"Katie, how ideal that you should call right now."

"I did call the Ark, didn't I?"

"Yes, I was just leaving, but no one else was available to answer the phone. Listen, I'm planning a graduation reception at our home and want to order the invitations this week. Do you know how many people you would like to invite?"

"Invite? I don't understand."

"I thought Rick would have mentioned it to you."

"Actually, Rick and I—"

"It doesn't matter. Let me tell you what I was thinking. Since you, Nicole, and Eli are graduating this year, I thought I would host a party at our home for all your family and friends."

"Um, I don't think that's such a good idea. I mean, thank you for thinking of doing this, but—"

"Katie, you know it's impossible to talk me out of hosting a party. I already have worked through the details with Nicole and her mom. Now, do you have an idea how many invitations you would like? I can help to address and send them for you, if you would like. That would take some pressure off you, which I'm guessing would be helpful right about now."

"You have no idea," Katie murmured.

"Good. Okay, well, email and let me know how many you want to invite. I'm really looking forward to having everyone in our home. Aside from Thanksgiving and Christmas, we've hardly entertained since we moved here. This is going to be wonderful."

After an awkward pause, Katie found enough words to say, "Is Christy there?"

"No, she and Todd left about half an hour ago."

"Okay. Thank you." Katie hung up and pressed Christy's name on her phone.

Todd answered.

"Is Christy there?" It seemed the only line Katie could speak without her over-stretched brain snapping.

"She's right here, but the doctor just came in. Do you want her to call you back?"

Katie found the rest of her words quickly. "Doctor? Is everything okay? What happened? Where are you guys? Are you at the hospital?"

"No, we're at the River Rock Clinic. I'll have her call you back, Katie." Todd hung up before Katie could pelt him with any more questions.

At the next light, Katie turned left and headed for the River Rock Clinic. Her heart was pounding yet again. She was certain this was the last of the adrenaline her poor body could manufacture in one day.

Why would Christy be at the doctor? She's not pregnant, is she? Is that why Todd went with her? To find out if she was pregnant? Why couldn't Todd just tell me, if that was the case? Why is he always so noncommittal?

"Men!" Katie shouted out her open car window as she drove onto the freeway. "You drive me crazy! All of you!"

13

At 6:45 that evening, toward the end of one of the most emotion-filled days of Katie's life, she found temporary solace in a grande chimichanga at Casa de Pedro.

Todd and Christy sat across from her in the booth as the three of them made their way through a large basket of warm tortilla chips. Katie summarized the last week of her life for them.

Christy tilted her head. "So Rick walked away with the ring in his pocket and everything left unsettled?"

"No. I mean, yes, he walked away, but nothing was left unsettled. Everything has been said that needs to be said. We're broken up."

"And what about Nicole?" Christy asked.

"I don't know what's going to happen there. But, you guys, you have to promise me you won't say anything to Rick about Nicole. I mean, if there's some possibility for them to get together, I'm thinking it will find its way to the surface."

Katie sat back and held her glass of ice water to her forehead. "I'm really done with all the drama. You know what I'm saying? When I look back over the last ten years of my life, I'm embarrassed at how impulsively I act."

"You mean like driving to River Rock Clinic and pouncing on us when we stepped out into the waiting room?" Todd asked with a grin. "I'm glad your impulsive days are over."

"That was different. Someone, who shall remain unnamed, hung up before sharing the simple details that his wife was having a mole removed from her back. My imagination went a little wild."

"It wasn't that big of a deal, Katie," Christy said.

The waiter placed a large platter of fish tacos in front of Todd and a cheese enchilada plate in front of Christy. The monstrous chimichanga went to Katie. She took a big bite and let the warm cheese and shredded beef minister to her spent emotions. She realized all she had eaten that day was half a bagel with strawberry jam that morning. The rest of the day she had been going nonstop. Food was a wonderful thing.

"The part I missed," Todd said, "was why you decided to break up with Rick. What happened Saturday night?"

"I don't know. I was lying there, and all of a sudden, I just knew we were done. I couldn't go any further in my relationship with Rick. I think it hit me when I realized how you and Christy sleep together."

Todd sat up a little straighter and looked at Christy with a half-amused, half-bashful look. "What have you been telling her?"

"Nothing personal." Christy's face had turned red.

"Don't worry, Todd. All your secrets are safe with her. I don't mean that kind of sleep together. What I was thinking about Saturday night was how your hearts are knit together. You go home to each other every night, but then you truly are at home when you're in each other's arms. You know what I mean? You fit. Every part of your relationship fits together."

Christy gave Todd a warm, you're-my-beloved sort of smile.

Todd kissed his wife and grinned tenderly.

"You guys are cute. Did I ever tell you that?"

Christy gave her a contented smile, and Katie felt a sharp sadness over the reality that she and Rick were really, truly broken up.

"I can't let this get me down," Katie said as much to herself as to Christy and Todd. "It's over. Rick and I are through. And I'm really done, you know? Now I need to focus my energy on school. I'm running out of time. I'm so behind in my classes. All I need to do for the next five weeks is finish college."

Just as Katie took another bite, Todd said, "And then what?"

She shrugged and kept chewing, using the food as a good excuse not to answer.

"We might have an opening at the bookstore," Christy said. "I don't know if you would want to work there, but one of the guys said he wasn't going to stay on after school ends."

Katie had no interest in working at the Ark, even though it would be fun to be with Christy every day. Thoughts of the Ark reminded her of what Rick's mom said when Katie called earlier, looking for Christy.

"That brings me to another dilemma. Rick's mom is planning a big graduation shindig for the three of us."

"The three of us?" Todd asked.

"Nicole, Eli, and me. The three of us who are graduating. I'm sure she will cancel as soon as Rick tells her we broke up."

"What if she doesn't? What if she still wants to have the party?" Christy asked.

"It would be a little awkward, don't you think?"

"Not necessarily. Not with Rick's mom. Katie, try looking at the big picture. If she still wants to host this party for all of you, think of your friendship with Nicole and Eli and even with Rick. Don't make a decision only in light of what happened this week."

Christy pressed the side of her fork into one of the enchiladas and cut a ladylike bite. Before she put it in her mouth, she said, "You're a woman of options. You can do whatever you want."

Katie bit into her chimichanga. It seemed surreal that the three of them were sitting there, discussing her life in terms of the big picture and how she was a woman of options. She didn't know if she had expected Todd and Christy to be more surprised about the breakup, but something seemed off. Neither of them seemed as concerned as she thought they would be.

Moving her plate aside, Katie looked at Christy and then at Todd. "Did you guys know Rick and I were going to break up?"

"No," Christy said.

"Neither of you seemed very surprised." Katie reached for her water and took a long swig while her friends exchanged glances. They didn't say anything.

"What's the deal? Were the two of you holding secret prayer meetings with Eli, praying Rick and I would break up?"

"Of course not," Todd said.

"So what do you guys think about all this? Give me some feedback here. I'm having a hard time reading you."

Todd looked at Katie with kindness in his silver blue eyes. "I think you're listening to the Lord and going with whatever you believe he's telling you to do. That's the path of life, Katie. Keep listening and keep following wherever he leads."

"Is that what you think too?" Katie asked Christy.

"Yes. And Katie, I am sad that you and Rick broke up. It might not seem like it, but I do feel for you." She reached across the table and gave Katie's arm a squeeze. "I think you're handling all this extremely well."

"Thank you."

"I want you to end up with a guy who sees the real you, the real Katie. Someone who gives you plenty of space for that free spirit of yours and at the same time encourages you to stay centered in Christ."

"And you didn't see that happening when I was with Rick?"

"Sometimes," Todd said. With a grin he added, "You guys certainly had your moments."

Katie's emotions turned wistful. "Yes, we did."

She cast a weary glance at her half-eaten food. "I can't believe this, but I'm full. I was planning to eat this whole thing."

"You and Eli are the only two people I know who consider it a personal victory if they can down an entire one of those," Todd said.

"I've seen you eat a whole one," Christy said to Todd.

"But I don't set it up as a challenge. I just like to eat."

For some reason, Todd's comment linking her with Eli got to Katie. She didn't know why, but she felt as if the tightly wound strings inside her were about to snap. If she stayed there one more minute, what she did next wouldn't be pretty.

"You know what? I have to go." Katie tossed her portion of the check on the table. "Don't take this personally, but I'm fried. I'll talk to you guys later."

"Are you okay?" Christy asked.

"No, I'm not. But I will be. I hope."

Katie slid out of the booth and caught Todd's eye.

His expression was calm and strangely reassuring. With his trademark chin-up gesture, he said, "Later, Katie."

"Later."

Fueled just enough by her seven bites of the Casa de Pedro giant chimichanga and by the need to release the intensity of her emotions, Katie drove straight up the hill to Rancho Corona. She parked her car, strode into Crown Hall, went directly to Nicole's closed door, and knocked.

No answer. She knocked again.

"Nicole, it's Katie."

The door opened, and Nicole offered Katie a tight smile and casually said, "What's up?"

"I need to talk to you."

"Oh. Well, I'm actually trying to finish a—"

"I know; me too. But I need to talk to you now."

Nicole stood to the side, let Katie in, closed the door, and then went over to her bed and picked up her cell phone. "I'll have to call you back ... Sure ... Okay, I will. You too. 'Bye."

Nicole sat on her bed as Katie settled in the side chair where she often sat for long, leisurely conversations. Tonight she was determined to make this conversation short.

"Here's the thing," Katie started in. "I didn't mean to, but I was outside Julia's room earlier today, and I heard what you were telling her."

Nicole's face went gray. Her lips parted, but no words came out.

"Don't say anything, please. Just hear me out. I know this isn't a very good way to communicate, but it seems to be the only way I've been able to express my true feelings this week. Nicole, you are a great friend. You've been nothing but a great friend. I've never felt as if you were trying to steal Rick away from me, so don't feel you need to explain any of that. I know what it's like to love him. I've known what that's like for a long time. And I'm guessing I will keep feeling that way for an even longer time."

Nicole was crying silently.

Katie kept going, not knowing if this was a wise route or not. All she knew was that she would snap if she had to live on the same floor with Nicole and not be able to address this issue.

"So here's the other part you may or may not know. I broke up with Rick."

Nicole's hand flew to her mouth. "Katie!"

"It wasn't because of you. I broke up with him Saturday night. It didn't fully stick, I guess, so Rick broke up with me this afternoon. We're broken up. For real. Yes, I'm a bit of a mess, but I'm okay. I think Rick is okay too. Or at least he will be. He doesn't know how you feel about him. Well, maybe he knows, just in the way that guys know those sorts of things about girls, but they act like they don't know, you know?"

Nicole reached for a tissue. She looked like an emotional mess.

"That's it. I don't know what happens now, but you have my blessing. I'm not going to say anything to Rick. You don't ever have to say anything to me about this conversation if you don't want to. I'm exhausted. If anyone needs me for official floor business, I'll be in my room trying to figure out a way to accomplish the impossible and finish everything before graduation."

Katie rose and headed for the door. She paused before leaving. "Do you want to know the biggest surprise in all this? Truth can be pretty raw sometimes. And here's a truth I learned. It's possible to love someone, and I mean really love him, and not end up spending the rest of your life with him. Isn't that strange? It's like the antithesis of every fairy tale we've ever heard. But it's true."

A clarifying thought came over her. "You know, I guess I now know in a tiny way how God feels. Wow, this is a horrible feeling."

With one more last thought, Katie offered Nicole a sympathetic expression. "Sorry I delivered all that without much couth. You're going to be okay, though. You will. No matter what happens."

Nicole sat unmoving on her bed, blinking through a flood of tears. She offered a nod, and Katie let herself out.

Three women stopped Katie as she made her way to her room at the end of the hall. Two of them wanted details on the Spring Fling, the all-dorm social that was scheduled for the second-to-last week of April. One of them just wanted to talk.

Katie listened absentmindedly for about four minutes and then said, "Can we finish this conversation a little later? I really have to go to the bathroom."

It was the truth. But as soon as Katie sequestered herself in the bathroom stall, she didn't want to leave. She didn't want to face anyone on the floor. She didn't want to write any papers, nor did she want to go to class Monday and ask for another week on one of her projects that was already overdue. No way could she finish everything. She was exhausted. Mind, body, soul. Exhausted.

14

The alarm on Katie's phone went off at 8:00 Saturday morning, forcing her out of bed after less than five hours of sleep. She stumbled around her messy room looking for something to wear and jammed her toe on the desk chair. Hopping up and down on one foot, she wanted nothing more than to fling herself back into bed and sleep for another week. But Julia had hunted her down last night and insisted that they schedule their long-overdue appointment for this morning. Exhausted and bleary of eye and mind, Katie wasn't looking forward to all the words she would have to form to catch Julia up on her overturned life.

Pulling on a pair of crumpled jeans, a sweatshirt, and flip-flops, Katie put up her hair in a clip. Her head ached.

"I'd better not be getting sick, that's all I can say. Please, God, just a few more weeks. Then ... well, I don't know what then, but I'm sure it will be more convenient to be sick."

Katie stopped at the bathroom on her way down the hall and felt admiration for Christy. How she had managed last year to graduate and get married a week later was beyond Katie's comprehension. She was sure she hadn't been sufficiently helpful or sympathetic toward her friend at the time. Now she knew all too well what it was like to be in the final stretch.

Julia was waiting for her in the lobby with a brighter-than-usual smile. "You look like you could use some coffee."

"Yeah, about twelve cups of the strongest you can find."

"Do you want to drive, or should I?"

"You better. I didn't bring my wallet."

"That was convenient. Good thing I told you I was paying." Julia opened the door for Katie and followed her out into the bright new day.

"That rain last night really made everything clean and fresh."

Katie yawned. "Did it rain?"

"You've been in a cave, haven't you?"

"Worse than that. More like a coma. Are you sure you want to try to debrief with me this morning? I already know my final RA score for the year."

"No you don't. And yes I do—want to debrief with you, that is. We've put it off too long." Julia opened her car door for Katie. She crawled in and curled up sideways, as if she would go back to sleep.

Julia laughed. "I'll wake you when we get there, and you can answer my long list of questions. Between here and the coffee shop, all you have to do is listen. I have something to tell you."

Katie's eyes were closed for only ten more seconds. What Julia said next made Katie's eyes snap open.

"I'm getting married."

Sitting up, Katie spouted, "To whom? Trent?"

Julia pulled back, stunned. "How did you know about Trent?"

"You told me about him a few months ago."

"I did? What did I tell you?"

"You said you were in love with him when you were a student here at Rancho, but you obviously didn't end up with him. What you said stayed with me because you told me you still had feelings for him, that love doesn't go away just because people go away. Something like that. I remembered what you said. I also asked if he married someone else, and you said no."

Tears had formed in the corner of Julia's eyes and trickled down her face as she drove down the hill.

"Oh, no. I said the wrong thing, didn't I?"

"It's okay. Really. I forgot that I told you about Trent."

"So you're not marrying Trent."

"No, I'm marrying John Ambrose."

"Why does that name sound familiar?" Katie snapped her fingers and sat up all the way in her seat. "Dr. Ambrose? Are you kidding me? I was in his Old Testament history class a few years ago, right after his wife passed away. He is the coolest man ever. And that voice! I used to love it when he read Scripture to us in class like a benediction. But wait. When did all this happen? When did you find time to fall in love with one of the Rancho Corona professors?"

Julia smiled. "Last year. He gave the closing prayer in chapel for the missions conference, and I just opened my eyes after he said 'amen,' and I don't know, my heart was turned toward him."

"That's so beautiful! Then what happened?"

"It took John a little longer to discover me, but once he did, everything went pretty fast. We're getting married right after school is out. We have just enough time to squeeze in a honeymoon before he has to be back for summer session."

"Wow! Julia, I'm so happy for you."

"Thank you. I'm ecstatic. We both are. We chose to keep our relationship quiet for such a long time that now we're officially engaged, I'm practically giddy."

"As you should be! This will show that old Trent, huh?"

Julia's expression went from rosy beams of love to a downcast shadow.

"I did it again, didn't I? Sorry. I just don't know when to keep my beak shut."

Julia seemed to be thinking for a moment before she turned the car into the parking lot of a hardware store.

"Why did you pull in here? Are they selling coffee at hardware stores now?"

"No." Julia turned off the engine and adjusted her position so she faced Katie. "I want to tell you about Trent."

"You don't have to."

"No, I think I do. None of what I tell you is general information around campus, okay? John knows, of course, and when Craig hired me as a resident director, he knew. Now I want you to know."

Katie wasn't prepared to be invited into Julia's confidence this way. She wished she hadn't popped off with the comments about Trent and had just let Julia keep her secrets.

"Trent and I got engaged a few months after we finished college. We went on a water-skiing trip at Lake Tahoe with some of our friends that summer, and Trent was injured seriously in an accident with another boat while he was water-skiing. He had to be flown out to a hospital, and he went into a coma."

Up to that point in the explanation, Julia spoke at a normal pace. When she came to the next part of the story, her voice became low, and her words were stretched out, as if each one were painful to say.

"Trent lost his right leg and was in a coma for two weeks."

"How awful!"

Julia pressed on without receiving Katie's sympathy. "When he came out of the coma, he just wasn't himself. He didn't remember who I was. I moved so I could be near him and help with the physical therapy and the long recovery. He worked at it for about three months, and then his spirit just gave up, I think. The doctor said the damage to his brain was more extensive than was first suspected. Two years after the accident, Trent still didn't know who I was."

"Oh, Julia."

"He passed away three years ago from an aneurysm."

The two of them sat in silence for several moments before Katie spoke again. "That's why you told me that love doesn't go away even though people go away."

Julia nodded and reached for a tissue from a box on her car's backseat.

"You can really love someone but not end up with him forever." Katie repeated what she had said when she was in Nicole's room yesterday.

Julia nodded again. "Love is mysterious. It can be irreparably painful as well."

"I agree with that more than you can imagine. Christy talks about how real love is an unconditional commitment to an imperfect person. It's more than that, though, isn't it? Love has to be a lot about accepting what is true and going from there."

Julia tilted her head. "Would I be correct in guessing that you've been doing some extra credit studying on love lately?"

"Yes, but I don't want to talk about me yet. Keep going with your love story."

"I don't know what else to say. I've come to believe you have to be courageous to survive real love. Both John and I went through some very deep, dark valleys. John says all the pain and darkness we experienced now makes our love for each other so much more powerful and highly valued. I agree with him. We aren't going to be the sort of couple that argues over the small stuff. We know what a gift this is, having each other and feeling the way we do."

"That is so amazing, Julia. So beautiful. I don't know if I have the right words to tell you how happy I am for you. For both of you. It sounds like the biggest God-thing ever."

Julia offered Katie a smile. "You just said it all right there. Thank you, Katie."

"Hearing your story gives me hope."

"'Hope is the thing with feathers that perches in the soul, and sings the tune without the words and never stops at all.'"

"I love that! You didn't make that up just now, did you?"

"No, it's from a poem by Emily Dickinson."

"Do you mean Emily on our floor? The one who plays the guitar? I knew she wrote songs. Does she write poems too?"

"No, I'm talking about Emily Dickinson, the poet. Mid-1800s? Hundreds of short poems published after she died?"

"Oh. I suppose I should have known that, right? I mean, I am almost a college graduate. I'm supposed to be well versed now in arts, literature, science, humanities, and—"

"And the eternal mysteries of love," Julia added with a grin.

"That too."

"So start there. Tell me all about what you now know about the eternal mysteries of love."

"It hurts."

"Ah, then I'm guessing you and I have a few things to talk about."

"Yes, I guess we do."

Julia and Katie started their many-faceted conversation in the car while parked in front of the hardware store. About forty minutes later, after Julia had been given a fairly thorough overview of the last month of Katie's life, she started the engine.

"Are you going to drive me to the nut farm now?" Katie asked.

"No. I need coffee before I hear any more."

Katie turned the topic back to Julia and her wedding plans while they drove a few more miles down the road. She thought it was great that Julia and John were going to hold the ceremony on upper campus in the meadow where Todd and Christy had their wedding last May.

What Katie didn't think was great was the place Julia selected for their coffee.

Bella Barista.

It was a place Katie and Rick had visited a number of times. On their first visit, Katie initiated a fun tradition of kissing Rick on the cheek at the register. As soon as Julia and Katie walked inside Bella Barista and the swirling fragrance of fresh-roasted coffee came over them, Katie wanted to cry.

But she held steady and braced herself while standing at the register. *Don't think about Rick. Don't think about Rick. Don't think about Rick.*

"Do you know what you want?" Julia asked.

"Eli."

Julia looked at her, amused and surprised.

Katie looked back, just as stunned, and said, "What did you just ask me?"

"A better question would be, what did you just answer me?"

"Tea. I was trying to order some tea." Katie turned to the young woman behind the counter and said, "I'll have a hot tea. Large. And one of those cinnamon rolls."

Julia paid, and the two of them went over to a corner table. "Well, that was rather revealing."

"What? That girl's top? I know. Hello! Leave a little for the imagination."

"Katie, I meant your saying you wanted Eli."

"I didn't say that."

Julia took a long, slow sip of her latte.

"I was trying to say I wanted tea. 'Tea' comes out sounding like 'Eli,' I suppose, when you haven't had enough sleep. It's the long *e* sound. Teeee. Eeeeli. See?"

Julia kept her glowy, composed look as she nibbled on a corner of Katie's cinnamon roll. "You know, my mother used to say she grew to appreciate PMS."

Katie made a face. "What does that have to do with anything?"

"She said that on those days of the month her emotions were at their most vulnerable and rawest. That's when she discovered that the words coming out of her mouth were closest to her real thoughts and feelings. She didn't have the usual filters on when her hormones were on edge."

"Are you saying my hormones are on edge? You sound like Rick. I've already told you where that relationship went. If you know what's good for you, you won't call me out on my hormones. Or on my verbal skills when I'm ordering tea and I'm sleep deprived."

Julia didn't seem to see the humor in Katie's comments. With a straightforward expression she said, "Katie, do you want to hear my opinion?"

"Yes, of course."

"I think you did a fantastic job navigating all of it. All of it! Including the way you went directly to Nicole but didn't say anything to Rick. I agree with Christy. You should look at the big picture of this whole year and accept the invitation to the graduation party at the Doyles' home."

"If Rick's mom will still have me."

"I think she will. This is your community. These are your people; Rick's mom is one of your women. You need to stay connected to your circles for this important moment in your life."

Katie blew on her tea in an attempt to cool it some. "Do you think I should have waited? Before breaking up with Rick, I mean. Do you think I should just have rolled on through graduation and the party and whatever else, and then, after all the attention was off us, I should have broken it off?"

"No."

Katie waited for more words. "That's it? No? You think I did the right thing?"

"I do. What you did was messy, yes. But it was honest, and if there's one thing I do know about you, Katie, you don't fake anything. I can't see how you could have maintained the relationship with Rick after your heart changed toward him. You did the right thing. Besides, what if you had gone along pretending all the way to the graduation party, and everyone was there, and then Rick proposed in front of everyone?"

Katie sobered instantly. "That would have been tragic."

"I'm not saying that's what he was going to do."

"But it definitely is the way he does things. The café in Redlands was scheduled to open April 27, but I received a generic email from Rick's company saying the opening was delayed until May 25 or something like that. I felt all along that he was waiting until after the café opened before turning his attention to our relationship. He wasn't going to propose until he had the café checked off his list. Then he would set up a new timeline for us. That's how his brain works. One goal at a time. Me, I'm all over the place all the time."

"Talk to me about your classes and how things are looking for you now that it's crunch time."

"Disastrous. Next question."

Julia pulled out a notebook and flipped it open to a blank page. "I know how you feel about lists and schedules, but I'm going to ask you to put aside those negatives feelings for the next half-hour. You need a plan of attack, and I'm just the person to give you one."

For the next twenty-five minutes, Julia helped Katie to walk through a step-by-step schedule to complete her work in the few remaining weeks. To Katie's surprise, the process was a lot less painful than she thought it would be. In the same way that Julia and John's love story gave Katie hope for her future love life, the plan in front of her gave her hope that she might pull off all that was required of her before graduation day.

Julia pulled out the paperwork Katie needed to complete for her position as RA, and together they organized Katie and Nicole's list of responsibilities for the Spring Fling.

"I can't believe this year is almost over."

"Don't start saying that now," Julia said. "Wait until we're in the final week. When I hear students becoming nostalgic before we're even into the last month of classes, it's like hearing Christmas music the day after Halloween. We're not there yet."

Katie looked at the list in front of her. "Thanks for helping me think though all this. It's a lot."

"Yes, it is. But you can do it, Katie."

"You know what? I believe you."

They left Bella Barista, and Katie realized she really did believe it. She believed she could not only accomplish all the work and class responsibilities on the list but she could also find her way around to the other side of her relationships with Rick and Nicole.

"What are you going to say to Nicole?" Katie asked Julia as they drove back up the hill to Rancho Corona.

"Say about what? Her responsibilities for the Spring Fling?"

"No, about Rick."

"Nothing. Why?"

"You don't feel that you should tell her it's okay to call him or maybe even ask him to the Spring Fling?"

Julia looked surprised. "Why would I tell her something like that?"

"I don't know. You're her RD."

"Katie, that would be like my telling you to call Eli and ask him to the Spring Fling. Why would I do something like that? You're capable of making your own decisions about your love life, as you made clear in your relationship with Rick. I mean, who am I, besides your RD, to try to help you to see all the common ground you have with Eli Lorenzo? Why would I pelt you with the obvious evidences of the guy's interest in you? What would be the point of reminding you of the way the two of you worked seamlessly on the fund-raiser for water for Africa? Why would I do that?"

"Yeah, why would you?"

"Exactly. And why would I remind you of what happened when you had the flu and Eli brought you medicine on Valentine's Day? Not to mention the New Zealand glacier water."

"Did I tell you about the New Zealand glacier water?"

"Yes, you did. You told me when I was checking in on you when you were sick. If I remember correctly, all you wanted to talk about was Eli and the way he prayed for you."

"And how he told me not to operate heavy machinery." Katie felt her defenses lowering.

"Just pay attention to what God is doing, Katie. That's all I'm saying. Just pay attention and respond appropriately."

15

W ith uncharacteristic organizational determination, after breakfast with Julia, Katie posted her long to-do list in her room and systematically went down the list. Instead of check marks next to each task, Katie mixed it up a little. Sometimes she crossed off the words. Sometimes she drew a happy face or a sunflower at the end of the line. She had other plans for a few of them, such as her huge year-end project. When she finally finished that, she planned to write "ALLELUIA!" over the task.

Keeping to her list kept Katie from becoming involved in long conversations with anyone other than the women on her floor. She only interacted with other students who came by the front desk when she was on duty and a few friends here and there who stopped her as she trekked across campus to her classes.

All in all, Katie had to admit that in one week, under the pressure of checking items off her list, she accomplished twice what she had expected. But she felt a sudden stab of pain when she entered Crown Hall lobby late Friday afternoon and realized the weekend was ahead of her. For the past year and a half, her first thought for every weekend was how she might adjust her time so she could see Rick or at least set aside time for long phone conversations with him.

Thoughts of Rick toppled her off the wave of success she had been riding on in light of her list of accomplishments. Ironically the list that was making her feel so happy was the very sort of difference that had kept her at odds with Rick. She now felt as if she understood him a little better. Checking tasks off a list could be a pretty great natural high.

Katie stopped by the front desk to check the schedule for her weekend hours. Jordan, one of the RAs on the guys' floor, was on duty. He handed Katie the roster before she even asked.

"How did you know?" she said.

"You're predictable. Hey, did you and Nicole figure out the decorations for the Spring Fling tomorrow night?"

"Julia delegated the whole thing to Nicole. I'm in charge of the games."

"What did you come up with?"

"Twister. I picked up twenty of them at Bargain Barn awhile ago. We'll divide up into teams. Craig is going to run the video camera while everyone is twisting, then some of the guys will edit it as we eat. The grand finale will be watching the playback."

"Uh, Katie, you know it's formal, don't you? How are you going to convince the women to play Twister in formal wear?"

"It's not formal."

"Yes, it is."

"No, it's not. Where did you hear it was formal? It's not a ball; it's a fling. Your information is wrong."

"I think you're the one who's wrong. You weren't at the staff meeting when we discussed the details. I don't know where you got your info, but I'm telling you: It's formal."

Katie let out a huff and headed to her floor. Nicole would know.

The two of them had managed three neutral encounters since Katie's grand announcement about overhearing Nicole and Julia's conversation. One of their encounters was in the bathroom and two were while passing each other on campus. In each of the circumstances, they were both in motion when they saw each other. That meant they could keep walking and exchange a friendly "hello" without anyone around them knowing the trauma they had gone through.

As Katie approached Nicole's door, she was pretty sure they had both had enough time to mellow and think things through. It probably would be good if they sat down now for a second round of talks.

With a light-hearted tap on Nicole's half-closed door, Katie called out, "It's me. Okay if I come in?"

Before Nicole could answer, the door swung open, and there stood Rick.

Katie's heart did a flitter-flutter. She stared into his brown eyes and felt as if, for one moment, time had stopped.

Then she blinked, and she was on the other side of the fairy tale. She really was out of love with him. She still loved him in the deep-soul-friends-forever way, but she knew—somehow knew—that she truly was no longer in love with him.

"Wow," she said under her breath. *I'm not in love with you anymore, Rick Doyle.*

His face was flushed and his jaw clenched. "I was just leaving."

"You don't have to." Katie looked past Rick and realized Nicole wasn't in her room. "Where's Nicole?"

"How would I know? The guy at the front desk said it was open dorm hours; so I stepped in and left the box on her desk. Your box is by your door." Rick sounded robotic.

"My box?"

"Invitations for your graduation party."

"Oh, right. The graduation party. Rick, are you sure your mom still wants to do this? I mean, she knows that you and I are—"

"She knows."

"And she still wants me to come?"

"The party is on the calendar. She sent you a box of invitations. Looks like she still wants you to come." Rick started to leave.

"Rick, wait."

He stopped but didn't look at Katie.

"Are you okay?"

"What kind of a question is that?"

"It's a sincere question." Katie's tone matched the irritation in his. "And here's another sincere question. How do you feel about my coming to your house for this graduation party? Because if you're not comfortable with my being there, I won't come."

"It's not my house. It's my parents' house."

"But you'll be there, right?"

"I'll be there."

Katie wanted to reach over and touch his shoulder in a sympathetic, friendly way. She realized that she was further along in the bounce-back process than Rick was. He wasn't moving from the doorway, and he still wasn't looking at her.

"Hey, Rick, listen." Katie lowered her voice.

"You don't have to say anything, Katie. Really. I think both of us have said just about everything we could say."

"Except I want to say I'm sorry, Rick. I'm sorry for—" Katie started to tear up. "I'm just really sorry, Rick."

His shoulders seemed to relax and his expression toward Katie turned more sympathetic.

"You don't have to say anything, Katie."

"I feel like I need to say something. I just don't know what to say."

Rick ran his fingers through his dark hair. "Look, Katie, I've been thinking a lot this week about us. About you. I think I thought more about you during this week than I have maybe our whole dating relationship."

Katie's heart pounded faster. *Is he going to say that he hopes we'll get back together?*

"The more I thought about you, the more I saw why you reached the conclusion you did. I think that's because I was thinking about you. Just you. Not about us. Not about me. Not about how you could fit into my life. I thought about you, your dreams and goals, and your personality. That's when I knew I had to agree. You and I weren't going to be good together for the long term."

"But as boyfriend and girlfriend, we were really good together."

"I thought so too."

They stood awkwardly for a moment, looking at each other and then looking away. In the past this was the moment when they would hug or kiss or both. Now they just shuffled their feet.

Katie made the first move and smiled up at him. "I loved being your girlfriend, Rick Doyle."

Rick smiled back. It was a great smile. Just like the ones Katie remembered over the years when Rick was his truest self. Whether he was being ornery or tender, sincere or cool. This was his best smile.

"I'm glad I ran into you, Katie."

"Me too. Hey, you should come to the Spring Fling tomorrow night."

"Is it a date event?"

"Not really. You know how these all-hall events are. People come together but not as actual couples. You should come. Just come. For old times' sake."

He thought a moment and asked, "When do you need a final answer?"

"I don't. We're not selling tickets or anything. Just come. Seven o'clock. Here in the lobby."

"It's casual, right?"

"Ah, that's one thing I'm not sure about. I heard rumors it was semi-formal. That's what I came to ask Nicole. I can let you know once I find out. How would that be?"

Rick nodded slowly. "That would be good."

Katie nodded and suddenly felt a little like crying, but she didn't.

Rick turned to go when Katie remembered one more thing. "Oh, I saw the email about the delay with the opening of the café. Is everything okay?"

"We had a delay on the pizza oven's delivery and had to have one of the walls rewired. It made sense to slow it down another month. Everything else is going good, though. I'm looking to move out to Redlands by the first of June."

"You are?"

"I was going to wait until ... well, you know ... until I saw how our plans lined up. But I decided this week to go ahead and make the move. I really like what I do, Katie."

"I know you do. It's what you were created to do."

"Just as you were created to chase adventure until it catches you."

Katie's smile broadened. No one ever had described her so accurately. "Yes, that's what I was created to do."

"You weren't made for the deli sandwich assembly line. You can do it, but it doesn't fill up your soul."

Now Katie knew she was going to cry. It was the first time Rick showed he really understood how she was wired. "Thank you, Rick."

He gave her another signature, vintage-Rick grin. "I have to give the prize to Eli for naming it."

"Naming what?" Katie blinked away her skittering tears.

"Naming this feeling that comes from being around you. It's extraordinary. You, Katie Weldon, are unforgettable."

Rick turned and strode down the hall. Katie watched him go. If ever there was a good way or a right way to break up with one of your forever friends, this was it, right there. Finally.

Wiping her tears with the back of her hand and drawing in a deep breath, Katie started to go. She was about to close Nicole's door all the way when she heard her name whispered.

Katie froze. She listened more closely. *Did I just hear something? No, that had to be my imagination, right?*

"Katie!" the whisper came again, louder this time.

Turning back into Nicole's room, Katie tiptoed across the rug. She went over to the bed and looked around to the side that faced the window. There on the floor was a big lump under a blanket with just a nose and pair of eyes peeking over the top.

16

N icole, what are you doing? Have you been there the whole time Rick and I were talking?"

"Is he gone?" Nicole pulled down the blanket and let her whole face show.

"Yes, he's gone."

"Could you close the door?"

Katie strode back to the door and gave it a firm push. If she weren't so flustered over Nicole's having heard every detail of her heartfelt conversation with Rick, she would have found it humorous that Nicole had been playing possum behind her bed.

When Nicole stood up, Katie could see why she hid. All she had on was her underwear.

"I forgot it was open-dorm Friday. My door was open a few inches, like it usually is. I heard this loud knock and then Rick's voice, and I didn't know what to do. I dove behind my bed and hoped he wouldn't see me. Oh, Katie, I'm sorry I eavesdropped. I didn't mean to."

Nicole pulled on a pair of shorts that were on the end of her bed along with a hooded cotton shirt. She pulled the hood over her head like a repentant little monk. "I'm so sorry."

Katie's frustration melted. She knew what it was like to eavesdrop accidentally.

"Don't worry about it, Nicole."

The two of them stood a few feet apart, looking at each other and then looking away.

After a full minute and a half of the awkwardness, Nicole said, "Do you have time to talk?"

"Sure." Even though Katie said the word, she didn't feel ready to have a heart-to-heart with Nicole. Instead of sinking into Nicole's conversation chair, Katie kept standing.

"Actually," Nicole said, looking away. "I need to meet someone in a few minutes. I'm probably late. What time is it? You know what? It doesn't matter. You and I can talk another time. I should just go."

Nicole wasn't acting like her gracious, calm self. She was acting more like Katie—on the run, never quite sure what time it was or where she was supposed to be.

"Okay, sure. We can talk later. I'll be in my room all night studying. I have front desk duty in the morning."

"Oh, and it's casual."

"What's casual?"

"The Spring Fling. I don't know who told you it was formal."

"That would be Jordan, the big lug sitting at the front desk right now, telling everyone it's formal."

"I'll talk to him right now and ask him to send an email out to the master list." Nicole headed for the door.

Katie followed her. "If you need any help with the decorations, I'll have time tomorrow afternoon."

"That's okay. Julia delegated it to me."

"I know. But I can help." Katie reached out and touched Nicole on the shoulder before she slid out the door. "Listen, you and I don't have to do this. We don't have to pretend anything. I can't say I'm crazy about what just happened and how you heard everything, but then I'm sure you're still frustrated with me for overhearing what you told Julia. So we both goofed up. It's all out on the table now. Why don't we find a way to go forward from here?"

Nicole looked as if she might cry. As a matter of fact, she looked like she had been doing a fair amount of crying lately. Her eyes were puffy, and she had on no makeup, which was unusual for her.

"I need a little more time, Katie."

"Time for what? To decide if you're going to forgive me for eavesdropping?"

"No, I don't hold that against you."

"Then time for what?"

Nicole turned to Katie with a tight expression. "Time to figure out how to act around you and around Rick."

"I can help you with that. Don't act. Just be you. Be the wonderful, sweet Nicole who has been my close friend all year. Nothing has changed between you and me, Nicole. You didn't betray me or anything. And with Rick, just be your sweet self. He'll wake up one of these days and realize what a gem you are."

Nicole's tears were dripping silently. She looked doubtful of Katie's words.

"Hey, you and I both know that boys are slower at figuring out these things than girls. He'll get there. Give him time."

"Katie, how can you be so open about all this? If I were you, I would be devastated. I would hate me. I wouldn't be talking to me right now."

Katie shrugged. "It's just how I see it."

"You and Rick had such a close relationship. I mean, even here at the end he's hugging you and telling you how wonderful you are."

"Trust me, Rick and I had a few ballistic moments before we got to this. And a lot of tears. You didn't see the other conversations, which is a good thing. It's okay, Nicole. Like I said last week, you have my blessing. I told you I wouldn't say anything to him, and I won't. But don't you go comatose on your true feelings. Just be you. See what God does and take it from there."

Nicole wrapped her arms around Katie and cried softly into her shoulder. Katie, who felt like she was pretty much done with all the tears she wanted to see or feel or cry for the next decade, gave Nicole a comforting pat on the back. "It's okay. Go ahead, cry it out. All this drama right before graduation. How smart are we? Have you ever heard of Emily Dickens, by the way?"

Nicole stepped back and gave Katie an odd look. "Do you mean Em across the hall?"

"No, the poet."

"Oh, Emily Dickinson. Yes, I've heard of her."

"I thought it was Dickens."

"You were probably thinking of Charles Dickens."

"Whatever. Emily whatever-her-last-name-was wrote a poem about hope. I can't quote it like Julia, but you should ask her to tell it to you. It's sweet. And encouraging. And I guess that doesn't really matter since I don't know the poem. But did you know that Julia is getting married?"

Nicole's eyes grew wide.

"Okay, obviously you didn't know. Why did I open my mouth?"

Nicole said, "No, I knew, but I thought I wasn't supposed to say anything. She asked me to do the flowers for the wedding."

"Oh, that's nice. They're getting married in the upper campus meadow."

"I know. It's going to be beautiful." Nicole took the hood off her head and patted her final tears away. "Katie, are you sure that you're okay with Rick and with your dating relationship being over?"

"Yes." Katie tried to make the sincerity she felt show in her eyes.

"You are amazing, Katie."

"So are you, Nicole. And like I told you, it's only a matter of time before Rick catches on to that fact. He'll be at the Spring Fling tomorrow night; so wear your boy-catcher sweater."

"My boy-catcher sweater?"

"You know, the black fitted one. You wear that with a pair of jeans and any pair of your lovely assortment of cute shoes, and I predict you'll catch yourself a boy before the night is out. No, let me correct that. You'll be catching a man. A godly man."

Nicole gave Katie a final quick hug and a big smile. Katie went down to her room and found the box of invitations by the door, where Rick had left them. She unlocked her door, went inside, and took a good look at the mess. The mess was why she had locked her door. Unlike Nicole's, Katie's room was never ready for company on a moment's notice.

Deciding to try a tactic Julia had suggested during their coffee meeting at Bella Barista last Saturday, Katie set the alarm on her phone for twenty minutes. She worked against the clock. Could she clean her entire room in twenty minutes?

To her surprise, the timed cleanup worked. *Christy would never believe what I just did. What a different year she and I would have had together last year if I had managed to implement this little trick sooner.*

Turning off the alarm on her phone, Katie texted Christy to report the small victory.

A moment later Christy's response came back. "GOOD FOR YOU! BIOPSY BENIGN, BTW."

Katie thought for a minute. Then she remembered Christy's visit to the doctor and the mole she had had removed.

"YEAH!" Katie texted back.

"YOU DOING OK?"

"BETTER THAN OK." Then, instead of typing out the rest, she called to give Christy a quick summary of what had happened since Casa de Pedro. Katie ended by saying she was going to send Christy and Todd an invitation to the graduation party at Rick's parents' house.

"I hope you send one to your parents too," Christy said.

"I will."

"And your brothers."

"I still only know where one of my brothers is."

"Then send one to him."

"I will. I've come to be at peace with quite a few things lately, including that I have to go with what I have and not to worry about what I don't have. I mean, I still pray for Larry, but I can't do anything about his taking off and not leaving contact information with anyone in the family. I know God is watching over him, wherever he is."

"That has to be tough, Katie."

"It is. But I can't fix it, you know?"

"Speaking of fixing things, you'll never guess what we got yesterday."

"What?"

"A new microwave. Finally. Why don't you come over tonight and bring some of your garage sale popcorn? We'll see if we can catch this one on fire too."

"Very funny. You're too late, anyway. I threw out all the food I bought at that garage sale. I'm telling you, I'm a reformed woman, sitting in a cleanish dorm room with a load of clothes doing a little cha-cha in the washer."

"Then you're free to come for dinner tonight."

"You didn't say anything about dinner. What are you guys having?"

"I don't know yet. Todd should be home in about half an hour. Why don't you come over? We can finish the conversation we started at Casa de Pedro."

"I could come there instead of going to the cafeteria. As a matter of fact, I could stop at Casa de Pedro on the way and pick up a couple of chimichangas."

"And two fish tacos," Christy added. "Todd likes the fish tacos."

"Todd is a fish taco," Katie said playfully.

"For that comment, you now have to bring four fish tacos and ask them to add cilantro."

"Fine! Be that way, little Ms. Bossy Married Woman. I'll be there in half an hour with way too much food for the three of us to eat, so you'd better have the table set."

"I'm on it this very minute. See you."

Katie sprang into action. With the best of intentions, she gathered up her laptop and the box of invitations so she could address them at Christy's, if the opportunity occurred.

Precisely thirty-four minutes later, Katie arrived on Christy and Todd's apartment doorstep with too many items in her hands to knock. Instead she kicked the door and called out, "Candygram!"

Todd opened the door and rescued the bags of food that were teetering in the crook of her arm.

"Oh, that's it, go for the fish tacos. Don't save the laptop or the fancy invitations. By all means, save the whales!"

From around the corner came another pair of helping hands, reaching for the invitation box as well as the shoulder strap of the case that held Katie's laptop. The hands belonged to Eli.

Katie gave him a generous grin. Then she turned to Christy and gave her an are-you-kidding-me? look.

Christy appeared proud of herself. She sidled up to Katie and whispered, "You said on the phone you were bringing more food than three people could possibly eat."

Katie gave Christy an exaggerated scowl, but the truth was she had almost expected this. And why not? She was the one trying to fix up Rick and Nicole. Why wouldn't her friends try to pair her up with Eli? They wanted to show her kindness, and she knew she would be echoing the kindness if she went along with the plan. As long as Eli stayed his cool self, nobody would get hurt.

Katie wasn't going to rebound from one guy to another. She didn't need a new boyfriend to make her feel good about herself. Nor was she in any hurry to date again. Her goal was to finish college. Then she would figure out what was next.

For now, she was happy to be with friends who loved her, were looking out for her, and who wanted the same for Eli. These were her people. Julia had said it last week. This was Katie's circle. Her community.

She might as well relax and break bread with them in sweet communion.

Or in this case, break burritos.

17

A nd what about this?" Katie said, holding up a fork as she sat across from Eli at Christy and Todd's petite kitchen table. In front of them was a mess of leftover Mexican food wrappers.

"Tenedor." Todd jumped in with his answer before Eli had a chance.

"Oh, man, I knew that one," Eli said.

"Too bad, so sad. You snooze, you lose. Todd wins yet again." Katie leaned back in her chair and felt contentedly full from the grande chimichanga she had split with Christy.

"Todd definitely remembers more Spanish words than you, Eli. What did the two of you do the whole time you were in Spain, besides not learn Spanish?"

"Surfed," Todd said.

"We did more than that when I was there with you guys." Christy cleared some of the mess on the table. "You know what those outreach trips were like, Katie. You were in Ireland while the three of us were in Spain, but we all were doing the same sort of outreach to the kids in the neighborhoods and at the open-air gatherings. Eli did a lot with the older boys. He led most of the morning devotions for the team too."

Katie looked at Eli. She wasn't surprised by the outreach skills or that he gave devotions. She had heard him speak in chapel, and he had a commanding presence. His words were steady and intense, the way his staring habit had been when Katie first met him.

None of those pieces of information surprised her. But another piece was surprising.

"You surf?"

"I try."

"He surfs," Todd answered for him. "And he rocks at soccer."

Katie could have guessed that Eli was good at soccer from previous conversations, when he had talked about playing football where he grew up in Africa.

"What about you?" Eli asked Katie. "Do you surf?"

"Ah, that would be a no. Although, I shouldn't say that. Once I did get to a bona fide standing position on a surfboard."

"You did more than that. I watched you catch a couple of waves that day at Newport Beach when Doug proposed to Tracy," Christy said.

"I guess I did catch a couple of waves. But not enough to make me dream of riding the big ones at Waimea, like Todd did. Oh, and Doug taught me how to body surf, and I can hold my own on a Boogie board."

"Which is more than we can say for Christy," Todd teased, leaning over and reaching his arm around his wife's neck. He drew her close and kissed her on the side of her head while she assumed an exaggerated pouting expression.

"It's not as if I haven't tried. Many times. My coordination skills in sports have always been a bit lacking. Not like you, Katie. You're the softball star. And remember the houseboat trip we took to Lake Shasta with my aunt and uncle? You were the star water skier as well."

"Water skiing is fun. Snow skiing, however ... Will we ever forget our high school ski trip?"

"Never." Christy looked like the memory was painful.

Katie laughed. "We both were pretty humorous on that trip. Uber-klutzes!"

"That was because the rental place gave us the wrong skis. The ones we had were too long for beginners."

Katie turned to Eli. "At least that's the story we decided to go with. I mean, I've heard of beginners making face plants in the snow, but Christy here did a face plant into the ski instructor."

"I don't think I ever heard that story." Todd had a hold of his darling wife by the wrist and looked like he wasn't going to let her go. "The ski instructor, huh?"

"He was cute too," Katie added.

"I'm sure you heard that story, Todd. You just chose to forget about the fiasco, like I've tried to forget about it. Who brought that up, anyway?"

Katie raised her hand. "Yo. But you jumped right in, Little Ms. Innocence and Kittens."

Then, because Katie was on a mischievous streak, she added, "Note that I said 'kittens' and not 'cats,' as in Mr. Jitters, the freaky cat from the alternate universe of all things mangy."

Christy gave Katie a tweak-your-beak look. "Anyone want something more to drink? I think we have some orange juice."

"I'll have more water," Eli said. "Thanks."

"Hey, whatever happened to that mangy cat?" Todd asked.

"Nicole ran over it," Katie quipped.

"The cat already was dead," Eli added. "Nicole just sort of ran over it in the parking lot. That was last fall."

"Oh, yeah, I remember hearing about that." Todd called over his shoulder to Christy in the kitchen. "And I do remember hearing about the good-looking ski instructor. And the chocolate bars. Didn't you guys sell chocolate bars to raise money?"

"Tried to sell chocolate bars," Katie corrected him. "My supply mysteriously left my box and later appeared in my stomach. It was the strangest thing. Do you have any tea, by the way, Chris?"

Christy opened a cupboard and pulled out a box with a variety of tea bags. "I have Earl Grey, English Breakfast, and orange something. I can't read the label."

Eli stood up. "I have some Kenyan tea at my apartment. Should I bring back anything else?"

"Yeah. Bring Rick. Tell him to come down with you if he's just sitting there doing nothing," Katie said.

Christy, Todd, and Eli shot surprised glances at each other like darts flying across the room. Then they looked at Katie, as if she wasn't supposed to have noticed their flurry of glances.

"Listen." Katie pulled back her shoulders and spoke with a clear heart. "Rick and I have talked all this through. Several times. We're good. We want the friendship between us to continue, which is obviously a good choice since all of us are in the same circle. I invited him to the Spring Fling at Crown Hall tomorrow night, and I think he's going to come. Nobody has to walk around on eggshells. Nobody has to wonder who can be in the same room with whom. We're all good."

"Rick's not home," Eli said. "At least he wasn't earlier. But if he's there now, I'll tell him to come down."

"Good. The sooner all of us find a way to be normal, whatever that is, the better. All we have to do is be ourselves. Be 'us.' That's what I told Nicole too."

Another round of dart glances flew across the room.

"Okay, I'll be right back." As Eli, who was wearing shorts, walked out the door, Katie noticed what muscular calves he had. He was built like a soccer player. Not an ounce of fat on him. Well, except for maybe the lard that came with the chimichanga he managed to wolf down almost by himself, with minor assistance from Todd. Katie had been impressed.

"You sure you're okay with Rick?" The question wasn't unusual, but Katie found it unusual that Todd was the one asking it.

She smiled and nodded. "I really am doing great with all of it. I think Rick is too. At least he seemed to be a few hours ago. It's crazy, right? Half of a lifetime dreaming of being with him, a year and a half of floating around inside that dream, but now I feel like I'm awake.

Wide awake. God has my attention. I'm fully turned toward him. I'm at peace. I really am."

Todd smiled at Katie. He had such clear blue eyes. Christy used to describe them as "screaming silver blue." Whenever Katie looked into Todd's full expression, those honest blue eyes seemed to look into the truest part of her. She couldn't imagine Todd ever speaking anything other than the truth to her.

He reached across the table and put his hand on hers. " 'Point out the road I must travel; I'm all ears, all eyes before you. Teach me how to live to please you because you're my God.' "

"That's a great verse. Where is it from?"

"Psalm 143:8 and 10. You like that one?"

Katie nodded.

"Then it's yours. Free. Take it."

Katie smiled. This part of Todd's personality used to drive Christy nuts in their early years together. Katie wasn't always so crazy about his highly tuned spiritual dial either, but as the years had gone by, she had come to love that dimension of him. He had taken a lot of God's Word into his heart, and it resided there for him to tap into whenever he needed it. He seemed to have one ear open to the eternal, spiritual perspective of life, and viewed life from that angle first, before looking at it the way everyone else did.

A deeply settled part of Katie felt an unspoken happiness over her heart being in alignment with what she knew Todd was saying to her. She really had grown spiritually over the last few years. Her relationship with Rick had something to do with that, but mostly the change had come because Katie had redirected her thoughts. Or maybe a more accurate way to say it was that God was redirecting her thoughts.

All she knew was she felt more at home inside her own skin than she ever had before. She also felt the Lord was more at home in her heart than he ever had been before.

Christy placed an empty mug in front of Katie and one at Eli's place. "Are you going to ask Eli to go to the Spring Fling too?"

"No, why?"

"You asked Rick."

"That's different."

"Eli might enjoy going to an end-of-the-year party. Since he's not in a dorm, he doesn't get in on some of the fun stuff."

"Are you trying to be his mother, Christy? You guys are pathetic. You know that, don't you? I'm not going to switch my attention to Eli. I'm going to graduate. That's my only goal. Besides, he's leaving for Africa as soon as school is out. Should I remind you, Christy, how much you disliked your long-distance relationship with Todd the year you spent in Switzerland?"

"Eli delayed his return to Africa," Todd said.

"Why? A team is going over from Rancho to help his dad with the clean water projects this summer. I thought he would want to be in Africa while they were there."

"He said he has something going on here with a family member."

"I didn't think he had any family here."

Christy shrugged and returned to her chair next to Todd. "Maybe he means someone in his gathered family."

Katie knew what Christy meant by that. Katie also had a "gathered" family of friends who filled the place of the blood relatives who weren't interested in being connected at holidays and special times.

"Regardless," Katie said, returning to her point. "It doesn't matter how long he plans to stay here this summer. I'm not shopping for a new boyfriend. Okay? So can we end this discussion right here? I'm very much in need of friends and will take all the good times I can get. But can we drop these lame attempts the two of you are making to match me up with Eli? It's not going to happen."

Todd had a funny grin on his face as he reached over and laced his fingers with Christy's. "You can run, but you can't hide, Katie. Love is going to catch up to you, and when it does, you are going down big time. Trust me on this. I give Rick a lot of credit for the way he led in your relationship and planned each step. But love can't always be scheduled neatly."

Katie had felt lighthearted all evening, but now she was miffed. Did Todd think she didn't really love Rick? Didn't he understand what her heart had been through in the past eighteen months? She wasn't running from anything. She was running to a goal. The goal of graduating.

When Katie didn't respond to Todd's comment, Christy squeezed his hand. "I think that might have come across a little too strong, Todd."

He looked surprised and turned back to Katie. "Did it? Did I hurt your feelings?"

"No." She bolstered herself and tried to repair the small crack in her emotional armor. "I think I've learned, or at least I am learning, a thing or two about love."

Then, to try to return the evening to a lighter tone, she said, "I keep trying to tell you guys, I'm not as messed up as you think I am."

"We don't think you're messed up," Christy said.

Todd jumped in. "That wasn't where I was going with what I said."

Blessedly, Eli returned just then, and the conversation moved to tea and the box of graduation party invitations he had brought back with him.

"Rick wasn't home. He left these for me yesterday and told me about the party his mom is planning. The only problem is that I can only think of a few people to invite. Do you want to take the rest of these, Katie?"

"I have way too many too. What about Joseph and Shiloh? Did you invite them?"

"Yes."

"Good. I was hoping they would come."

Eli made himself at home in Todd and Christy's kitchen and prepared the hot tea. "Does everyone want some?"

"Pass," Todd said.

"I'll have some," Christy said. "You can use the white teapot there on the counter. Tell me again what kind of tea this is?"

"It's from Kenya. It came from a tea plantation run by some people we know. It's just outside of Nairobi. Beautiful, hilly place. High altitude. Vivid shades of green."

"I changed my mind." Todd stood and pulled a mug from the cupboard. "I'll try some of your Kenyan tea."

Katie had been watching Eli. She didn't know if it was the overhead lights, but from the way he was turned toward them, the backward L-shaped scar on his neck seemed to stand out.

"Eli, how did you get that scar? The one on your neck."

He stopped pouring the boiling water from Christy's kettle into the teapot. For a moment, he seemed frozen in place. Katie looked at Todd and Christy for clues. As soon as she saw Todd's expression, she knew she had put her foot in her mouth.

"You know what? I'm guessing I shouldn't have blurted that out. I take it back. Here's a different question. Have you seen any good movies lately?"

When Eli didn't answer right away, Katie turned to Christy for a bailout. "How about you guys? Anything worth recommending?"

Neither Todd nor Christy played along with Katie's change-of-topic move. Both of them sat at the table, looking at Eli. Katie couldn't tell if their attentiveness was an indication that the two of them already knew the story and were waiting to see if Eli would tell Katie, or if they didn't know.

Could it be that Todd and Christy were just as curious, but neither had blurted out the question before?

Eli picked up the lid to Christy's teapot. He put it in place and carried the pot over to the table where he set it in the center of the table along with a tea strainer.

"It's best if you let it steep for about four minutes," he said. "That allows the tea leaves to open all the way and release the good stuff. But then, you know all that already, Katie."

Katie, who loved tea, nodded. "Four minutes," she repeated. "Do you have any milk, Christy?"

"Sure."

She hopped up, but Eli said, "I can get it." He returned to the quiet gathering at the kitchen table and placed the milk carton unceremoniously next to the teapot.

"I'm pretty sure my aunt and uncle are going to come to the graduation," Christy said, encompassing Eli and Katie in her statement. "If you send them an invitation to the party, I think they would love to come."

Katie nodded again. She had Bob and Marti's address and had already planned to send them an invitation. It seemed pointless to add another comment about the party or the invitations. That topic wasn't going anywhere.

Katie's dangling question had encompassed all of them. She wished she could think of something, anything, to kick them all back into the ebb and flow of a different conversation.

"I'd like to know too," Todd said. His statement sat there, waiting for Eli to pick it up.

Eli didn't reach for it. He let it sit there, steeping, as it were.

After a long moment, Eli drew in a deep breath, but still he didn't speak. His gaze was fixed on the teapot in the center of the table.

Katie felt for him. She knew all too well what it was like to be the target when Todd was stuck on a topic. Not more than ten minutes ago Katie had felt she had been in that same place as he tried to convince her that love was on the hunt for her and was going to take her down. The longevity of their friendship gave Katie the feeling that she could talk her way out the back door of Todd's direct comments.

She didn't know, however, if Eli had that same sense of freedom with them.

Without speaking, Eli reached for the teapot and the strainer and served each of them, pouring the steaming tea into their cups.

Katie watched with reverence for the way Eli carried out this ceremony that represented friendship's simplicity to her. She could see that the tea leaves had unfurled during their four-minute soak. The water had turned into tea. Its unmistakably rich yet delicate fragrance rose to encircle them.

"I was eleven," Eli said in low, even words.

Katie knew that what was about to unfurl at this table was a deep, fluttering part of Eli's heart and life. Part of her wanted to be excused. She wanted to leave now and not listen to what Eli was about to say.

That was because her gut told her this communion between these gathered friends would be neither delicate nor fragrant. But it would be true. And truth has a way of staying in the heart for a very long time.

18

W e lived in Zaire." Eli told his story in steady tones as he finished pouring the tea. "Our home was inside a medical compound."

Katie's mind flashed back to something Eli had said at Thanksgiving dinner when they were all feasting at the Doyles' home. He said his favorite birthday was when he was nine, and it rained that day after a long drought. School was let out at the compound, and all the children ran around in the rain and danced in the mud. The image from that story had stayed with Katie; she had filed it away as one of her favorite virtual pictures of Africa.

Eli kept going with his story. "Our family was relatively safe on the mission compound. We lived right next to the medical facilities. People from the villages came into the compound every day. Individuals from warring groups put aside their differences, and all came to the same place for treatment."

He looked at Katie and then at Todd.

"I was supposed to be in school, but I was feeling sick, so the teacher sent me home since she knew my mom was home that day. She sent a note with me. I read it, even though I wasn't supposed to. The note said that if I was faking it, my mom was supposed to send me right back."

Christy smiled softly.

"I went into the house, which was small but one of the more sturdy structures on the compound. I called for my mom, but she didn't answer. I thought she might be out back hanging up laundry or in the vegetable garden. She loves growing carrots and tomatoes."

Eli paused. He kept his gaze on the untouched mug of tea in front of him.

"My mother wasn't in the garden. She was in the bedroom. And a man ... a man from a different village ... intended to rape her."

The stillness that fell on them seemed to draw their hearts together. Katie sensed all their pulses were beating in inaudible unison.

"I ran at him. I didn't know what I was doing, but I jumped on his back and ... he had a knife." Eli stopped there.

Katie felt awful on many levels. From the way Eli weighed each word before speaking it, it was clear he hadn't offered this story to many people in the past. She wished she hadn't voiced the question that caused him to tell them. Katie also felt horrible about what she had thought of Eli last May when she first saw him at Christy and Todd's wedding. When she noticed the backward *L*, Katie had made one of her familiar notes to self from that season and quipped that the *L* stood for "Loser."

Oh, how wrong she was.

"Was your mom ... okay?" Christy asked.

"Sort of. He cut her throat too. Then he ran off because a woman from our village came over just then. If she hadn't come ... A visiting surgeon was there that day, and he was able to work on my mom and me right away, which was incredible at that clinic. My mom needed more stitches. For me, the problem was the cut. It was deep and close ... close to my jugular. Less than a quarter of an inch, the surgeon said."

Katie could barely breathe. She couldn't imagine going through anything like that.

"We both contracted infections afterward. The compound didn't have the right antibiotics, but they eventually got what we needed and ... we just went on."

"Wow, Eli." Todd's voice was tight with emotion. "You and your mom ..."

"I know," Eli said quickly. "God had his hand on our lives. We know that."

Obviously Eli had been around Todd enough to know his bent toward the spiritual side of every situation. Eli's comment didn't carry any hint of irritation.

Katie had nothing to say. She waited for Eli to look her direction so she could offer a look that expressed her heartfelt sympathies.

He glanced around the table briefly. "I don't like to talk about this much."

Christy, Todd, and Katie all gave agreeing nods.

"Actually, aside from you guys, my uncle is the only one I've talked to about it. He's my mom's brother; so of course he knew about everything when it happened."

The pace of Eli's words picked up now that the story had gotten past the rocky place and was on a more level path. "My uncle was the one who convinced me to come to Rancho Corona. When we moved from Zaire to Nairobi, I think my parents figured being in a city would help me get over being so withdrawn and hesitant with people. I'm not sure exactly why they thought that, but my uncle told me a number of times that I needed to experience life outside of Africa. That's why I joined up with the missions outreach project in Spain. It was the first possibility that came up, so I went. It was good, and coming here to school has been good. But I don't know if my uncle really understands that you can leave your home and live somewhere else, but when you love a certain place, it never leaves you."

Todd nodded. "I feel that way about Hawaii."

"Do you think you'll always live in Africa, then?" Christy asked.

"I don't know." Eli wrapped his hands around the mug that still brimmed with untouched tea that had now cooled. "Since I've told you guys all this already, I might as well tell you something else. I've been meaning to say this for a while. Todd, I wanted to thank you for including me in your life. Ever since I got here you've been a solid friend to me. I appreciate your connecting me with Rick and getting me into this apartment complex. It's been good."

"Where did you live before you moved in with Rick?" Katie asked. "You weren't in the dorms, were you?"

"No, I lived with my uncle. That worked out okay last summer, but I was ready to move on. And Katie, I wanted to thank you for inviting me to the pizza night last fall. I don't know if you remember giving me your etiquette tips that night, but I really appreciated them. What you said helped a lot."

Katie definitely remembered how she had briefed Eli on socially approved ways to enter into the group, such as not to stare so much. She felt bad now that she had been critical of his rough-around-the-edges ways. The guy was dealing with a lot. Culture shock as well as trying to fit in on campus and work on campus security.

"If we're turning this into a true-confessions time, then I have to say a few things to you, Eli." Katie took a quick sip of her tea for courage. "I have to apologize to you for being so rude. I know I was more than once."

Eli's expression was returning to his good-humored self. He calmly said, "Do you mean the first week of school when I gave you a parking ticket?"

Katie scowled. "Oh, I forgot about that time. No, I don't think I want to apologize for yelling at you in the parking lot. I think you should have given me a little more grace."

"I think you should have given me a little more respect."

"Why? Because you were wearing a uniform and looking all campus-security macho? I'll tell you something; if the powers-that-be at Rancho want their campus security guy to be treated with more respect, then they are going to have to do something about those beat-up golf carts. I mean, seriously! Those carts look like reject clown cars from the circus. You might as well put one of those oooga squeezy horns on the steering wheel and hang a bunch of balloons out the back."

"Baboons?" Christy said, squelching a laugh.

"No, I said balloons. Not baboons."

"I heard baboons."

"Me too," Todd said.

"Oh, you always take Christy's side. What did you hear me say, Eli?"

"It could have gone either way. How about if I say balloons just to even the score?"

"Thanks. I don't know what's going on lately. Julia misunderstood me the other day when I was trying to say the word *tea*."

"What did you say instead?" Eli asked.

Katie suddenly remembered the entire incident at Bella Barista and lowered her eyes. "It was just something crazy. I don't know what's going on with my brain. Study overload, I think."

"Not to overdo this topic or anything," Eli said, moving back to his previous conversation. "But I wanted to finish saying thank you to all three of you for helping me to find a place here in California and at Rancho."

"No problem, man." Todd extended his hand across the table and exchanged the brawny sort of handshake that men give by clasping each other by the wrist. "Christy and I are here for you anytime. You know that, don't you?"

"I do. Thanks."

It seemed like a good time for Katie to echo Todd's sentiment and say that Eli could count on her as well. Anytime. Katie didn't quite know what to say. Her view of Eli had been tilted in a new direction, but she didn't want to indicate she had a vulnerable soft spot in her heart for him.

Instead of adding words of renewed allegiance to their friendship, Katie took another sip of tea and said, "This sure is good tea. Thanks for bringing it over and sharing it with us."

"Anytime."

Katie relented just slightly and added, "And, Eli, I mean this more than I think it's going to sound, but thank you for sharing about your life with us. I can't imagine what it must have been like for you. Or for your mom. This might be too personal of a question, so you don't have to answer, but did you get any counseling? I mean, have you resolved all this internally?"

"That's part of the reason my uncle wanted me to come here. He set up a counselor for me and paid for it. I started last summer and went to him for about six months. So, yeah, I think I've resolved some of this."

Katie was impressed with how open Eli was being.

Quiet settled around the table for a moment before Eli added, "The one piece that helped me the most from the counseling was getting ahold of being a victim. A victim of grace."

None of them responded right away.

Todd leaned back and nodded. "A victim of grace. That's intense. It's true, though, isn't it? All of us are victims of grace. We don't usually ask for good things to happen to us. We don't see it coming. We certainly don't deserve all of God's love and kindness, but he keeps pouring it out on us. That's strong stuff, Eli. Instead of being a victim of evil, you see God's hand in it all and name yourself a victim of grace. I'm going to remember that one."

"I love that phrase," Christy added. "It really flips around the concept of seeing yourself as being a helpless victim of all the bad stuff that happens in life."

Eli nodded. "Once I reframed it that way, I started to feel again, you know? I'd shut down in some ways, and I think the counseling helped me to get my heart back on track with God. I don't know how to explain it. All I know is that I feel like a whole person now."

Katie felt bad all over again that she had been so judgmental of Eli last summer and fall. Here he was, dealing with so much stuff, and Katie was treating him as if he should have been her idea of a normal American guy who came from a cushy, middle-class home and had gone to a private school and received whatever he wanted each year at Christmas. She wished she had this year to do over again. Not that she wanted to do her relationship with Rick over or do it differently, nor her year of classes or her RA position. All of those parts of the past year had been good. Even the breakup with Rick felt right. What didn't feel good was that she had judged Eli and kept him at a distance for so long.

Katie decided there, at Todd and Christy's kitchen table, that she was going to be kinder to people, especially when she didn't know why they were acting the way they were. She definitely would treat Eli with more kindness and respect from here on out.

Her personal pledge to show Eli more kindness and respect was put to the test the next evening when he showed up at the Spring Fling uninvited. He entered Crown Hall's lobby with Rick.

Katie waved to both of them but found she was glad she couldn't go over to greet them because she was "on duty" with Nicole and responsible to make the party happen. She felt a little uncomfortable and unsure of what to say to either of them.

Her idea of passing out the boxes of Twister to the teams was a big hit until all the groups opened their boxes and found the reason they were such a great price at Bargain Barn was that the spinners didn't work. Some of them didn't spin. Others were missing the arrow piece altogether.

"Listen up!" Katie called out to the restless crowd. When they didn't turn their attention her way, Katie whistled shrilly. That got their attention.

"How many of you can't make your spinner work?"

Every one of the groups responded in the affirmative. Katie was about to say they should skip the game altogether, go for the food, and call it a party. But before she could pull the plug, Nicole appeared at her side, just as she had been all school year.

"Call out the combinations," Nicole said to Katie. "Like a big Bingo game. You can call them out, and each team does the same moves at the same time."

"Great idea! Okay, everyone, we have a Plan B, thanks to our fearless and fabulous Nicole. Here's what we're going to do." Katie issued the revised instructions, confiscated one of the defective spinners as a reminder of the colors, and called out, "Let the games begin!"

For the first few minutes all the teams managed Katie's call-outs with ease. As soon as one person toppled or crumbled, the next person in line took the first player's place. From where she stood on top of one of the coffee tables, Katie saw everyone was mixing it up nicely.

Then she decided to spice it up and added, "Right ear to green!"

"Ear?" everyone called out.

"Yes, ear! Go!"

The noise level kicked up a notch, as the teams faced the challenging job of deciding who was really out because that person had fallen and who was just trying to get his or her ear to the ground.

"Okay, forget the ears. Here we go. Left elbow to blue."

More pandemonium ensued as those with their ears dutifully touching the green tried an anatomically impossible move.

"Forget the ears!" Katie called out, waving her hands, trying to restore some semblance of order. "Take your ears off the green. Or the blue. Or whatever I called. Just put your right elbow on blue."

"I think it was left elbow." Eli had come alongside Katie.

"I think this game is about to tank," Katie said to him.

"No, it isn't. You're doing fine. Everyone is having a good time. Keep going."

"I'm not good at this. Here, do you want to do it? You be the caller. Everyone listens to you, Eli."

"That was in chapel."

"So? Here." She thrust the spinner at him and called out, "Get ready for a real treat, my twisted friends! Eli Lorenzo is your new caller. Hit it, Eli."

His speaking voice rolled out nice and loud and commanding. Not high and bossy and squeaky like Katie's was getting. Eli brought a faster pace to the game, which the players appreciated so they didn't experience muscle cramps waiting.

Eli jump-started the party, from Katie's point of view. She went over to the sound system and turned the speaker back on. When everyone was congregating in the lobby at seven o'clock, Nicole had the music going to make them feel like this really was a party and not just a lame sort of meeting for those who wanted to get away from studying. Nicole also had put up a banner that read, "Spring Fling," and had dotted the area with brightly colored gerbera daisies, Nicole's favorite flower.

Katie adjusted the volume of the music so it was in the background and not competing with Eli, but just enough to bring back the party atmosphere. Nicole came over and said, "Great idea to put the music back on. I think it's working out."

"Yeah, thanks to Eli. By the way, I noticed you went with the boy-catcher sweater. Good choice. Has it worked its marvels yet?"

"No, not even a tiny bit. I went over and said hi when he came in. He said hi back and asked if I thought the paint color in the men's bathroom at the café was too dark."

"That's all he talked to you about? Paint in the men's bathroom? He can be so clueless sometimes."

Nicole looked a little forlorn, but the hint of disappointment quickly vanished. "It's no big deal, Katie. I talked with Julia about it some more, and I'm okay. Ever since she prayed with me, I've felt settled. As least more settled than I have been the past few months."

Katie knew Nicole was switching to more generic statements because Carley, one of the girls from their floor, had slid up close to the two of them. Carley had a history of being divisive and flat-out ornery. Nicole was wise not to reveal any specifics, especially about Rick, when it was possible that Carley could hear.

Katie and Nicole turned their attention to the group. Things were going much better with Eli than they had with Katie at the helm. Katie wasn't the only one who noticed the improvement. Rick wandered over to where Katie and Nicole stood and said, "You can go ahead and say it now, if you want."

"Say what?" Katie asked.

"Say that you're glad I brought Eli. Say that I saved the party by making him come. Anything along those lines will be considered acceptable."

Widening her eyes and putting on a playful baby-doll face, Katie entered into the flirty fun with Rick like she used to back in high school. In an overly lollypop-and-rainbows voice, she said, "Oh, thank you, Rick Doyle. You're so wonderful. I don't know what I would ever do without you. You're my hero."

The last line unexpectedly caught in Katie's throat.

She and Rick locked glances. A last twinge of pain and loss seemed to exchange a whisper between their two hearts. She saw it in his face too.

Katie and Christy had long challenged each other to "hold out for a hero" when it came to their love lives. Christy had held out for Todd, and he definitely was her hero.

Katie had held out for Rick for a long time. And while he most certainly had turned into a hero, he wasn't her hero.

Katie couldn't swallow. She blinked rapidly and turned to the side. "Nicole, take it from here, will you? I'll ... I'll be back."

19

A week and a half later, when Katie met with Julia for another one of her evaluation meetings, she expected to get reamed for leaving the Spring Fling and not returning to finish her part of the program. Nicole had covered beautifully, and no one at the event knew that Katie was supposed to close out the evening by passing out humorous year-end awards to select students.

When Katie stepped into Julia's room, she dipped her chin in a humbled posture. "Go ahead. Let me have it. I can take it."

"What are you doing?" Julia asked.

"I'm repenting for leaving the Spring Fling."

"Don't worry about it, Katie. Nicole told me what was going on, and I understand. You had a heart moment with Rick, and you needed to tend to it right then."

"A heart moment? Yeah, I guess that's exactly what it was. Where did you hear that?"

"From Nicole. I also heard from others that Nicole covered beautifully. They said they had a good time. So don't worry about going AWOL. The event was a big success. I'm the one who should be repenting for not being there with you."

"You told us ahead of time that you had the big faculty dinner. Of course you needed to be there with John. Nicole and I understood, so you don't have to apologize."

Julia's expression lightened. "Speaking of John and weddings and maids of honor ... John and I are each having only one attendant at our wedding, and I'd like you to be my maid of honor."

"Me?"

"Yes, you."

"Why me? I mean, I'm honored to be your maid of honor, but are you sure?"

"Yes, very sure. I've thought about it a lot. John and I talked about it a number of times, and I would like you to be the one who stands up with me. Part of the reason is because most of my close friends were there for me over all the years I went through everything with Trent. They are great friends and have been supportive. But they're woven into my first love story. None of them has been part of this new journey with me as I've fallen in love with John. We kept it all very quiet and private."

Katie could see why Julia had done that. News of an RD and a professor getting together would open up opportunities for lots of rumors, no matter how much integrity was infused in their relationship.

"Another reason I wanted to have you be part of this next season of my life is the way you took me into your confidence with the inheritance. I think that whole process put you and me into each other's lives in an intense way. I feel very connected to you, Katie."

"I know. I feel the same way. All year, Julia, more than with the inheritance stuff, you've been there for me at just the right times."

"And now I want you to be there for me."

"You got it. Like I said. I'd be honored to be your woman of honor."

"Good. I like that: woman of honor instead of maid of honor."

"I know, huh? That's a much better title. Let's start a revolution and change that out-of- date term. Who wants to be a maid? It always makes me think of the Christmas song with the 'eight maids a-milking.' Seriously, who needs that image in her head at a wedding?"

"I had never thought that before, but thanks for planting the image in my head. I'm sure it will stay with me now whenever I hear the term *maid of honor*."

"Not if we're successful in our mission to retrain brides every-where to call their first attendant her 'woman of honor.' Or even 'best woman.' Why not? The groom gets to call his wingman his best man. Why can't the bride have a best woman?"

"I like the term *woman of honor*. That's what I now officially label your role in our wedding. So it's a definite yes, then?"

"Yes. Definitely, yes! I am your woman of honor." Katie gave a little half-bow. "Bring on the details."

"Okay. First, I'd better ask you, what have you decided you'll do after you graduate?"

"I don't know exactly. Find a job somewhere doing something. I thought I would see if I could move into Rick and Eli's apartment."

Julia looked surprised. "With the two of them?"

"No. Rick is planning to move to Redlands. I don't know when Eli's leaving, but when he goes back to Nairobi, I'm guessing that would leave their apartment open."

"But Eli isn't going back to Kenya until after our wedding."

Katie wasn't sure why Julia knew that little detail, but it didn't seem important to pursue.

"When is the wedding?" Katie asked.

"The week after graduation. Didn't I tell you that yet?"

"Maybe, but I might have forgotten. Homework overload. Wow, that's fast."

"I know. When John and I decided we wanted to get married on upper campus, we had to go with one of the few remaining open dates. Ever since Christy and Todd held their wedding in the meadow last year, it's become a popular location for lots of Rancho students, past and present. They really started something."

"Don't let her aunt Marti hear you say that. She'll want a cut of the profit from all the events held there. She was the one who went all out with the setup, the caterers, and the flowers."

"Our wedding won't be that elaborate. And it won't be that large, either. We're trying to keep it to about fifty people. Seventy-five at the most."

"That is small."

"We realized we both know a lot of people. It could practically be an all-school event, if we opened it up. We decided we wanted just family and close friends. Since John and Patricia never had children, it's not as if we need to be sensitive to blending our extended families."

"Will the reception be there too, in the meadow?"

"Yes. It's going to be simple. Cake and punch. A friend of mine is providing the cake as a gift to us. Did Nicole tell you she's doing the flowers?"

"She did. I'm sure she'll make it beyond beautiful for you guys. She's so gifted that way. What about your dress?"

"I'm going to wear my sister's wedding dress. She's sending it to me."

"Is she coming to the wedding?"

"No, she's in her third trimester of a difficult pregnancy, and the doctor said she couldn't fly. We talked about postponing the wedding until after the baby comes and both of them are able to travel. But then it would be well into September, and John would be back in classes."

"Are you okay with your sister's not being there?"

Julia nodded. "She was the one who urged us to go ahead and get married."

"Well, tell me what you need me to do, and when you need it done, and I'll be all over it."

"I'm working on a list. If you have time now, we could go over some of the details."

"Sure. But wait. Aren't you supposed to give me my year-end review?"

"Oh, right. Katie, you've done a good job this year. Keep it up for these final weeks."

"Okay."

"Any particular problems?"

"Just the usual."

"Okay. Good. End of review."

The two of them laughed. Julia went over to a little desk that fit nicely in the corner of her apartment and pulled out a big binder.

"Whoa! I thought you said it was going to be a simple wedding."

"This is simple. Everything is right here. This is my brain. If I lose this, I'm sunk." As Julia put the book down on the coffee table, a business card fluttered out and landed on Katie's shoe.

She picked it up and read the front of the card. " 'Animals R Us?' What kind of a wedding are you guys having? Did you forget to tell me about the Noah's ark theme?"

Julia looked at the card. "Oh. That was one of John's ideas. We crossed that off the list awhile ago."

"What? Two-by-two giraffes coming down the aisle instead of flower girls? A zebra for a ring bearer?"

"No, doves. Lots of doves. John wanted to have them released at the end. You probably remember from having taken his Bible class that he's big on doves' symbolism in Scripture."

"Oh, that's right. The dove that was released from the ark and flew back with the olive branch showing that the floodwaters had receded."

"And the Holy Spirit in the form of a dove coming down at the baptism of Christ," Julia added. "Also the two doves being the poor man's sacrifice that Mary and Joseph offered in the temple right after Christ was born."

"What exactly did Dr. Ambrose want the doves to symbolize at your wedding?"

"Our uniting as one in peace now that the waters of all our painful years have receded. The presence of God's Spirit. Offering ourselves as set apart to God. He had a few other dove connections, but I don't remember now what they were."

"I think it's a beautiful addition to your wedding. Why don't you do it? I wanted Christy to release hundreds of butterflies at her wedding. I had a hard time finding a place that would sell enough butterflies for her to do it. Does this company rent the doves, or do you have to buy them?"

"I don't know. We didn't pursue it. I think the man who runs Animals R Us was a former student of John's, and he now trains animals for TV and film. You can throw away the card. Do you want something to drink?"

"Sure. Just water."

As Julia went into her small kitchenette for the water, Katie tucked the card into her pocket. She had a plan.

Before the day was out, Katie had made a strategic phone call to Animals R Us. The quote she received on the cost of one hundred doves was astronomical. She had to buy them since, unlike homing pigeons, these doves weren't trained to return to their cages. The cages and delivery costs were almost as much as the cost of the birds. So much for that idea.

Then, while working on her ridiculously overdue final project the next night, a brilliant thought came to her. Julia and her beloved didn't need one hundred doves. Only one.

Dashing down to Nicole's room, she found her friend already in bed.

"Hey, wake up. It's only eleven-thirty. What are you doing?"

"Sleeping. You really should try it some time." Nicole turned on the light next to her bed, squinting at Katie.

"This is the best idea ever. I couldn't wait till morning to tell you."

"Katie, I thought something was wrong!"

"No, something is right. Or at least it is going to be right. Beautifully right." Katie launched into a rundown of how Dr. Ambrose wanted doves at the wedding and Julia had said to throw away the card, but Katie had called for information.

"Here's my stroke of genius. When you design the flowers, you can make my bouquet so that it has a hidden cage big enough for one dove."

"Katie ..."

"No, listen, it's perfect. I'm not talking about a bunch of doves. Just a single dove. This will be my surprise for them. I'll release it from the bouquet right after they say 'I do.' Or after they kiss. Or maybe right before they go down the aisle. It will be perfect! Don't you see? Dr. Ambrose will love it. The single dove symbolizes, when Julia came down the aisle, that she and Dr. Ambrose were two separate people with two hearts. The mystery of marriage is that the two become one. One dove. One heart. United as one. Don't you love it?"

"Actually ..." Nicole was sitting up now and had stopped blinking in the bright light. "I do love it. What a great idea, Katie."

"Told you it couldn't wait till morning."

"I don't think it would be that difficult to incorporate a small cage in the center of the bouquet. As long as the dove is a magician's sort of dove that doesn't mind being confined to a small space."

"We'll ask for a nonclaustrophobic dove. How will that be?"

"You'll have to have a big bouquet. That's fine because Julia's bouquet is going to be big too. She left it up to me to decide on your bouquet, so she probably wouldn't question what I design for you. How fun!"

"I know. Dr. Ambrose will love it."

Katie and Nicole sat together on her bed for the next hour going over Julia's wedding plans.

"I could use some help shopping for my woman of honor dress too. Any ideas you have would be greatly appreciated."

"What style or color does Julia want you to wear?"

"She said it's up to me since I don't have to match anyone else. I was thinking of going with basic black. What do you think?"

"I think that's a good way to go. We should be able to find something stunning for you. When do you have time to go shopping?"

The two of them figured out when they had open time on their calendars and then moved on to graduation party plans.

"I sent my invitations last Monday," Katie said.

"So did I. I have extras, if you need any more."

"No, I have a lot of extras too."

"You sent one to your parents, didn't you?"

"Yes. I doubt they'll come. I didn't order graduation announcements or anything, so the party invitation served double duty for me. At least my parents will know that I graduated. That is, if I finish everything in the next few weeks."

"I hope your parents come, Katie. You said things were a little better with them at Christmas."

"Yeah, Rick and I went down late on Christmas day. I told you that, didn't I? We took them some presents. My mom made some soup, which is about as fancy as my parents ever get now with food. Our time with them was okay. Not jolly but okay. We were there for a total of about two hours. My dad thanked us for coming to see them, so I think it was worth it."

"Maybe he'll think it's worth it to come up for your graduation."

"Maybe."

Nicole yawned and politely covered her mouth.

"I should let you sleep," Katie said, getting up. "Thanks for listening. I'm glad you like my idea."

"You buy the dove, and I'll design the bouquet with the hidden cage."

Katie trotted down the hall to her room, stopping to talk to two other night owls who were still up, roaming the hall in their pjs. Katie recognized their spacey, stress-incited looks. She encouraged both of them by saying they would make it through the semester. "Get extra vitamin C in you whenever you can."

"Thanks, Mom," one of the women said with a grin.

"Your immune system will thank me for this."

When she returned to her room, she took her own advice and went looking for her supply of vitamin C. Taking three of the chewable tablets, she plugged in her hot pot. She wasn't particularly interested in tea, but a box of instant Thai noodles sounded good. Within six minutes she was back at her laptop. The steaming bowl of noodles wafted their spicy fragrance like a blessing over her middle-of-the-night study session.

"This is going to happen, isn't it? I'm going to finish this tonight at long last. I'm going make it through finals, and I'm going to graduate." She slowly sipped the noodle broth, feeling warmed inside her belly as well as inside her spirit.

Taped to the wall beside her desk were five cards on which she had written some of her favorite verses. Her glance landed on a verse she had written out over a year and a half ago, when she and Christy were roommates. She had fixed her thoughts on that verse before she started going out with Rick.

Psalm 138:8 — The Lord will fulfill his purpose for me.

"I believe you did that, Lord. You still are fulfilling your purposes for me."

The verse on the card next to that one was from Exodus 20:24:

Build altars in the places where I remind you who I am, and I will come and bless you there.

She remembered that she had come across that verse last August during the RA retreat on Catalina Island. In response, as her own unconventional act of worship, Katie had built a small altar and dedicated the coming year to the Lord.

Reaching for a third card, she pulled it off the wall and smiled. This one, from Psalms, was the verse some women from her floor had selected especially for Katie for the year. It also was written out next to her photo in a collage that had been up on their wall since the beginning of the school year. Katie had walked past that wall so many times and had read all the verses by the photos so often that she had become immune to "her" verse.

The Lord will guard your going out and your coming in from this time forth and forever.

"You did that too. You guarded and blessed all my months of going out with Rick."

Katie knew it was extraordinary to feel so at peace about how everything had turned out with Rick. "You blessed my going out, and now I believe you're going to bless my coming in. Coming into what? Coming in for a landing on this long flight called the College Express. All I ask, Lord, is for a safe landing. After that ... what? What do you want me to do?"

Katie pulled a blank index card from a stack on her desk and wrote a note to herself. All school year she had been making up mental notes to herself. It seemed fitting that she at long last should write out one of those notes with real paper and ink.

Surprisingly, the note ended up not being written as if she were the one doing the speaking. She didn't plan to, but she wrote it as if God were writing it to her.

> Dear Katie, I have it all figured out. Keep trusting me and stay tuned for coming attractions. Don't forget: You too are a victim of my grace.
>
> Love, God.

20

The day before Katie's graduation, her cell phone rang at 3:05 a.m. At first she thought she had set her alarm and tried to turn off that feature on her phone. When her phone kept buzzing, her eyes adjusted to the glow of the screen, and she saw that Eli was calling.

"Eli, what's going on? Are you okay?"

"I'm good. Do you want to do something a little crazy to celebrate that we're about to graduate from college?"

"Crazy? Eli, I think it's crazy that you're calling me at three o'clock in the morning on a day that I could have slept till noon if I wanted!"

"You can sleep all you want next week. Come with me. I'm going to watch the sunrise."

"Where are you going?"

"To the mountains."

"It will take two hours to get there." Katie was sitting up now and wrapping her mind around the spontaneous idea.

"Which is why we need to leave right now if we're going to catch the first light. Are you in?"

Katie hesitated only a moment. "Yeah. Why not? I'll go with you." Even though she was responding calmly, Katie felt her spirit stir with anticipation. After all the pressure of the past few weeks, this was like a get-out-of-jail-free card.

She was the one who usually suggested outlandish adventures to her friends, so it felt good to have someone else invite her to a crazy outing in the middle of the night.

"Where do you want me to meet you?"

"I'll come over to Crown Hall and meet you out front."

With a blast of energy, Katie was up and pulling on warm clothes. By the time she stepped out of the lobby and into the dark chill, Eli was climbing out of the campus security cart.

"Tell me we're not driving that clown-mobile anywhere." Katie pulled a beanie cap from her shoulder bag and tugged it over her head.

"No, I just got off duty. I was hoping you would drive. I still haven't gone for a ride in your new car. Or should I say in 'Clover.'"

"Yes, my little green Clover. Sure, I'll drive. I think Clover is up for an adventure too." Katie fished around for her keys and fell into stride with Eli. They walked to her car in steady measure and got in. Katie started the engine and backed up.

"Do you know where we're going? Big Bear? Lake Arrowhead?" she asked.

One of the things students from other states loved about Rancho Corona University was its location. A person could drive an hour west and be at the beach, an hour southeast and be in the desert, or two hours northeast and be in the mountains.

"I printed a map," Eli said. "Have you been to Crestline or Rim of the World before?"

"Maybe. I'm not sure."

"One of the guys I work with used to live there. He said to go to a place called Strawberry Peak Fire Lookout. The map says it takes an hour and fifty-five minutes from here."

"I've never heard of Strawberry Peak Lookout. But I've been sledding at Big Bear. Or maybe it was Lake Arrowhead. Anyway, how about if I get us on the freeway, and you tell me where to go from there?"

"Sounds good. Thanks for coming with me, Katie."

She glanced at him and offered a contented smile. "Thanks for asking me to go. I do love an adventure."

"I know you do. So do I. I was making the usual rounds tonight in my clown-mobile, as you call it, and realized I've been here for almost a year, but I haven't gone to the mountains."

"It's too bad you didn't decide to go during the winter when there was snow. Have you ever seen snow before?"

"Of course I've seen snow."

"Well, your being from Africa and all ..."

Eli looked amused. "We have a few mountains in Africa too, you know."

"Really? Like mountains that get snow?"

"Have you heard of Kilimanjaro?"

"Maybe."

"It's across the border in Tanzania, but it's not far from where my parents live. The summit is almost 20,000 feet."

"Twenty thousand? Wow, it would catch a little snow at that height."

"Kilimanjaro is the tallest mountain in Africa. My dad and I hiked it two years ago. Not all the way to the top. You need to be expedition outfitted to trek to the summit of the highest peak. We went far enough to freeze our tails off and take some awesome pictures."

"Oh, yeah, now that I think about it, I did see some of those pictures in the presentation you did for chapel."

"That was Kilimanjaro."

"I want to go to Africa someday."

"You do?"

Katie glanced at him. "Haven't I ever told you that?"

"No. I'm surprised."

"Why?"

"When the outreach team met a few months ago, you went to the first meeting but walked out after twenty minutes."

"I received a text saying I needed to go back to the dorm for a problem that came up. I don't remember now what it was. I didn't attend the next meeting or sign up for the trip because of Rick."

"Why? Didn't Rick want you to go?"

"He didn't come out and say it, but I knew he wouldn't understand why I wanted to go. At the time, things were so great for Rick and me that I didn't want to do anything to jeopardize our relationship."

Katie paused a moment before adding, "How pathetic is that? I held off going to Africa, and look how everything turned out."

"I don't see your decision as pathetic."

"Thanks, Eli, but in a way, it was."

"How is it pathetic to be committed to someone you deeply care for? I think the level of loyalty that both you and Rick showed toward each other and your relationship was impressive."

"Impressive, huh? Is that what we were? Rick would probably like that description."

"I can't think of another couple I know who tried so hard for so long to make each other happy. What you guys worked through was impressive."

Katie wasn't sure how to take Eli's comment. She knew from one of her classes this semester that, when a person puts on a false front to let another individual get his or her way, the relationship is unhealthy. Eventually the stronger personality wins out in making the decisions, and the other person is falsely compliant, ending up stifled and frustrated.

The class instructor had applied that relational model to politics and the misdirection of funds to developing nations. However, while studying for her final, Katie put herself and Rick into the model. While she didn't think the concept fit them exactly, she did see similarities. She wanted to believe she had stayed true to her personality throughout their relationship and not put on a false front, but she wasn't sure Rick had done the same.

"I still don't see why you say that what Rick and I did was impressive."

"Because both of you tried so hard."

"I take it you don't think a good relationship requires a lot of trying or a lot of hard work."

"Sure it does. But I also think a good relationship rolls out natu-rally and unforced. Like waves. Love comes on its own schedule. It's inconvenient and organic, and that's what makes it real."

Katie squirmed in her seat and adjusted her rearview mirror. Eli's words made her heart do a little skip, and that made her uncomfort-able. If she were to be honest with herself and with Eli, she would blurt out that she agreed with him. These were things she had tried to express to Rick for months, but he was too set on weighing, measur-ing, and scheduling every step of their relationship.

She couldn't bring herself to jump in with an affirmation of Eli's comment. Instead, she challenged him. "So tell me, what's your idea of a successful relationship?" Katie hated the word *successful* since that was a defining term for Rick, but it seemed the best word to use if the conversation were to stay on a more impersonal level.

Eli settled deeper into the passenger's seat. "I'm not big on mea-suring things by success."

"And why is that?" She knew she was presenting the opposite side of her feelings on the subject, but she wasn't about to let down her guard. Not here. Not now.

"I don't think many of us know how to accurately measure suc-cess," Eli said. "That's because God's ways aren't our ways, and his thoughts aren't our thoughts. So much of the kingdom of God is measured on a different scale than the one the world uses to measure value. I should warn you, I just turned in a final paper last week for my doctrine class on the Law of Christ, so stop me if you don't want a lecture."

"We have over an hour. Go ahead, spill your knowledge. Prove that you're almost a college graduate."

Eli seemed to like her challenge. "The title of my paper was, 'Love God and Do What You Want.'"

Katie had heard that line a year ago in her doctrine class. She even vaguely remembered what she had written for the essay question. Something about how Christ fulfilled the Old Testament command to "love the Lord your God with all your heart and with all your soul and with all your mind" and that he added, "love your neighbor as yourself." That meant people needed to love themselves so that they could treat others with the same love and kindness they showed themselves.

She had received a 78 out of 100 on her paper and was guessing Eli's paper had been along the same lines.

However, as his voice picked up speed, she saw how passionate he was about his ideas. In a way, Eli reminded her of Todd, with the spiritual side of life being Eli's default setting on any given topic. That especially showed up in his subtle but commanding air when he was in front of people.

Rick's good looks gave him a commanding presence no matter where he was. When he gave instructions at the café, everyone took it as coming from their commanding officer. His words were often sharp and direct. And they were obeyed.

With Eli, the commanding air was different. He looked average on the outside. Better than average, actually. Especially now that his hair had grown long and curly. He had a handsome face, not chiseled like Rick's, but more approachable and unintimidating. While Eli appeared average and accessible on the outside, once he stood in front of a group and spoke, his presence became surprisingly powerful. His words flowed clear and steady, like a pristine underground spring that found its way to the surface and watered everything around it.

"Love starts in the heart," Eli said. "Not just in the head. All love engages the emotions."

Katie tuned back to what he was saying.

"So, if I love God, and I mean really love God with abandon, then I must come to love myself, my life. I need to love my story at the heart level. That's what I believe life is for all of us. A story being written by God. He is the Author and Finisher of our faith. When I start to love my story, with all its messed up twists and turns, then I can love other people who are living out their own stories with all their messed up twists and turns."

Katie jumped in. "I've been learning to make peace with my story this past year too. Or, I guess I should say, the story God is writing in my life. I have my share of messed up twists and turns."

"We all do. If we didn't, why would we need a Savior? Why would we need God's grace? And in my story, why would I need the power of forgiveness if I could simply work out my anger on my own?"

"Do you think you've really forgiven the guy who attacked you and your mom?"

"Yes. Not all at once. It's been a process. But, yes, I've forgiven him. I don't hold an account against him anymore."

"Did he get arrested or anything?"

"No. He wasn't arrested or tried or even caught. Not in that part of Zaire. Some things will never be brought to justice. At least not on a human level. That's why I said I don't hold out a case against him anymore. If there's going to be any justice, it will be measured out by God, not by me."

"That's pretty intense."

"I know. It's like I was saying about our stories. I don't know that guy's story. Why would he do that? What demonic force pressed in on him to act in that way? I mean, if I'm going to go around saying I love God, then I have to trust him and believe that everything in my life first passed through his fingers. Nothing happens outside of his control. He alone will bring all things to justice one day. All I'm supposed to do is love my own story so that I can love that guy's story too."

Katie felt a swirl of emotions at Eli's words. She agreed with him in theory and even knew personally some of the freedom of forgiveness. Early in the semester Julia had helped her to go through a process of forgiving her parents for being so emotionally disengaged in her life. She also forgave Rick for the ways he had hurt her during their high school years. She knew what it was like to no longer carry the weight of that unforgiveness.

But forgiving someone who had done what Eli's attacker had done? Katie had no way to relate to the depth of that sort of forgiveness.

"You kind of amaze me," Katie said awkwardly.

"Why do you say that?"

"For starters, I don't think I've ever heard you talk this much. And this is deep stuff, Eli."

"It's the stuff life is made of. The world is a dark place."

Katie felt a somberness covering her. She had listened to many women on her floor as they told pieces of their stories. She knew a lot of darkness filled this world. Terrible things happened to very good people.

She tried to remember how she had felt a few weeks ago when Eli said he was a victim of grace. She wanted to return now to that same feeling of hope.

Eli's voice lowered. "You know, I think the best thing I learned this year was when I helped to put the strings of lights around the palm trees on upper campus."

Katie was amused and touched. She loved the lights on the palm trees. She loved the way they had transformed upper campus.

"And what did you learn from the palm tree, O Sage One?"

"I didn't learn anything from the palm trees. What I learned was that light transforms darkness. The first time we hit that On switch, I couldn't believe how much difference a little touch of light made in the middle of all that darkness. We're all a bunch of small light bulbs, you know? We just hang in there, and when God's power comes on, it's amazing. The darkness is transformed. Especially when we stay connected to each other."

Katie glanced over at him again. A half-dozen thoughts scrambled inside her, trying to line up with everything she knew about life, love, and God.

Could it be that simple? We just stay connected, and God is the one who flips the On switch with all the power?

She was feeling strangely jittery, and her stomach was clenching. Returning her view to the road ahead, Katie still couldn't believe how open Eli was. He seemed like a different person than the Eli she had first seen at Todd and Christy's wedding.

"Hang on a minute." Eli pulled out a small flashlight and looked at his folded-up map. "You're going to want to take the next exit. Not this one, but the next one. Waterman."

"Okay." Katie put on her blinker and changed lanes, ready to make the turn to exit the freeway and head for the mountains.

For a moment she flashed back to a conversation she had had with Rick while they were driving on a freeway several months ago. At the time she was exasperated over being in the slow lane of their relationship for so long. She wanted Rick to put on the dating blinker and move them over to the fast lane.

At the time Rick wasn't willing to make the move. Their relationship stayed in the same, straight, slow lane for what seemed like an unbearably long stretch to Katie.

Symbolically, she liked what was happening now. It felt much better to be exiting the straight lanes of the freeway and taking the winding side streets that led to destinations not yet explored.

"I can't believe how we've come so far so quickly." Katie was referring to the distance they had traveled in the car. Eli apparently took her comment to mean how far the two of them had come as a result of their open conversation over the past hour.

"I know," Eli said. "I wish you and I had been able to talk to each other like this last summer. It would have been a completely different school year. I wasn't there yet."

He paused and added, "But I am now."

21

K atie refused to read anything into Eli's comment about "being there now." She looked at him out of the corner of her eye. Was he indicating that he was ready to pursue a relationship with her beyond what it was now?

No, that couldn't be what he meant. Why would he even hint at such a thing? He's going back to Kenya, and I'm on an indefinite fast from all dating relationships. No way am I going to let myself tumble headlong into another dead-end crush. I've done that far too often.

As soon as Katie thought that, she felt her heart beat faster. She knew Eli would never be a crush. No, not a crush. She realized that if she opened her heart to him, life as she knew it would be over. This guy would love her back with more kindness, intensity, and freedom than she ever had experienced. Except for maybe the relationship she had with Christy. And now with Julia. Katie knew what if felt like to be knit together at the heart with true friends.

But she refused even to consider a relationship on that level with Eli. Stopping the car at a light on Waterman Avenue, she felt a frown coming over her face. She didn't like the conclusion she had just arrived at while straightening the wiggly line that had been her connection with Eli for the past year.

Basically, you just told yourself that if you're going to have a relationship with Eli, it has to be all or nothing. He cares about you. You know it, but you just won't admit it. If you allow yourself for one minute to care even one pinch about him, he'll get in your heart, and you know it.

Katie reached over and turned on her car radio. She pressed a button that switched to her own music selection and went for something on the jazzy side.

"Have you heard this group before?" Katie had to talk loud over the music. Her voice sounded urgent. She needed to redirect the conversation. Pronto!

"It's not African dance music like you had on when we went to the desert," she added. "But it's good for waking us up. Do you want to stop for coffee, by the way? I'm sure we can find a gas station convenience store somewhere around here that's open."

Eli seemed to be studying her, trying to understand the abrupt change in her demeanor.

Katie glanced at him and then back at the road. "Not to be rude or anything, Eli, but you've got that staring thing going on again."

He was quiet for a moment. Then he countered with, "Not to be rude or anything, Katie, but you've got that nervous defense mechanism thing going on again."

Katie felt a rush of blood to her face. She looked straight ahead and clenched her teeth. No one called her out on her stuff. No one!

She didn't know what to say.

Unmoved by her discomfort or her silence, Eli shuffled through her music. He changed to a different song that had a more defined drumbeat. Flipping on his handy-dandy little flashlight, he checked the map again.

"This road will take us up the mountain," Eli said. "Stay on Waterman."

"Okay." Her voice came out solid even though her flapping heart felt wobbly. She drove another few miles and calmed down. Eli was calm. Why shouldn't she be calm? There was no reason to get upset or start a small war here in the car.

But Katie felt odd, letting the topic float there around them without forcing a resolution or conclusion. She also felt safe. That was the oddest part. Katie knew she didn't have to adjust her temperament or personality when she was around Eli.

They stopped at a gas station before heading up the hills into the San Bernardino Mountains. Eli went for a big cup of coffee while Katie selected a bottle of New Zealand glacier water and stood in line behind Eli.

"I'll buy that." He reached for her bottle of water.

"No, that's okay. I have money."

A guy came in with three boxes that looked like they contained donuts and headed to the back of the store. As soon as he walked past, Katie caught the scent and knew her suspicions were right.

"Are those for sale?" she asked.

"They will be as soon as I put them in the case."

"I'll take one."

"So will I," Eli said.

A few minutes later the two of them were back in Katie's car, sinking their teeth into early-morning-fresh-from-the-bakery donuts.

"Oh, man," Katie cooed after her first swallow. "They're still warm."

"Good stuff," Eli said. "We sure never had junk food like this when I was growing up."

"You want another one?"

Before Eli could answer, she was out the door with her donut between her lips and her wallet in hand. She bought three donuts. Two of them were for her and Eli. The third one she gave to the cashier and said, "Merry Christmas."

He looked amused and chomped into the donut before she was out the door.

"You didn't need to buy me another one, Katie."

"Yes, I did. You only had Glazed Donut 101. If you're going to learn the ways of American gluttony and the delights of warm lard, then you really need to go for this advanced course. Donut 201. Chocolate-covered, old-fashioned buttermilk. This is the reason aliens keep trying to land on planet Earth. They want this recipe."

Eli took a bite. "Oh, yeah, this is dangerous."

Katie joined him in the Donut 201 class, letting the still-warm chocolate melt on her tongue. "Every now and then, you gotta' live dangerously. That's what I say."

"Especially on our official last day as college students. Tomorrow you and I will be college graduates."

"Yes, we will. Here's to us!" Katie held up her half-eaten donut, inviting Eli to toast with her.

"Yes," Eli echoed. "To us."

They tapped donuts and took a bite in unison.

Their eyes fixed on each other in shared merriment. Eli didn't blink. His eyes were speaking to her, but Katie refused to listen.

She looked away and felt a strong rumbling inside.

Is my stomach telling me it's too early for so much sugar? Never. Not my stomach. Why do I feel as if a herd of buffalo is stampeding through my gut?

She put down her donut and took a long drink of water. Pressing the back of her hand to her forehead, she checked to make sure she wasn't running a fever.

"You okay?"

"Yeah, I'm fine. Just throwing it down too fast, I guess. Smaller bites, right? Good stuff, isn't it?"

"Good stuff," Eli agreed.

Katie put her attention back on driving up the mountain. As she sipped her water, the buffalo stampede calmed down. The music came on as soon as she started up the car, so that provided safe conversational topics for them. As long as she didn't make eye contact with Eli, she felt fine.

Worrying about eye contact wasn't a problem because Katie needed both eyes on the road and both hands on the wheel, as the mountain road wound higher and higher. They both said their ears were popping. Eli directed Katie on which turnoff to take once they were in Crestline. The valley floor below was a vast field of twinkling lights in the remains of the dark night. The only light ahead came from Clover's headlights and an occasional streetlight.

"Are you sure this is right?"

"I think so. The directions say we stay on this road for another three miles and then look for a sign for Strawberry Peak Lookout on the left."

"What's with the 'strawberry'? This elevation has to be too high to grow strawberries."

"I have no idea where the name comes from."

Katie kept her focus on the road. They found the sign as predicted, turned up a steep road, and drove to what looked like a huge microwave tower. Turning off the engine and clambering out, they were caught off guard by the chill in the air.

"I have a blanket in my trunk." Katie went for the small fleece blanket she had put in there soon after she bought the car. "You going to be warm enough?"

Eli zipped up the front of his sweatshirt and put the hood over his head. "Yeah, I'm good. How about you?"

"I'm good too." With the blanket wrapped around her shoulders, Katie put the car keys in her pocket and reached inside the car for her camera. She had remembered it was in her purse and was glad. From this lookout she could take some great shots of the valley below and all the dots of lights.

In the predawn silence, as they walked around the open area near the tower, Katie snapped photos of the twinkling lights in the dark valley. She took some of the myriad of stars that presented themselves in shimmering glory. She took one shot of Eli's profile as he looked to the heavens with his hands in his sweatshirt's pocket and the hood falling back.

Then it happened. The song of a bird twittered in a tree overhead. A singular call to worship.

Katie looked to Eli to see if he had heard it. He was looking at her, and the features of his face suddenly seemed more defined. Katie looked to the east, where Eli had turned his gaze. The wide panorama of spacious sky had turned a pale shade of lavender.

Another bird joined the morning song and then several more.

Do you do this every day, little birds? Do you sing the morning into the sky?

The bird song and the dawn seemed sweetly connected, as Eli and Katie stood several feet away from each other, both transfixed on the changing sky welcomed by the symphony. Neither spoke. It would have ruined the moment to try to comment on what they were witnessing.

How do you say, "Oh, how pretty!" to something as magnificent as this?

Katie couldn't remember ever witnessing the birth of a new day like this before.

You do this every day, don't you, Father? Who notices? You're performing sunrise to a nearly empty house. I'm so glad we're here to see this. I applaud your work, God. Bravo!

A half dozen shades of blue appeared like streams of satin ribbons in the endless sky before them. Faint tinges of rose and pale daffodil yellow touched the celestial canvas. A wayward fleet of rusted silver clouds sailed into the south. Their meager number seemed to dissipate as the outline of the hills came into view.

All around them the landscape began to show off its complex layers of hills and valleys. The ridges revealed their wealth of tall fir trees. Above them, in the tallest tree, an expanded chorus of birds sang their little hearts out.

Katie's heart pounded with expectancy and awe.

Silently, unnoticed by the majority of God's vast creation, the new day came. The sun floated heavenward over the edge of the horizon and in streaming golden glory sent instant beams of light to cover them.

She had forgotten to take pictures because she was so caught up in the moment. With a steady hand, Katie tried to capture the beauty. Turning to the west, where the mountain still shaded the new day's sun from the sleeping valley, all was dark and gray except for the determined electric lights. Human efforts toward lighting the world never could compare to God's singular, spectacular orb of brilliance.

All the stars wearily tucked themselves in for the day as the sun rose.

Katie whispered her worshipful thoughts to God. She felt comfortably alone with her heavenly Father at that moment, even though Eli was standing only a few feet away. He seemed caught up in his own thoughts. They stayed that way for some time, waiting until the sun had taken center stage in the morning sky and was well into its eternal climb into the heavens.

Katie took more pictures of the amazing views of the valley below. She didn't feel the need to say anything. She loved this solace, this sacred space, and the beauty they just had witnessed.

Eli came closer and whispered something, but she didn't quite catch it.

Was he completing a thought? A prayer? Or was he talking to me?

Katie asked, "So what do you think? Are you ready to go?"

"Sure."

They drove down the mountain in silence. Both of them seemed to have a lot on their minds. Katie didn't know how to process everything she had just witnessed, so she redirected her thoughts. At the top of the list was thinking through how she was going to move the last of her things out of her dorm room. She had another week that she could stay in her room since she had agreed to remain on duty after graduation to finish her RA job and check out all the students who were moving out of the dorm.

The only problem was that she didn't know yet where she was going to move her belongings. She had several offers. She could move into an apartment three miles away along with two other women RAs who had gotten jobs on campus for the summer. Christy said she could stay with them in their little apartment if she didn't mind an air mattress in the living room and as long as it was only for a few weeks.

Nicole hadn't decided yet what she was going to do either. She said she could always move back to Santa Barbara and stay with her parents until she found a job somewhere, but that possibility depressed her.

Katie had considered the same sort of less-desirable option of moving in with her parents in Escondido. At least she assumed she could do that. She hadn't asked.

Financially she had enough money to rent her own place, and that was her preferred option. She knew she should have had all this figured out a month ago, but she had been busy passing her classes. Some of them with flying colors. Katie had a lot to celebrate tomorrow when she walked onstage and received her diploma. She would celebrate first and figure out where she was going to live later.

"This is where to turn to get back on the freeway." Eli's voice broke into her thoughts.

"Oh, thanks."

"Are your parents coming to the commencement ceremony tomorrow?" Eli asked.

Katie wondered where he had come up with that question.

"I don't know. Probably not." She wondered if he was regretting that his parents wouldn't be able to come and added, "I'm sure your mom and dad would be there if they could."

"They would. My parents met here, at Rancho Corona."

"Did they really?"

"My dad was roommates with my uncle. My mom's brother. He introduced them, and they got married six months later."

"Wow! That was fast."

"They said they just knew so why delay the inevitable?"

"Had they graduated from college yet?"

"No, they were still in school. They worked on campus, went to summer school, lived on rice and beans. It's one of those stories that expands and gets embellished with each telling. I think one of the versions includes them walking uphill in the snow barefoot to get to class."

Katie laughed. She was grateful that the conversation between the two of them was on a lighter subject than it had been for the drive up the mountain.

"What about your parents?" Eli asked. "How did they meet?"

Her laughter dissipated. Katie didn't particularly want to respond to that question. She knew the answer, but it wasn't one that fit with the typical Rancho student's answer to that question. She also knew that whatever she told Eli she could feel safe entrusting it to him. This was part of her story. Her messy life story. She decided she might as well own it.

"My parents met at a bar."

Without a hint of judgment, Eli asked, "Was it love at first sight?"

His question caught her off guard. "No, I don't think so. I don't know. My parents are older. They're in their sixties now. I think my dad is sixty-eight. He might be sixty-nine. Anyway, I was a surprise baby, obviously. I can't say I exactly had a normal childhood, whatever normal means."

"Does it make you feel uncomfortable talking about this?"

Katie glanced at him. "Yeah, a little."

"That's good," Eli said.

"Good?"

"Yes, good. It's good to talk about things that make you feel uncomfortable. Getting them out gives you a lot of freedom. It allows you to move around inside your life and get comfortable."

"Okay, you can stop now. You're beginning to sound like one of those group therapists on TV."

"So what if I do? It's true, Katie. You wouldn't believe how much it helped me to talk to you, Todd, and Christy about what happened in Zaire. Even saying aloud that I had gone to counseling was a big step for me. I've held so much in for so long. Are you hungry, by the way?"

Katie followed his line of sight and saw that he was looking at a sign for a fast food restaurant they were passing. "Yeah. Actually, no.

I mean, I was thinking I would eat in the caf once we get back on campus. Old times and all that."

Katie wasn't sure why she had said the part about "old times." She felt no compulsion to eat in the cafeteria ever again. It was more of a protective response. If she and Eli stopped somewhere to eat at a restaurant or even at a drive-through place, she wasn't sure she would be able to keep a lockdown on her vulnerable emotions that had been bouncing all over the place that morning.

"We should get back to campus." She hoped her words came out solid and convincing. As long as she could keep the sunrise moment of worship separate from any sunrises of deep-hearted feelings inside, she would be fine.

"Okay. Well, if you change your mind about stopping for breakfast, you will let me know, won't you?" Eli asked.

"Sure. If I see a pancake house I can't resist, I'll pull over. And I'll make you pay. How's that?"

"Fine."

They rolled along for another mile or so before Eli said, "And if you change your mind about the other thing, you'll let me know too, won't you?"

"What other thing?" She could feel him looking at her.

"You know," he said. "The other thing."

They were stopped at a red light. Katie looked over at him, hoping her expression looked as clueless as she was trying to make it appear.

Eli's gaze was on her. He placed his hand on his chest and said one simple word. "Us."

Katie felt the herd of buffalos in her stomach.

22

Katie avoided Eli's comment and heartfelt gesture.

She pulled onto the freeway and put the music back on. The really hard part of avoiding where Eli was trying to take the conversation was that she no longer felt the freedom to talk to him. Their free exchange had been so great before.

Consider this loss of conversation a casualty of your present campaign, Katie. The campaign to keep all the wiggly lines of your life nice and straight and untangled. It's better this way. You'll see.

Eli took her silence as he had taken all the other curves she had tossed at him. He wasn't miffed. Or if he was, he didn't show it. He didn't bully his way back into the conversation or badger her until she responded.

Eli seemed to be at rest. At ease, so to speak.

His lack of aggression gave Katie the space to move around without having to step on the unaddressed topic. She thought that was gracious of Eli, to let sleeping topics lie.

They drove a long time with only the music making words between them.

After Katie had pulled into a parking spot in the lot by Crown Hall, she turned off the engine and reached for her purse. "Thanks for inviting me to go with you, Eli. It was amazing. Really, really amazing."

"It was. Are you going to the caf now for some breakfast?"

"No, I think I'll crawl back into bed."

A tense pause followed. Neither of them moved. Eli's expression made it clear that he was no longer completely at ease.

Did he think I would open up to him once we were back on campus?

Katie felt the tension but didn't know what to do. She didn't see any point in opening up her heart to any possibilities with Eli. She wasn't going to poke around to see what sort of feelings for Eli might be dormant, waiting for a springtime whim to give them freedom to burst into bloom.

No, Eli's unrequited feelings for Katie would have to remain frozen and covered in their seed stage. He would soon return to Kenya, and Katie was certain she would fall to the bottom of his list of things to think about. If Eli were the man she thought he was, he could handle that.

Apparently he could because he said good-bye and left Katie without pressing her any further.

Good. That was good. All of it. Settled.

Katie returned to her room and crawled back into bed and slept less than an hour before two women on her floor came to her room in a fluster. Both of them had lost their room keys. Katie got up, solved their dilemma, and ate some cereal in her room while staring out the window.

Get it in gear, Weldon. Come on, you have things to do today.

The rest of the day Katie spent walking in circles. She had paperwork to file with student services and banking to do down the hill.

Next to her bank was a chain drugstore with a sign in the window announcing free flu shots. Katie paused. The sign looked as if it had been posted since last December. She wondered for a moment what other immunizations could be obtained at the pharmacy inside the drugstore. She knew from the brief time she had spent in the meeting with the outreach team that, if she ever did want to go to Africa, she would need some shots. And malaria pills. If she could take those shots now, she would be ready to go to Africa whenever she wanted. She would have the malaria pills too.

It seemed logical. Be prepared for future adventures. Get stuff checked off the list.

Katie finished her banking business and went into the drugstore. Before she had time to change her mind, she went to the pharmacy in the back to ask a bunch of questions.

Twenty-five minutes later, Katie left the drugstore with a small Band-Aid on her left arm and a filled prescription for malaria pills in her hand.

She hurried back to school for commencement rehearsal at four. Eli waved at her during the rehearsal, and she waved back.

Good. No hard feelings.

She noticed when she lifted her arm that it was sore.

Afterward Katie dashed into town with three of the women on her floor, who had arranged for a special dinner for the four of them, saying they wanted to do something extra with Katie to celebrate her graduation. They laughed over some of the experiences they had shared. Vicki teased Katie about the time Katie hid Vicki's shoes in the oven for a prank and they melted.

What humbled Katie was the way all three of the underclasswomen said that she had encouraged them, motivated them, and inspired them this past year. Katie never would have given herself as high of an evaluation as an RA. She told them she felt as if she were running all year and never quite finished anything she started.

"Speaking of finishing things," Vicki said. "We heard you finished your relationship with Rick."

Katie nodded. She didn't add any details because she didn't feel like going down that conversational trail.

"That had to be hard," Emily said.

"It was. But the decision was right. It was true. It came from my heart. So!" Katie drew in a breath. "On to the next topic. Tell me what all of you are doing this summer."

Their dinner ended without Katie giving any further details about her adjusted love life. In a small way she felt as if she better understood why Julia had kept the details of her engagement quiet for so long. Nothing like a community of college students living in close quarters to spread around a juicy bit of love-life information.

Once Katie returned to campus, she headed to Julia's for the pre-graduation party for all the Crown Hall RAs and RDs. Katie was late, but it didn't seem to matter. Everyone seemed weary, mellow, and not quite ready to celebrate the graduation milestone.

After an hour and a half, the low-key conversations and the closeness in the small space got to Katie. She left while the party was still going, saying she had laundry to do, which was true. Surprisingly, she stopped herself right before announcing to those gathered in the room that she really wanted to have clean underwear to wear to graduation. Instead, she slipped out of the room with her lips sealed.

Note to self: Way to finally demonstrate a little prudence.

Striding down the hall back to her room, Katie thought, *So where were you, Miss Prudence and Miss Temperance, at the beginning of this year? You decided to show up a little late in my college career, didn't you? Are you by chance a little graduation present for me? Feel free to stick around, will you?*

Once her clothes were in the washer, Katie returned to her room and loaded the photos from that morning onto her computer. She had promised her friend Sierra a nice long email before graduation day, and here Katie was, right down to the wire, as usual.

Sierra and Katie had met in England several years earlier when both of them were volunteering with a mission outreach organization. It was the same organization Todd and Eli had signed up for when they met in Spain.

After a year at Rancho, Sierra went to Brazil last summer and hadn't come back. According to her last email, Sierra told Katie she didn't plan to return to the States anytime soon. Originally intending to take some classes and do some outreach work, once Sierra had settled in with her host family and their church, she took a position helping a teacher teach English to high school students at a private school.

Sierra loved what she was doing and, according to her bubbly reports, had learned to communicate in Portuguese, the language of her Brazilian students. She wasn't fluent, but she could get by.

Selecting three of the best sunrise photos, Katie attached them to her brief but newsy email to Sierra. Katie had a lot to cover, starting with her breakup with Rick, babysitting darling baby Daniel, and her new car. She left out any mention of Eli. She knew by the time she wrote Sierra again Eli would be only a lovely memory.

With a push of the Send button, Katie looked at the clock: 1:15. As much as she wanted to step into one of her online social networks and check in on all her pals near and far, she turned off her laptop and turned out the lights. Her thoughts were all over the place, and she knew she needed sleep more than she needed any more socializing, real or virtual.

By the next morning she felt she was getting her brain back.

Christy called right after Katie returned to her room from her shower. "Good morning to my favorite college graduate! I wanted to be the first to congratulate you."

"Thanks, Chris. You guys are coming to the ceremony, aren't you? It's going to be in the gym."

"Yes, we'll be there. Bob and Marti are coming too. I called Tracy last night, and she said she and Doug would try to make it. They weren't sure Daniel could handle being quiet through the commencement service; so they might go directly to the Doyles' house afterward. This is going to be so fun, being all together again!"

"I know. I can't wait. I have to dry my hair now. I'll see you soon."

A few weeks ago, Katie and Nicole had managed to squeeze in a two-hour shopping trip. Katie found the perfect black dress to wear for Julia's wedding and decided it would double for her graduation dress. Nicole talked her into some fun black shoes by saying, "You won't be able to borrow my shoes that day because I'll be wearing them."

With her hair dried, her dress on, her new shoes in place, and wearing just enough make-up to feel pretty, Katie tried to decide if she should add some jewelry. That's when she remembered the expensive brooch Rick had presented to her. She needed to give it back.

Tucking the box in her purse, Katie figured she could find a convenient time at Rick's parents' house that afternoon to return the brooch. She didn't want to draw any attention to the transaction, so she knew she would have to be sensitive about the timing.

Katie took the garment bag with her commencement gown and cap from the closet. Leaving her room in high spirits, she trotted down the hall to Nicole's room, where she tapped on the door.

"Bring out your graduates!" she called.

Nicole opened her door. She had a quizzical look on her face.

Katie knew that indecisive look. She immediately said the same sort of thing she had said to Nicole on other occasions. "You look wonderful. Don't even think about changing. Come on. Let's go."

"Are you sure? I had this skirt on earlier with this top and—"

"Nope. The dress you're wearing is perfect. Let's go." Katie reached for Nicole's garment bag containing her cap and gown.

"But I was thinking—"

"Aha! That's your problem right there. Don't think. Go with your gut. Look at yourself in the mirror. Turn around. See? Do you look amazing? Go ahead. Say it."

"I do like this dress and the way it hangs from here. But ..."

"See? You like it! That's your final answer. Go with it. Come on. Besides, you're going to wear a generic robe over your dress for the first half of the day."

"I know, but at the party we won't be wearing our robes."

"We could if we wanted to. We could start a new tradition."

"Okay, fine. I'll go with this one."

"That's the Nicole I was waiting for. Come on, grab your purse. It's over there. You need anything else?"

"Oh, I almost forgot." Nicole reached for a gift bag. The striped bag had yellow and pink polka-dotted tissue paper peeking out the top.

"For me? You shouldn't have."

"No, sorry. It's for Rick's mom. A little thank-you gift."

Katie hadn't even thought about buying a gift for Rick's mom. She knew better too, because in the past social etiquette required that she show up with a thank-you gift whenever they went to his parents' house for a special occasion. Nicole had joined them last Thanksgiving and presented Rick's mom with the perfect potted flowers while Katie came with a too-large box of too-expensive, hand-dipped chocolates that Rick's mom didn't even open because she was trying to watch her weight.

"And by the way," Nicole added, "I signed the card from both of us."

"You did? Thanks, Nicole. You covered for me once again. You're wonderful."

The two of them started down the hall.

"So what did we buy her?"

"Bath salts."

Katie laughed. "No, really, what did you get her?"

"It's a special sort of bath salts and lotion. The brand she likes is hard to find. I think it's because the bath salts are from the Dead Sea."

Katie, who had never used bath salts in her life, knew she would never have come up with such a gift. Who knew salts from the Dead Sea, of all places, would constitute a highly valued gift?

Katie thought about how Nicole fit so nicely with Rick's family. Too bad Rick hadn't yet come to that conclusion. She thought about going back on her original decision of not nudging him toward Nicole. It had been almost seven weeks since she had broken up with him. Rick and Nicole had been together on several occasions, but the dense Doyle hadn't given any indication he was interested in her.

Katie decided that when she took Rick aside to give him back the brooch, she would find a subtle way to find out what was going on. Not that subtle was one of her strengths.

A sudden thought hit her. Maybe Rick hadn't pursued Nicole because he was interested in someone else. Someone he had hired for the new café, perhaps. If that were the case, Katie wanted to know about it.

As they approached the swarm of other graduates gathering by the side door of the gym, both Nicole and Katie stopped in their tracks.

"Katie, I thought we were supposed to bring our gowns, not wear them."

All the grads standing there were capped and gowned.

"I thought so too. We can put ours on here and toss the hangers and bags in the bushes or something."

"We can't leave our purses in the bushes. I don't know what I was thinking, bringing my purse or this gift. We have to go back to the dorm. Fast!"

"If we do, we'll be late," Katie said.

"Not if we hurry. Come on!"

The two friends took off for Crown Hall at an admirably fast clip, considering they were wearing not-so-comfortable shoes. They had just turned past the cafeteria when they saw another graduate in a cap and gown coming their way, riding on a white security golf cart.

"Eli!" Katie waved her arm in the air. "Stop! We need a ride!"

He pulled up, looking rather heroic in his flowing gown with the dark blue tassel on his cap swinging back and forth. His curly brown hair was doing a crazy jig under the tilted cap. His smile was just too cute.

"I always knew one of these days you would come to appreciate my classy mode of transportation around campus."

"Drop it, Lorenzo. This is no time to gloat over, at long last, managing to talk two cute girls into going for a ride with you in your convertible. Now, put this baby in gear and drive us to Crown Hall as fast as you can!"

It immediately became evident to all three of them that the cart wasn't used to carrying so many passengers, especially while going uphill. They puttered along at a maddening sputter.

"Seriously, Eli, is this the fastest your clown-mobile can go?"

"Seriously, Katie, is that the best gripe you can come up with?"

"Oh, no, I have plenty more gripes. Which do you want to hear first? How about the gripe that these brand news shoes already rubbed a blister on my heel? Or do you want to hear the gripe about my left arm? It's so sore I can hardly lift it."

"Why is your arm sore?" Nicole asked.

"I got some shots yesterday."

"What for?"

"Yellow fever. Typhoid. Oh, and tetanus because it had been over ten years since my last tetanus shot."

"Why in the world would you get all those immunizations?" Nicole asked. "And why would you have them the day before graduation?"

Katie shrugged. "It seemed like a good idea at the time."

Eli turned to Katie with a wide grin. He looked like the happiest kid on the planet.

She knew that he knew what that combination of immunizations meant. She wished she had kept her mouth shut. It was too late now. Eli knew.

Come on, Miss Prudence! Where are you when I need you? Try to keep up with me, will you?

They were in front of Crown Hall then, and Nicole and Katie jumped off the cart to hurry to Nicole's room.

"Katie, I can't believe you got all those shots at once! No wonder your arm is sore. Why in the world did you do that?"

"I wanted to be prepared. The guy at the drugstore said they would be good for the next five years. Except for the tetanus. That's good for ten years."

"You got those shots at a drugstore? Not at a doctor's?"

"The sign said they specialized in travel immunizations. The guy who gave me the shots said it cost a lot less than what they charge at a clinic or a doctor's office. He said he gave shots all the time. Especially for older people who go on cruises to sketchy places around the world."

"Why would anyone go on a cruise to a sketchy place?" Nicole dismissed her own question and said, "Katie, I can't believe you put all those diseases in your body at one time. Is your immune system up for that?"

They had slipped into their graduation gowns and were sharing Nicole's full-length mirror, trying to balance their caps just right on their heads.

"I guess I'll find out."

"So are you going on a cruise?"

"No, I just thought I should catch up on all my immunizations in case I ever wanted to go on a last-minute missions trip to someplace like Malaysia or India."

Nicole turned to her and said, "Or Africa?"

"Sure, Africa is a possibility. They have mosquitoes there, you know."

"And yellow fever." Nicole leaned toward her until Katie had to give in and look at her. Nicole's flawless skin made it easy to read every expression. This time it was her since-your-mother-never-told-you-this-I-get-to-be-the-one-to-nail-you-right-now look.

"Don't torture him, Katie. Eli's feelings for you are so obvious. You have to know that he's smitten with you big time. Please." Her voice grew softer. "I know a thing or two about feelings of love that aren't returned. So, please, don't give him hope like that unless you mean it."

Katie felt the weight of Nicole's velvet hammer. If they had had any more time, Katie would have let a tear break free from the fortress she had built around her heart.

But they had no time. Nicole knew it as well.

"Promise me," Nicole said firmly. "Promise me you won't mess with Eli's feelings."

Katie nodded. "I promise."

"Good. Now lean over." Nicole reached for Katie's cap. "You need to tip it down more in the front. Like that. No, here, let me do it. Hand me some of those bobby pins. There. You ready? Let's go."

They hurried down the hall and through the lobby, each with her robe flapping and a hand on top of her cap. Katie couldn't help but think how fitting it was that she was running so she wouldn't be late for graduation. That summarized her entire senior year.

Eli was waiting in the cart. "We'll pick up some speed going downhill. Hold onto your hats."

Katie didn't place a hand on her cap the way Nicole did. The cart picked up speed, but certainly nothing impressive. The bobby pins did their job, or Katie would have had to run back uphill to retrieve her cap as the golf cart dashed down to the gym.

Eli parked in one of the campus security zones around the back of the gym. The three of them ran to their spots in line where the rest of their classmates were already in alphabetical order.

"Cutting it a little close there," one of the organizers said as Katie slid into the back of the three other *W*s, followed by one *Y* and two *Z*s. The students were already walking into the gym. Nicole was in place with the rest of the *S*s, but Katie couldn't see if Eli had made it in with the *L*s.

She felt a surge of anticipation. Or maybe it was just the adrenaline from the last fifteen minutes. Whatever it was, Katie felt as if she were sweltering under the long robe. The warm air inside the gym and all her bundled up feelings made her feel faint. She never had been a swooner, but at the moment she wished she had a fan or a drink of water.

The chairs for the graduates lined the center of the gym floor, while the photo-snapping guests were on the perimeter as well as filling the bleachers. It was a full house. Katie looked around and knew it would be impossible to spot any of her friends. She was just grateful to be in place, standing in front of her assigned chair when the dean of Rancho Corona opened the ceremony with a welcome and a prayer.

Then everyone was seated. The best part was, since Katie's last name started with *W*, she could sit for a long time before she had to rise again. The choir sang beautifully. A short man in a long robe gave a speech and ended by telling the graduates they could accomplish anything they put their hearts and minds to, by the grace of God. One of last year's graduates played the piano while a graduate from this year sang a solo. The applause was invigorating.

Katie kept looking around. She couldn't see where Eli was sitting, but she had settled with herself during the ride down the hill that she was going to keep her distance from him physically and emotionally. Everything Nicole said was right. It wasn't fair for Katie to say or do anything that would boost his hopes.

Her scanning had moved on into the bleachers. She wanted to find Christy and Todd or maybe Uncle Bob. But so far she hadn't spotted them in the masses.

The president of the university took his place at the podium to give his final thoughts before the graduates stood row-by-row and walked onstage to receive their diplomas. Katie gave up looking for her friends and turned her attention to the stage.

The first row of graduates stood and vacated their chairs. Katie watched them walk toward the stage and felt a sense of satisfaction rising inside her. In a few moments she would be walking up there too, to receive her diploma. She had done it!

Now that some of the grads had stood, Katie could see the attentive family and friends seated on the ground level in the first few rows. She knew those people had to have come at least two hours before the ceremony because no seats were reserved for guests. The people in those rows were the parents with either the most patience or the most pride in their sons or daughters. Maybe the families felt a combination of both.

Suddenly Katie stopped smiling. She blinked and leaned forward as far as she could to see more clearly. There was no mistake.

Seated in the first seats in the front row were the last two people she expected to see. Her mother and father.

23

Katie was a mess. She had held in her feelings ... well, for most of her life. Long ago she had told herself, *If you don't care, then you can't be hurt.* That was perhaps the strongest lesson her mother had taught her without ever saying a word.

Yet here was Vivian Weldon, breaking all her own rules, sitting in the front row with Katie's dad, demonstrating their unspoken pride and care for their only daughter.

Katie let the tears come. She didn't care who saw her. Let them think she was happy to be graduating.

She watched as her classmates walked across the stage. She applauded and kept wiping her tears on her robe's sleeve. When it came to the *L*s, Katie watched Eli take strong, confident steps to accept his diploma. She smiled, cried, applauded, and laughed a little when she heard Eli's Ghanaian friend, Joseph, from somewhere in the bleachers let out a wild whoop.

All the while, Katie thought of how her parents were waiting for her to stride across the stage. This, their presence, might be the single best gift her parents had ever given her.

Katie clapped when the name "Nicole Sanders" was called. She wasn't the only one. Nicole seemed to receive more applause than any student so far. In the mix, Katie thought she heard one of Rick's shrill whistles. It made her smile softly because she could whistle better than

Rick and had on several occasions tried to teach him how to improve his feeble skills.

The row in front of Katie stood. The guy who had been seated directly in front of her glanced at her right before marching off. She knew him from the coed softball games she had been involved with her first year at Rancho. He broke into a grin when he looked at her. "That's a good one, Weldon."

She had no idea what he meant. Nor did she have time to try to spout out some joke about their softball days.

When her row was to stand. Katie composed herself. She checked that her cap was in place just as Nicole had arranged it for her. Her gown was zipped up all the way. Her tears had stopped. She still could feel the dampness of the sleeve that had doubled as a tissue, but she didn't care. All she had to do was walk down the aisle, go up the steps without tripping, shake with her right hand, receive the diploma with her left hand, and make it down the steps on the other side of the stage.

This was her moment. Every step signified success. She denied herself the pleasure of looking over at her parents when she reached the end of the row. Her emotions were right on the edge, and she didn't want to do anything that could cause her to burst into tears.

Looking straight ahead, Katie made it up the steps in her new shoes. She felt like a pageant princess, floating across the stage to the podium. She waited one, two, three seconds. Then, right on cue, her name was called.

Katie held out her right hand, shook with the president of Rancho Corona University, received her diploma in her left, and suddenly was aware of the applause for two reasons. The first was because her brain clicked into the sound of clapping, with some whistles and a Ghanaian whoop thrown in. The second reason was because of the stunned and almost disapproving expressions on the faces of the president and the professor who handed her the diploma.

At the beginning of the ceremony, a request was made that all applause be held until the end, but after the first two or three students, someone sneaked in a cheer, and after that, everyone applauded for his or her favorite graduate. It was a tradition.

Katie couldn't tell because her heart was pounding in her ears, but perhaps she was receiving more applause than other students, and therefore her friends and family were overzealous in their violation of the no-clapping request.

She wasn't sure why she was met with not-so-masked expressions of disapproval, but at that moment, it didn't matter. She had her diploma in hand! Raising it high and giving a wave, she turned to the audience and let out a modest but meaningful, "Woo-hoo!"

Several people laughed, and a few pointed. That was puzzling because a couple of the students had done their own controlled version of a happy dance as they exited the stage, so Katie knew she wasn't overdoing her celebratory expression. Let the faculty look at her with disdain. Let the audience laugh and point. She didn't care. She was a college graduate!

Returning down the aisle, Katie felt as if all other grads' eyes were on her. She beamed and waved her diploma at Nicole when she made eye contact with her.

Nicole looked stunned. She pointed to her cheek and then anxiously pointed at Katie.

Katie touched her cheek. She didn't have anything stuck to her face. *What was Nicole trying to say?*

By the time Katie was back at her seat, the remaining students had gone through the line, and the dean had returned to the podium. He asked all the graduates to rise. In the solemn moment, all the graduates did as they had been instructed the day before in practice. They reached for the tassels on their caps, moved them to the other side, and recited in unison Psalm 23, which had been selected for their class at the beginning of the year during senior chapel. Katie stood with her chin up and recited boldly with the rest of her class.

" 'The Lord is my shepherd; I shall not want. He makes me to lie down in green pastures; He leads me beside the still waters. He restores my soul.' "

The sound of so many voices as they recited the rest of the chapter was powerful in the echoing gym. This was Katie's favorite tradition in Rancho Corona graduation ceremonies. Now she, a graduate, was participating in the recitation of her class's closing benediction.

When the grads reached the final lines of "Surely goodness and mercy shall follow me all the days of my life," Katie quickly pulled out the bobby pins from her cap. As soon as the final words, "dwell in the house of the Lord forever," were uttered, the graduating class was introduced to the audience. Then all the caps were tossed into the air.

A happy flurry of cheers broke out as the guests were reminded to exit the side doors to meet with their graduates out on the lawn and not in the gym.

Katie watched her tossed cap as it came down. She snatched it and looked around.

"Way to go, Katie!" one of her friends said.

Another patted her on the back. "I knew if anyone could pull a prank, it would be you."

The guy next to her said, "Subtle but point made. Were you going for linebacker or quarterback?"

Katie had no idea what any of them were talking about.

Just then she felt someone grab her arm. It was Nicole.

"Hey, congratulations!" Katie went to hug her, but Nicole nearly knocked over a chair pulling Katie away from her seat.

"Katie, your face! Come with me. Right now. Don't look at anyone. Just keep going."

"What's wrong?"

"I'll show you in a minute."

Nicole pressed through the massive crowd and headed for the workout room restrooms on the side of the gymnasium instead of the more obvious ones at the front that probably would be packed. Nicole practically shoved Katie into the restroom and pointed at the mirror.

Katie turned to look, and her mouth dropped open. Across both cheeks were dark black patches that resembled the black "war paint" football players wore. Hers wasn't subtle. It was dark and wide across her cheeks.

"What happened?" Katie reached for a paper towel.

Nicole turned on the warm water and wet the paper towel. "Look!" Nicole pointed to a dark swirl in the sink. The sleeve of Nicole's robe had tagged the stream of water from the faucet when she wet the paper towel. As she squeezed the sleeve to wring it out, the dye from the robe created a dark puddle in the sink.

"I was crying," Katie said, holding up her sleeve. "I used my sleeve for a tissue."

"You must have been crying a lot."

"I was. Nicole, my parents are here."

"So are mine. Come on; try to hurry." Nicole then seemed to catch on to what Katie had said. "Wait. Your parents are here? Katie! Wow."

"I know. Help me scrub this off. I can't believe this. Now I know why I was getting the dirty looks. I can't imagine what the president and the dean thought of me. Oh, man!"

Nicole helped her to scrub. Even with the liquid soap and warm water, not all of the stain came off. But at least it was down to looking like a shadow and not a bold stripe.

"When we go back to my room to pick up our purses and the gift, I have some mineral powder that will cover that up. But for now, we really need to get out on the lawn and have pictures taken before everyone leaves."

They hurried out the back way, and the first person Katie saw was Eli. He was standing with Joseph, Shiloh, and their little daughter, Hope. Katie waved at Joseph and Shiloh, and they both waved back.

As soon as Eli saw Katie, he strode across the field to her, wrapped both arms around her, and gave her a tight hug. Eli had never hugged her like that, and all she could think was, *Wow, this guy can hug!*

He smelled good too.

In her ear he said, "Congratulations, Katie girl."

"Thanks." She pulled back, feeling red in the face for several reasons. "Congratulations to you too."

"Thanks."

Looking over the top of his head, she said, "My parents are here somewhere."

"They are? Katie, that's amazing! Where are they?"

"I don't know. I have to find them."

"I'll go with you."

"No, that's okay. You have people here for you." Katie turned and saw that Joseph and Shiloh had moved on through the crowd. That's when it struck her. Eli had no one else here for him.

"Actually, Eli, why don't you come with me? Maybe my parents found Rick or Todd and Christy."

Nicole had disappeared into the massive group. It was just Eli and Katie wandering through the sea of people. They were separated while trying to move past a large group in the midst of organizing family photos with twin girls who had graduated. Katie instinctively put out her hand behind her and motioned for Eli to follow a little closer.

Eli took her flapping hand in his and held it tight. His hand felt rough and stronger than she would have imagined.

Right on cue, the herd of buffalos showed up and stampeded through her gut. Katie would have dropped Eli's hand except she felt paralyzed. Or maybe it was more like hypnotized. She couldn't let go. Actually, she could let go, but she didn't want to.

Eli was the one who released the grip as soon as they were past the human traffic jam and into a good spot to view the open area.

"There's Todd." Eli pointed to the left.

Katie saw Uncle Bob and Aunt Marti standing with Todd and Christy. Rick was with them, as were Nicole and her parents. But she didn't see her parents anywhere. Her heart was still fluttering.

"I hope they didn't leave." Katie told herself the fluttering was due to the nervousness she felt over seeing her parents. Or maybe it was the effects of the immunizations.

"Were they planning to go to the party? Maybe they went on to the Doyles' house."

"I doubt it."

Katie bit her lower lip and tried to think like her parents would. This sort of crowd would be way too much for them. Even though the announcement had been given for everyone to congregate on the field, Katie suspected her parents would have stayed away from the crowds.

"Maybe they're still in the gym."

Before Katie could decide if her conclusion was a good possibility, Eli had taken her once again by the hand. This time he was leading the way back to the gym with swift steps. Katie let him lead her and mentally told herself, *This doesn't mean anything. We're just trying to move through the crowd on a hunt for my parents.*

Eli led Katie to the front opening of the gym and let go of her hand. She felt the rush of his warmth and support leave her at the very moment she saw her mother.

Dressed in the same floral dress Katie had seen her wear ten years ago, Vivian Weldon stood by the wall with both hands on her pocketbook, as if someone might snatch it from her, here on the campus of this nice Christian university.

Katie tried to form the simple word *Mom*, but nothing came out. Deep emotions tugged at her, causing her lips to curl up into a vulnerable, little-girl smile. With ten deliberate steps forward, she stood, dressed in her graduation robe with her hat in her hand and the little girl wiggly smile frozen on her lips, in front of her mother.

Her mom looked up, startled, almost as if she hadn't expected to see her daughter in that moment.

"You came. You came to my graduation."

Her mother didn't seem to know what to do with the greeting. "Well, you sent us an invitation."

"I know. But you didn't have to come, and you did. Thank you."

"We're not going to the party," her mom stated. "Your father hasn't been feeling well. I think it's his gallbladder. He's in the restroom. The women's restroom had a terrible line. There always is. I see you took the ink off your face. What were you doing, trying to play a joke?"

Katie's spirits plummeted, and so did her smile. "No. I was crying. I used my gown's sleeve, and the dye came off on my face. I didn't know it was there. Honest."

"Well, why would the color come off? Do they recycle the robes by redying them?"

"I don't know. It doesn't matter about the robe. The point is I wasn't trying to be funny or anything. It was an accident."

"You certainly are the one for accidents, aren't you?"

Katie tried to brush aside the old, familiar jab. She drew in a deep breath and glanced over her shoulder. Eli was still standing in the doorway of the gym. He wasn't alone, though. He was talking to Julia and her fiancé, Dr. Ambrose.

"Mom, come with me. I want you to meet some of my friends."

"I told your father I would wait right here for him. I'm not going to move."

"Okay, I'll bring them here." Katie swished over to Julia's side. "I'd really love for you guys to come meet my mom."

The three of them followed Katie over to the wall across from the men's restroom where her mother stood, still clutching her purse with both hands.

"This is my friend Eli, my RD, Julia, and..." Katie tried to decide if she should say, "Dr. Ambrose" or "Julia's fiancé," when she introduced the third member of the trio.

Eli took the decision away from Katie by picking up the introductions from there and saying, "This is my uncle, John Ambrose."

"Your uncle?" Katie turned to Eli in surprise.

Eli nodded.

Dr. Ambrose was wearing his impressive-looking robe with professor's cap and doctoral ribbons. He shook hands with Katie's mom. "You must be quite proud."

Katie's mom looked flustered. Her curly hair had gone gray over the years, and she kept it short in a puff. Her face was long, and her glasses were the same round saucer style she had worn for as long as Katie could remember.

In response to Dr. Ambrose's question, Vivian Weldon put her nose a little higher in the air. "I thought pride was a sin for you Christians."

Right then and there Katie knew the three of them had been given a glimpse into her life. Before Dr. Ambrose or any of them could respond, Katie's dad came out of the restroom using a cane.

"Hi, Dad." Katie greeted him cautiously. "Is your knee acting up again?"

"It's my feet. Didn't your mother tell you? I have something wrong with my heels. Walking all the way here from the parking lot just about did me in."

"I can give you a ride back to the parking lot," Eli said. "I work for campus security. I can take you in the golf cart."

"I'm ready to go now," Katie's dad said. "Where's the cart?"

"I'll bring it around right up front."

"Thanks, Eli," Katie said as he turned to go. He glanced at her over his shoulder and gave her a grin. A wonderful, warm, forever-friend sort of grin. Katie wished she had a photo of him just then, whooshing out the door, still wearing his robe, hair every which way and a great twinkling light in his eyes. That's the picture she would like to have taken and sent to his parents with a note saying, "You have a wonderful son. I wish you could have been here to see him graduate. You would be proud of him."

Somehow, Katie knew Eli's parents would be proud. They wouldn't snap back with statements about pride being a sin.

Turning to her parents, Katie remembered how Eli said that forgiving his attacker was a process. Katie knew she had forgiven her parents last summer. Julia had been there with her. But this felt like yet another step in the process. Without reservation, Katie breathed out her disappointment and frustration over her mother's comment to Dr. Ambrose. She breathed in and hoped the fresh air would give her an equally fresh feeling in her spirit.

Katie looked at her disgruntled mother and her father, who was obviously in a lot of discomfort, and decided this was a graduation moment for her of another sort. Stepping closer to her mother, Katie gingerly wrapped her arms around her and gave her a small kiss on the cheek.

Taking a step over to her dad, Katie wrapped her arms around him more tightly. He responded by patting her on the back, as if she were a great big dog and had just fetched a duck.

Katie put that image out of her mind and said in his ear, "I really appreciate your coming, Dad. Thank you. It means a lot to me."

Both her parents appeared to be touched by her expressions of affection, yet neither of them seemed to know how to respond. That wasn't unusual. Katie, though, felt that the way she was acting right now was the closest she had been to her real self since she was very young.

"I have my camera with me," Julia said. "I was wondering if the three of you would like a picture taken together."

"Not by the bathroom," Katie's mom spouted.

"How about over here?" Katie walked seven feet away to a big, blank wall. It was boring as a background, but at least her mom couldn't complain.

With some effort her parents came over to where Katie stood. She wiggled her way in between them and put her cap back on.

"Make sure you put the tassel on the correct side," her mom said.

"Very observant, Mother. Thank you." Katie made the switch and gave Julia a big grin.

Julia took several shots and said she would make sure Katie got copies so she could send them to her parents. Julia and Dr. Ambrose slid out, leaving Katie and her parents alone in the gym entrance. Katie knew Christy and the others must be wondering what had happened to her. She wished she had brought her phone so she could at least text them.

It didn't matter. Eli was at the door in the golf cart, and Katie could see him coming toward them, ready to usher her parents to the parking lot.

With one final opportunity in front of her before the curtain closed on this moment, Katie remembered how Eli had said that real love comes from the heart. It's spontaneous, organic, and not planned. He also said love was inconvenient.

Katie turned to her parents, and with a deep and sudden sincerity rising in her voice, she said, "I love you, Mom. I love you, Dad. Thank you so much for coming."

Katie's mother looked away. But before she did, Katie was certain she saw something she never had seen before on her mother's face. A tiny smile like a crescent moon was accented by a silver tear coming toward that moon.

If Katie had never believed in the beauty or the power of love when it was birthed from grace, she believed in it now.

24

"You do know that we almost gave up on you and went on to the party." Aunt Marti made it clear she was in quite a snit by the time Katie joined the group on the field. Many families already had dispersed, including Nicole's and Rick's families. Doug and Tracy were still there, jostling little Daniel between them.

"She's here now," Bob said. "Go ahead and present her with the lei. I have the camera ready. Then we'll take some group shots."

Todd and Christy presented Katie with a beautiful orchid lei. She sniffed at it, but it didn't have a fragrance. Over the past few years, leis had become a symbol of honor for many Rancho grads. The school website had a picture of a graduating student from Hawaii who was being congratulated by his family that had come from the islands. Many leis were stacked up to his chin. After that photo was posted, graduates wanted to share a taste of what it was like to be congratulated with a fragrant or colorful circle of flowers.

"It's a wonder this didn't shrivel up and dry out completely." Marti had a rose and carnation lei looped on her arm. She placed it over Katie's head and made a kissing sound next to Katie's ear.

Katie couldn't blame any of them for not wanting to get too close. She still was warm from running out to the field after helping her parents board Eli's cart. Her face felt glowy from perspiration. Not to mention the scrub job she had done, trying to rub the dye off her cheeks.

Christy touched Katie's cheek. "So what was that about? I didn't get it."

"Can you still see it?"

"Just a little. Not like when you were on stage."

"Smile!" Uncle Bob called out.

"What was it supposed to mean?"

"Nothing." Katie gave a big grin to the camera. "I didn't do it on purpose. The dye came off of this ridiculous robe."

"Why was it only there, on your face?"

"I was crying. My parents came, Chris. That's where I was just now. Talking to them in the gym. Can you believe they came?"

Christy threw her arms around Katie and hugged her tight. "Katie, that's wonderful! I'm so happy for you!" Pulling back, Christy did a double take to make sure the robe hadn't rubbed off on her clothes. It hadn't.

"Yeah, it was good that they came. It's really, really great that you guys came. Thank you so much. I'm sorry I kept you all waiting."

"Understandable," Uncle Bob said. "Glad to hear that your parents made it. Congratulations, Katie."

"Thank you." She beamed her best smile, as Bob raised his camera and took the shot.

The photo-taking then began in earnest. Katie with Christy, Katie with the entire group, Katie with just Daniel, who squirmed and stretched out his arms for his daddy to take him.

The moment was much like she had dreamed it would be, only so different since her parents had come and gone. She was with her people. Except Nicole wasn't there. Or Rick.

Or Eli.

Katie could feel the perspiration dripping down her back and from her forehead. "Do you mind if we finish with the photos and then find water somewhere? I'm burning up. I want to take off this robe."

Bob obliged, and the group headed back to the gym. Doug gave Katie one last hug and said they would see her over at the Doyles'.

"I have to pick up something from my room before I go to the party," Katie said. "From Nicole's room, actually."

"We'll meet you there." Marti decided. "We have a map. Come, Robert. We parked over this way."

Christy and Todd kept in stride with Katie as she went in the side door of the gym and took a long drink from the nearest drinking fountain. She unzipped her robe and, took off her cap. "I'm burning up. Do you guys want to go on ahead too?"

Christy and Todd looked at each other. Todd shrugged.

"We'll wait for you," Christy said. "You can ride over with us, if you like. I have something I want to give you, and I'd like to do that before we get to the house."

The long-time trio headed for the parking lot and slipped into Todd and Christy's car so they could drive Katie to Crown Hall. On the way Katie told them how Eli came riding in on his white golf cart and saved the day for her and Nicole a few hours earlier.

"Eli told us about the trip the two of you took up to the mountains yesterday," Todd said.

"Did you see any of the pictures?" Katie asked. "I posted some of them. It was beautiful beyond description. I'm so glad we went."

"I haven't seen any of your pictures, but I'm thinking of taking some of the students from the youth group up there this summer," Todd said.

"If you do, I'd love to go with you," Katie said. "As a matter of fact, I'd love to help out with the youth group this summer in any way you need help."

"So you're going to be around this summer?"

"I think so."

"What have you decided?" Christy asked.

"You mean, where am I going to live and work and everything? That I haven't figured out yet. I do have one more week in the dorm."

"Our offer still stands," Todd said. "You can camp out with us anytime. As long as you don't mind sleeping on an air mattress."

"I think I'll rent my own place before I impose on you guys. But thanks for the offer."

Katie was perspiring like crazy in the warm car. She couldn't wait to slip into the dorm, where it was bound to be cooler. She retrieved the master key from the front desk, went to Nicole's room, and unlocked the door. Her purse lay on Nicole's bed along with a note saying that Nicole had gone on to the party at the Doyles' with her parents, but the mineral powder she had mentioned was on her desk with the application brush.

Katie decided to leave her makeup untouched and just go on to the party. Then, taking a quick glance in the mirror on her way out, Katie stopped. She looked awful. Her face was pale and moist with perspiration except for her cheeks, which looked bruised. Her hair had a ridge from the cap that had been held securely in place with Nicole's bobby pins. And her dress felt hot and itchy.

Katie called Christy's cell phone. "If you guys want to go ahead, it's going to take me a few minutes here. I can drive over in my car."

"We don't mind waiting. It's your graduation party. You can be fashionably late if you want."

"I'll be as quick as I can." Katie dashed to her room. She grabbed what she needed for the shower and did a lightning fast wash-over. A facial scrub improved on the job the paper towel had started in the gymnasium's bathroom. She quickly rinsed her hair, figuring it would air dry with the windows down on the way to the party.

Applying an extra layer of deodorant, Katie was about to put her new dress back on until she caught a whiff of what her perspiration had done to the garment.

"Great. What am I going to wear?"

Opting for the first skirt and top she could find, Katie dressed. It might not be as stylish or cute as the dress, but the outfit was fresh and clean, and so was she.

Right before she ran out the door, Katie grabbed her new tube of mascara with the intent of putting some on in the car. Noting the immunization card next to the mascara on the dresser, she realized the profuse perspiration and fever could be the shots' side effects.

Practically diving into the backseat of Todd and Christy's Volvo, Katie said, "To the party, James. And I hope you guys don't mind if we drive there with the windows open."

"Did you take a shower?" Christy asked.

"Yes. Believe me, you should be glad I did. Could you smell me before?"

"No."

"Well, that's good."

"Here, open this." Christy handed Katie a wrapped package. "This is my graduation gift to you."

"It's from both of us," Todd said.

Christy gave him an amused look.

"Hey!" Todd returned her look. "I watched you work on it. And I told you what a great job you were doing."

Katie opened the gift. "A scrapbook? Christy, I love it! I can't believe you did this for me. No one has ever done anything like this for me. I've always wanted a scrapbook. Thank you, thank you, thank you!"

"You're welcome."

"Yeah," Todd echoed. "You're welcome. Glad you like it."

Christy playfully gave him a punch in the arm.

Turning to the first page, Katie burst out laughing. The photo was really old. Their high school friend, Janelle, had taken the picture of the two of them in their pjs at a sleepover. That was when Christy and Katie had met. It was also the night the group had gone out in the middle of the night and toilet papered Rick Doyle's house in Escondido. That was the start of Christy and Katie's friendship.

"I can't believe you have this picture!"

"There's more. Lots of really good ones. It took me awhile to round them up. Wait till you see the ones of us from the Lake Shasta water-skiing trip."

"This is one from our yearbook, isn't it?" Katie held up the book and pointed to a photo of her playing volleyball for the Kelley High team. "I remember this because you were on yearbook staff, and I was so into being with Michael that semester that I was late for the team photo. Or did I miss it altogether?"

"I'm not sure. That was a rough stretch for our friendship, but we survived."

"Yeah, I was a little on the obstinate side back then."

"Back then?" Todd asked.

Katie ignored his teasing and turned the page. "Oh, this is a good one. Did you take this on our ski trip or on a snow day?"

"That was from the ski trip. Keep going. There's a great shot of us from the Christmas you worked as an elf at the mall."

"You have one from that Christmas?" Katie turned a few pages until she found the photo of her wearing the pointy elf ears and equally pointy elf shoes. "This is hilarious! How come you're not dressed up too?"

"I worked at the pet store, remember?"

"Oh, right. Hey, that reminds me. Do you think that pet store is still there? I need a dove. I was going to rent one, but turns out the guy only sells them. I think he's charging too much. I thought maybe your old boss would give me a break."

"What do you need a dove for?" Christy asked.

Katie told her about the plans she and Nicole were formulating for the secret compartment in the woman of honor bouquet.

"Great idea," Todd said. "Love the symbolism. We should have done that, Kilikina."

Even though Todd's use of Christy's romantic-sounding Hawaiian nickname seemed to soften his suggestion, Christy shot him another tell-me-you're-joking look and made no comment.

They were at the Doyles' house by then. Cars lined the street, so Todd pulled up to the driveway and dropped the two of them off, saying he would go down the block to find a parking place.

As Christy and Katie walked up to the front door, Katie complained that she had forgotten her camera.

"I have mine. I'll take some pictures for you. Did you happen to get a shot with your parents?"

"Yes, Julia took a couple."

"That's good."

"I know, but I wanted to get a picture of Eli. I thought he should have a photo to send his parents."

"Maybe Julia took one of him as well."

Katie wasn't certain she had seen Julia snap any of Eli, but then Katie had been wrapped up with her parents at the time.

"I'll make sure I take some pictures of Eli here at the party," Christy said.

"It won't be the same." Framed in Katie's imagination was the image of a grinning Eli in his cap and gown. First on the cart during their wild ride and then when he was leaving the gym in his act of kindness toward her parents.

"The same as what?"

"The same as when he had on his cap and gown. His hair was going every which way and he had that grin ..."

Christy stopped and put her hand on Katie's arm. Her eyes were wide. "Katie!"

"What?"

"Hello!"

"Hello to you too. What did I miss?"

"Apparently quite a lot. Or maybe I was the one who missed it."

"What are you talking about?" Katie checked the bottoms of her shoes. "Did I step in something? Is the black still showing on my face?"

"No." Christy stared at her, a little smile playing on her lips. "All I have to say to you, Katie girl, is stay tuned for coming attractions."

Katie gave her an odd look in response. She remembered using that phrase with Rick months ago, although she couldn't remember why.

Hearing Christy say it now, Katie said, "That line sounds like it's from the start of an old DVD or something."

"Oh, it's the start of something, that's for sure."

Christy turned and walked up the steps, leaving Katie standing in the Doyles' driveway with both hands on her hips. Katie wasn't tracking with Christy at all. But that didn't surprise her. Her head and her heart were a bit on overload at the moment. Shaking off her friend's odd behavior, Katie joined Christy at the front door.

Christy rang the doorbell, and Katie thought of how far all of them had come since the night she and Christy toilet papered Rick's old house and then scrambled to run or hide in the bushes.

Right now, hiding in the bushes sounded like something Katie wanted to do. She just wasn't sure why.

25

Rick's mom had once again outdone herself in throwing a first-class party. That was good because it meant that, due to the nice-sized crowd that had collected at the spacious home, Katie and Christy slipped in without its being obvious they were among the last to arrive.

It also meant that Marti had cozied right up to Rick's mom in a lengthy conversation about everything from appetizers to spa treatments. Katie could hear them chatting as she filled a plate with delicious nibbles from the dining room table, which was bubbling over with good things to eat.

All seemed to be going great until Marti spied Katie. Changing the subject, Marti said, "Of course, when the time comes for Rick and Katie to make their special announcement, I would love to host a party for them at our home."

Rick's mom looked stunned. She turned to Katie.

Katie quickly moved over next to Marti and said, "We won't be making any special announcements. Rick and I aren't together anymore."

"What!" Marti's exclamation shut down several nearby conversations, as half a dozen guests looked to see what was going on. "You and Rick broke up? When? Why wasn't I told?"

Katie was aware that a number of people were listening for her answer. She tried to choose her words carefully and kept her voice low. "We broke up a couple of months ago."

Marti looked enraged. "And you're telling me now? Do you have any idea what I went through to secure the Newport Beach Yacht Club for you? I have them holding three separate weekends for you. Two in November and one in October."

"The Yacht Club? For me? Why in the world did you reserve the Yacht Club for me?"

Marti pointed her finger at Katie. "When you were a guest in my home, you distinctly said you and Rick were waiting until after graduation to make your announcement. You said six months was a good length of time for an engagement. That means a fall wedding. I was right there when you said it."

"I never said that!" Now Katie was the one whose voice was elevated. "You were the one who said that. All of it. All those plans and dates were something you came up with in your own little mind. Rick and I never said anything more than that we were going to wait until after the café opened and I graduated before we made any decisions about what was next."

"That is not what you said."

"Marti, no one asked you to make reservations at any yacht clubs for any reason!"

Rick had appeared at Katie's side and slipped his arm through hers. In his smooth, authoritative voice, Rick said, "We both would like to apologize for not communicating with you, Marti. We had no idea you were working on any arrangements for us. We're very sorry for the inconvenience we've caused you. Isn't that right, Katie?"

She felt his arm tighten as he flexed his muscle.

"Yes, very sorry."

Other partygoers had shuffled into the dining room area to find out what all the ruckus was. Rick kept his arm linked through Katie's, as he turned to the extended crowd. "I guess this is my oversight. I apologize. Apparently, I have an announcement I should have made earlier. Since Katie is right here and since she and I are in agreement on this, we have an announcement to make."

Katie looked up at Rick with a skeptical expression and extracted her arm from his. Either he was finding a way to graciously take the focus off of Marti, or he was in league with her, and the two of them had come up with a plan to trap Katie into getting back together with him.

She knew the second option was highly unlikely so she stood back and let Rick speak for both of them.

He glanced at her, and she gave him a "go ahead, I trust you" look.

"Katie and I have been friends for a long time. As a matter of fact, both of us have been friends with many of you in this room for a long time. We appreciate your friendships more than we can say. This is a time to celebrate a milestone for Katie, Nicki, and Eli."

Katie spotted Nicole and Eli in opposite corners, both looking at Rick, waiting to see what was going to happen next.

"Nicki? Eli? Could the two of you join Katie and me over here?"

Nicole and Eli made their way over to the table.

Rick had the crowd under control. At least fifty people were filling up the large dining room area and spilling into the living room. All were turned to Rick with rapt attention. Even Marti.

"As many of you know, our family's tradition is to offer a toast at celebrations, and this is definitely a celebration for my three friends. If you have a glass nearby, would you raise it with me in a toast?"

Nearly everyone had a glass to lift.

"Here's to Eli Lorenzo, my excellent roommate, and to Nicki Sanders, my mother's excellent design assistant, and to Katie Weldon, my once-girlfriend and now my excellent forever friend."

His gaze encompassed the gathered crowd. "Toast with me, will you? Congratulations to the graduates!"

The guests cheered and took a sip of lemonade, iced tea, or whatever was in their glass, and the near spectacle between Katie and Marti dissolved. Conversations started up again. Some of the guests shuffled back into the other room. Eli was receiving lots of attention from a few older people, who were obviously friends of the Doyles.

Rick, however, wasn't done. He turned to Katie and said, "Will you go upstairs and wait for me in the room over the garage? I need to talk to you."

He then leaned closer to Marti where she stood with a glass of something sparkling in her hand. She was looking up at Rick, as if she weren't sure exactly what had just happened. Katie watched as he tilted his chin and in his suave way took responsibility for not notifying Marti about the status of his relationship with Katie. Katie heard him offer to pay for any room deposits Marti had put down at the Yacht Club.

Once again, Rick, there you go, being the perfect gentleman.

Katie exited the dining room with her plate of finger foods in hand. She felt like she was doing something naughty, taking food out of the designated eating area and waiting for Rick upstairs.

She went back to where she had left her purse and took it with her. This may not be the way she had hoped to set up a private time when she could give back the brooch, but with Rick, she had to take whatever time she could get with him.

The room over the garage was a combination of a workout room with a treadmill and of a den with an old television and a loveseat.

Katie didn't have to wait long before she heard Rick coming up the stairs. When he appeared, he nearly filled the doorway.

"Good save, Doyle. Has anyone told you your skills are being wasted in the field of sliced deli ham and mocha lattes? You should be an international negotiator. Or at the very least, a divorce lawyer."

By the look on his face, she couldn't tell if he was going to scold her or take her compliments and wear them like a medal of honor.

Katie decided to try her own attempt at redirecting the topic. "Hey, before you say whatever you're going to say, I want to give this back. It's your grandmother's brooch. I'm sorry I didn't get it to you sooner."

Rick took the box from her. "It's okay. Thanks."

He seemed preoccupied with something. Katie guessed it was what had just happened with Aunt Marti.

He crossed his arms. "Katie, I thought you and I should talk. I'm trying to do what's right here for all of us. That's what I've aimed for in our relationship all along, and I'm still aiming for that."

"I know, and I appreciate it, Rick. What you did downstairs in smoothing out what could have been a huge disaster with Marti was really great. Thanks. I'm sure Eli and Nicole appreciated being honored too."

"I hope so." He looked nervous. "Listen, I have to tell you something. I'm not sure how to say this, so I'll just say it. I'm having a difficult time being around her now that things aren't the way they used to be between you and me."

Katie realized she was the one who had pressed Bob and Marti to come to her graduation. If she hadn't done that, the confrontation in the dining room wouldn't have happened. "Do you wish she hadn't come?"

"No," Rick said quickly. "I want her here. She's a big part of your life. That's what makes it so complicated. When you and I were together, it wasn't that hard to ... I don't know if this is the right word, but it wasn't that hard to ignore her. Now whenever I'm around her, I go out of my way to avoid her because she ..."

"She drives you a little crazy, right?"

"Exactly." He looked relieved. "Katie, I hope you don't mind my talking about this with you."

"No. Are you kidding? You can talk with me like this anytime you want. You said it yourself in the toast—you and I are forever friends."

He offered her a grin. "Thanks. I don't know why I feel this way, but whenever I'm around her, I just ..." Rick put out his hands as if at a loss for words.

Katie filled in for him, transferring all her feelings about Aunt Marti to him. "You want to stuff an egg roll in her mouth and show her to the door. Believe me, I feel the same way."

Rick's jaw went slack.

"Why? What do you want to do when you see her?"

"To be honest, I want to ask her out."

Katie nearly jumped off the loveseat. "You want to go out with Christy's aunt? That's twisted, Rick!"

Rick took a step back. "Marti! You thought I was talking about Marti?"

"Yes, of course. You said she drives you a little crazy; you try to ignore her when you're in the same room. Who else would you be ... Oh. Oh!"

"Not Marti," Rick said slowly.

"No, not Marti," Katie quickly agreed. She covered her mouth with her hand so she wouldn't let out a small shriek.

"I was talking about Nicki," Rick said.

"Right. I knew that. I was just trying to make a dumb joke about Marti. Scratch that joke off my list of stand-up material. It obviously bombed. Sorry. Bad choice. Bad, bad choice of comedy material. Won't happen again."

Rick lowered himself into the old recliner in the corner of the room across from Katie. He looked irritated now, as if he really did believe Katie had been making a bad joke.

"So, yeah." Katie hoped they could keep talking about this. "Nicole. Or Nicki, as you call her. She's great. But then, you know that. I think you should ask her out. I mean, it seems like you said, you've done a good job of ignoring her whenever she's in the same room. So now maybe you should talk to her and see what happens."

"I want to do what's right, Katie."

"This is right, Rick. Really, I'm sure this is quite right."

"I thought it would be wise to wait."

"Wait until what? Until she moves back to Santa Barbara and you have to drive five hours in traffic to see her?"

"Is that what she's doing? Did she decide? My mom said she hadn't decided yet."

"She's thinking about moving to Santa Barbara. She has this week to figure it out and then ... who knows?"

Rick rubbed the back of his neck. He always did that when he was stressed. Katie wished she could just spill the truth about how Nicole felt about him so he wouldn't be so uptight about asking her out, or at the very least, talking to her about something other than the paint color in the men's bathroom.

"You know, I thought six months in between relationships would be a good space. Especially since you and I went together for so long. But now I'm thinking—"

"That's your problem, right there, Rick Doyle. I mean, if you don't mind my being blunt, you think too much. It's time for you to go with your gut. Your heart, Rick. Go with your heart. I know your heart is steadfast. Listen to it. Love is a mystery. It can't be planned. It comes on its own schedule. It's inconvenient and organic, but that's what makes it real. Really good relationships are the ones that come naturally and are unforced. Like waves."

Katie realized the words she used had all come from Eli.

Rick looked surprised.

Katie leaned forward. As long as she had Rick's attention, she might as well tell him everything she was thinking. "Listen, Rick, I know that your goal in our relationship was to do everything right. And you did. You accomplished that goal. You were a wonderful boyfriend, and you did everything according to your head. Your plan. Your logic. It worked."

"Thank you, Katie. Thank you for saying that."

"Now I'm telling you to move forward without a plan. Go, find Nicole, look into her eyes, and see what your gut tells you. What do you already know in your heart? Start from there and then go and do everything right from the heart out. Don't do this one from your head."

Katie felt herself choking up as she added, "You two are already more knit together at the heart than you even realize. You're just being too logical to see it. Don't blow it, Doyle."

Rick looked stunned. He went over to where Katie was sitting. Offering her his hand, like a true gentlemen, he pulled her to her feet.

Katie heard the sound of people coming up the stairs. If she and Rick had any last words to say to each other, this was their chance.

Looking at her and gently smoothing down the side of her hair, Rick seemed to search her eyes for something.

His touch felt foreign to her now. Tender, but not especially romantic. Katie didn't feel an urge to kiss him, nor did she hope he would initiate a kiss with her. The close friendship remained. The romantic feelings had played themselves out.

Whatever it was Rick seemed to be looking for in her eyes, he apparently didn't find it. He nodded slowly, and in a nice, friendly soccer coach sort of move, he put both hands on Katie's upper arms.

"No, Rick, don't!" Katie shrieked as Rick gave her upper arms a friendly squeeze.

Todd, Christy, and Eli all stepped into the room as Katie crumbled back onto the loveseat in response to the pain in the tender flesh around her immunizations.

Eli rushed over to her. He looked at Rick and then at Katie. "You okay?" Eli's hand was on her shoulder, ready to comfort her.

Katie lifted her babied left arm a few inches. "Yeah. It's my arm. It's still really sore. I had some shots yesterday, Rick. You didn't know."

Rick gave Eli an eyebrow-raised look and said, "Anything else I don't know?"

"No," Katie answered. "That's all. Just a sore arm."

Rick was still looking at Eli. He dipped his chin. As if no one else were in the room, Rick said to his roommate, "You knew last summer, didn't you?"

Eli stared at Rick for a moment before responding with the slightest of nods.

The two of them continued to size each other up. Katie wasn't sure what was going on.

Then Rick's expression relaxed into one of his wry grins. "Well, it looks like we're in agreement then, aren't we, Katie? Both of us are ready to move on."

"I think we should move on downstairs," Christy suggested. She had a little bit of her aunt Marti's organizational nudge in her voice, only in a much more gracious way.

"We want to take some pictures of everyone," Christy said. "Who knows when we'll all be together in the same place like this again?"

The five of them exchanged flash glances in response to the reality that hung on Christy's last statement. This was the end of a peculiar season for all of them.

"We need pictures together." Katie rose from the loveseat. "Lots of pictures."

26

K atie spent the next three days feeling sicker than she had since Valentine's Day. She perspired an unladylike amount. She barely ate. Her appetite was gone, and her stomach remained in knots.

Blessedly, her on-duty hours were minimal, which gave her time to sort, organize, and pack her room. It also gave her time to work on where she was going to live and work. However, by Wednesday morning, Katie still hadn't taken any steps to figure out her housing or her work. She was lost. Floating on a vast sea of possibilities in her tiny, buoyant raft of indecision.

It seemed the only way to get unstuck was to talk things through with Julia. Trying to set a time with her was tricky because Julia was caught up in the dash of last-minute wedding details. Katie felt bad about that too, because she was the woman of honor, but she didn't feel she was doing much assisting.

Katie and several other RAs had hosted a successful shower for Julia, but that had been the sum total of Katie's involvement with the wedding. Now the wedding was only three days away, and Katie had one self-imposed task remaining. She needed a dove.

Her first call was to the pet store in Escondido where Christy had worked in high school. The store's owner remembered Katie. Maybe a little too well. Why, she didn't know.

"Listen, Jon, I'm trying to find a dove. A nice, quiet one that will fly out of a bridal bouquet when I open the door of the cage. Can you help me out?"

No response.

"Hello? Jon, are you still there?"

"You know, if this were anyone else calling, I would have hung up. But since it's you, Katie, I believe this isn't a prank call."

"Of course it's not a prank call! I'm serious; I need a dove."

"Okay, not a problem. When can you pick it up?"

"Really? You have one?"

"I don't have one in the store, but I can get one and have it here by next week."

"No, I need it right away. The wedding is Saturday."

"Saturday. That's cutting it close."

"Yeah, I know. Story of my life. So what else is new? Can you get me the dove?"

"I'll work on it and call you back. By the way, who's the lucky groom?"

"His name is Dr. Ambrose. Well, John. John Ambrose."

"A doctor, huh? Good for you, Katie."

"No, I'm not getting married. I'm the maid of honor. Well, actually, the woman of honor. We decided 'woman' sounded better than 'maid.'"

"It's all the same, isn't it?"

Katie was feeling irritated with Jon's ribbing. She wasn't a little high school girl in a Christmas elf costume anymore. She was a college graduate and felt she should be treated with more respect.

"Just get me the dove, Jon, will you? By Friday at the latest."

"I'll see what I can do."

Katie hung up, muttering to herself. She gathered her shower things and headed down the hall. When she entered the bathroom, Nicole was there, brushing her teeth.

"Hey, grad," Katie quipped. "Haven't seen you for a couple of days."

Nicole demurely spit in the sink and rinsed out her mouth before turning to Katie with a hesitant expression. "I was avoiding you."

"Why?"

Nicole raised an eyebrow. Her skin took on a soft glow. "Rick asked me out."

Katie dropped her towel and shampoo and lunged toward Nicole with a big bear hug. "Fantastic!"

Nicole pulled away. "You're sure you're okay with this?"

"Absolutely. Blessings on you, blessings on Rick, and blessings on all your future children, grandchildren, and great-grandchildren!"

Nicole scrutinized Katie's expression more carefully. "You're not having some reaction to all the immunizations, are you?"

"No, I'm happy for you, that's all. As of last night I stopped the sweats, by the way. I think my immune system met the tetanus, yellow fever, and typhoid challenge and won."

"Have you decided yet where you're going to go?"

"Not yet. What about you?"

Nicole hesitated.

"Why are you looking at me like that? Where are you going to live?"

"Rick's mom invited me to stay in their guestroom for the summer or until a permanent job opens up. She said I could help with the family business, if I wanted, and I said I would. I didn't have anything else opening up. My parents talked it over with them at the graduation party, and they think it's a good option."

"Wow."

Even though Katie was happy for Nicole, she was feeling twinges of regret. Or maybe they were touches of jealousy. If Katie and Rick still were together, Katie could see herself setting up camp in a luxurious guestroom at the Doyles'. She would have wonderful things to eat every day and lots of comfort. She would have a stream of kindness and affirmation from Rick's gracious mother, and Katie would belong.

But she didn't want to be absorbed into the expanding Doyle enterprises. Of that she was certain. There was nothing wrong with their wonderful and successful endeavors. The Doyles were a generous and kind family. But their world just wasn't the one Katie wanted to live in long term.

"That's great, Nicole." Katie hoped her expression matched her words and didn't reflect the aftershocks rumbling through her heart as she spoke.

"Thanks for being so supportive, Katie."

"So where is Rick taking you for your big first date, and when is it?"

"It's tomorrow night. We're going to the opening of an art exhibit in San Diego and then to a restaurant at the top of a high-rise on the bay."

Katie gave a low whistle. "Swanky."

"He said to dress up." Nicole smiled. "I might need some help deciding what to wear."

Katie had to draw the line there; her feelings were too tender to venture that deeply into Nicole and Rick's relationship. "I'm not sure I'll be able to help you out there, Nicole. I have a pretty tight schedule today. And tomorrow. And Friday too, for that matter. Then the wedding is Saturday, and by the way, I ruined my new dress during graduation. I have to come up with something else for the wedding."

"Can't you have it dry cleaned?"

"Maybe. But I'd rather get something else for the wedding."

"Do you want me to go shopping with you?"

"No, that's okay. I have to go down to Escondido later this week, so I thought I would have a look at the mall there."

"If you get stuck, you know you can borrow anything of mine that you want."

"Thanks." Katie knew she was done borrowing Nicole's clothes. Something strong and slightly sad had happened to her during this conversation. Even though she was in agreement that Rick and Nicole should go out, she didn't feel quite the same about things like sharing clothes and secrets. When the day came that Rick kissed Nicole, Katie didn't want to hear about it.

"I'd better get rolling." Katie made her way to the shower. "Have a great time on your date."

"Thanks, Katie. You're the best of the best." Nicole was beaming.

Even that was a little hard to take. While Katie agreed with all of this in principle, the loss of Rick in her own life caused her heart to sag a little.

At least he gets to take her to high-class places I never wanted to go to like the art show and the fancy restaurant.

Katie stepped into the shower and turned on the warm water. *When Rick took me to San Diego, we went to the zoo and a Brazilian barbecue.*

Right then and there Katie decided she wasn't going to start a list of comparisons. If she planted a whole field of those seeds in her heart, nothing good would grow from them.

Father, clear my heart from any jealousy or unwarranted hurt. I'm not the castoff woman in this scenario. I'm a victim of your grace. You have other plans for me. Plans for good and not harm. You have something custom designed for me. So what is it? Where do you want me to live? What do you want me to do?

Katie was careful not to ask God if he had any guys in mind for her now that Rick was out of the picture. She knew that a relationship with any guy right now wasn't where her focus needed to be. She had more important needs to be fulfilled, like housing and a job.

Returning to her room after her shower, Katie saw that she had missed a call. Jon had left a message saying he had a dove for her. She could pick up the bird anytime after two that afternoon. The price was much more than she had expected, but when she thought about it, she realized she didn't mind paying what he asked.

Katie scrounged around her room for something to eat. Her odd assortment of snacks was depleted, and her small refrigerator held only half a tub of strawberry cream cheese and an unopened bottle of soy sauce. Not exactly a winning combination when she had no bagels or noodles.

Her easiest option was to be first in line for lunch at the cafeteria. Then she would check to see if she could do anything for Julia. After that, she would put her thoughts toward finding a place to live.

When Katie arrived at the cafeteria, she wasn't the first one in line. But she was definitely the only graduate. It felt funny being there. Yes, it was all so familiar that she could go through the line and find everything she wanted, plus make a frozen yogurt cone from the machine, while blindfolded.

She knew that feeling uncomfortable there was more of a mental thing. In her head, she was done. Time to get a life. Time to make her own turkey sandwiches on white bread with her own jar of mayonnaise from her own refrigerator in her own apartment.

Katie had just filled her all-too-familiar plastic cafeteria cup with milk from the never- empty metal cow, when she saw Eli standing by the salad bar in his security uniform.

"So you've been promoted, huh? Official guard of the cherry tomatoes?" She intended to keep walking, but his serious expression made her pause.

"No, it's the croutons," he said with a straight face. "We had a report of unauthorized hoarding of croutons by a subversive group of disgruntled freshmen."

Eli said it so convincingly that Katie paused before catching on that he was messing with her.

"Don't mess with me, Lorenzo. I'm a college graduate."

"Don't mess with me, Weldon. I'm a college graduate, *and* I know the tribal call of the Masai warriors."

"And what exactly happens when you give this tribal call of the ... whatever warriors?"

"That's for me to know and you to wonder about."

She squinted at him and shook her head. "You're just a bundle of mysteries. For instance, 'Oh, surprise! Dr. Ambrose is my uncle.'"

"Why does that matter?"

"Well, he's marrying Julia. My RD. My friend. I guess that means you're going to be at the wedding Saturday."

He nodded. "Do you have anything against my uncle?"

"No, I think he's wonderful. Although he did give me a B- my first year here, and I think, if he had searched his heart, he could have found his way to make that into a nice solid B. But I'm not complaining. I managed to graduate anyway and choose not to hold that temporary slip in his grading abilities against him. We all have our weaknesses."

"My uncle is an extremely generous man," Eli said. "Maybe not in grades, but in other ways. He doesn't know that I know this, but he found a way to pay off my tuition. All of it. He did it anonymously, but I know it had to be him."

Katie swallowed hard and tried not to let her face show any flicker of disagreement. No way was she going to spout, "That was me, Eli. I paid for your college tuition." This was much better all around. Let Eli think it had been Dr. Ambrose.

"Is he the uncle you lived with last summer?" Katie asked calmly.

"Yeah."

"So that makes him the uncle who went to school here ages ago and introduced your parents to each other."

"That's right. You remembered."

Katie pulled up a smile. "Well, I have to be going; I'm in a rush. As usual, I have lots to do and not enough time to do it all."

Eli took a step toward her and looked her in the eye. "Before you run off, I want to ask you to do me a big favor."

"Sure." Katie felt his gaze coming at her like a wave she couldn't escape. When Doug taught Katie to surf, he showed her how to hold her breath, dive down under the wave, and float through the less turbulent waters before popping up on the other side. Subconsciously, she held her breath and dove.

Eli said in a low voice, "In Africa we have a saying. 'If you want to go fast, go alone. If you want to go far, go together.' "

Katie popped up on the other side of her heart-dive, blinking.

That wasn't so overwhelming. Actually, that was a beautiful saying.

Then the real wave hit her full on.

"Before I go back home, I want you to consider us, Katie. Ponder what it would be like if we went together. Not alone and fast but together and far."

Katie had no words. No quips, comebacks, or clever jives.

When it seemed clear she wasn't going to respond, Eli turned and walked away.

She watched him go; she was treading thoughts but refusing to call out to him.

Then he turned around. An ocean of humans bobbed between the two of them. He looked at Katie, placed his open palm on his chest, and pounded three times.

K atie suddenly lost her appetite. She made her way to the dishwasher carousel in the cafeteria and placed her tray of untouched food on the conveyor belt.

Making a straight line to her car, she took off, heading for Escondido. Driving helped. Driving down the hill, away from Rancho. Away from everything. Away from Eli.

I can't do what you asked, Eli. I can't ponder "us." Pondering happens in the heart. I can't go there. No, not now. You'll go home to Africa, and you'll see. It's better if we don't open any of these pondering places of the heart.

Katie turned on the music and tried to find something to sing along to. She wanted to get something else stuck in her head besides the mesmerizing image of Eli thumping his palm on his chest. Annoying lyrics would be fine.

Nothing seemed to stick.

She pulled onto the freeway and made a to-do list aloud. "Find a dress for the wedding, pick up the dove from the pet store, call Julia to see if she needs help with any wedding details, go on duty at the desk at seven o'clock this evening, maybe eat something eventually."

Katie went on lining up a second list for Thursday. And another for Friday. She knew she could find plenty to occupy herself Saturday with the wedding. Then Sunday she would have to move somewhere. That would keep her busy. Monday she would look for a job.

That probably would take a few days. By then, a full week would have passed. Although she didn't know when Eli planned to return to Kenya, she thought a week might cover it.

Just one more week. Then he will be far away, and I'll be able to focus on what God wants me to do next.

Ignoring the sensation of the hoof-stomping buffaloes in her stomach, Katie kept driving. When she arrived at the old mall in Escondido, she thought of how this place used to be such a familiar hangout. Like most things in life, it had changed. Many of the smaller shops had either gone out of business or moved to another section of the mall.

Surprisingly, the old pet shop now was located in the happening side of the mall and had expanded to twice the size it had been when Christy worked there. When Katie walked in, she noticed that it still had the same rabbit-pellet and hamster-shaving fragrance.

Jon was behind the register and didn't recognize Katie at first. When he did, he acted like they were hanging out at a party, chatting away.

"So you're not married, huh?"

"Nope."

"Living with anyone?"

"Jon."

"Hey, you wouldn't be the first one who recited all her Christian principles to me at sixteen and changed them by the time she was twenty-one."

His statement churned her stomach even more and for reasons she didn't want to think about. She knew she was among a small number of her friends who had stayed strong in her walk with Christ, kept to her moral commitments, and was holding out for a hero.

"Then I guess I'm one of a rare and nearly extinct breed of God-lovers who still lives and breathes what she believed back then. Only now it's more real than ever because it's in me. God's Spirit is in me, changing me. Not just around me, influencing me."

Her direct response seemed to startle him. He had no comeback.

"So do you have the dove?"

Jon pointed at the clock on the wall behind him. "It's not two o'clock yet."

Katie saw that it was only 1:20.

"Okay, fine. I'll come back then."

She went to the food court and walked by each of the fast food booths to see what her poor stomach might handle. She went for a healthy fruit smoothie with a booster of vitamin C. Then she hit the main department store and three smaller chain clothing stores before finding a classy black dress that fit and didn't make her fidget. All that in less than two hours.

Katie felt pretty victorious when she returned to the pet store with her new dress on a hanger inside a garment bag.

"It's after two o'clock," Jon said with a sour curl on the end of his words. "I've been holding the bird for you for more than an hour."

"Well aren't you Mr. Sunshine? Is this how you treat all your paying customers? I said I'd be back; I didn't say when. I had some shopping to do." Katie held up the garment bag in case he hadn't noticed the obvious. "So what are you waiting for, mister? Hand over the dove, and nobody gets hurt."

Jon reached behind the counter and lifted a small cage with a lovely white dove that greeted Katie with a rapid string of coo-cooing.

"She's so sweet," Katie said. "I'll need some food for her. Just a couple of days' worth. And you are sure that she's okay in the wild, right? I mean, when I release her she's not so domesticated that she won't know how to find food and take care of herself."

"She'll be fine."

Katie paid Jon the agreed amount for the bird and the food. She was about to go when he said, "I think you'll be fine too."

Katie gave him a funny look. "What's that supposed to mean?"

"If you ever spring outta that cage of yours and flap your wings out there in the wild, I think you'll be fine, Katie. You might be an endangered-species sort of Christian, but survival of the fittest, you know. You'll hold your own in the wild."

"Jon, that was outright poetic. Thank you. And here I thought you were turning into an old grump. Take it easy, Mr. Sunshine. I'll tell Christy you say hi."

"Tell her to come in and visit sometime."

"I will." Katie left with the caged dove in one hand and her new and improved bridesmaid dress in the other.

She felt better driving back to school than she had on the drive to Escondido. Jon's comment about her holding her own in the wild kept floating around in her thoughts. That was a pretty nice thing for him to say. She wondered if he thought her cage was the Christian college she had been living at for the past few years. Or was he alluding to more? Like she could spring out of the comfy western lifestyle to which she was so accustomed and hold her own living in a developing country.

It didn't matter what he meant. She was feeling pretty good at the moment, and food was sounding interesting once again.

Instead of going directly to school, she drove through a fast food restaurant and ordered a grilled chicken sandwich. Taking the long way back to school, Katie nibbled as she drove. The dove had taken to cooing from its position on the floor on the passenger's side.

"Are you hungry too, little friend? I'll feed you something as soon as we're back at school. But first I need to make a stop. Here." Katie tore off a corner of the bread from her sandwich and pressed it through the wires. The dove pecked at the bun and appeared only mildly interested.

"I'll give you your own food soon. I promise."

Pulling into Todd and Christy's apartment complex, Katie went to the office. The less-than-friendly manager remembered her from when she had reported the dead cat, Mr. Jitters, last fall.

"I was wondering if you had any open apartments."

"Not until the first of the month."

"I'd be interested in it."

He went through the rundown of the requirement of first and last months' rent and what was included and not included in the rates. He gave her an application to fill out and stressed the need for her credit report to be clear.

"Got it," Katie said. "Thanks. I'll drop these papers back tomorrow."

"Not only the papers, but also a cashier's check. I don't take personal checks. First and last plus security deposit. And it's extra for pets."

"How much extra?"

"Depends on the pet. Whatcha got?"

"No pets. I was just curious."

Katie drove back to campus, counting the days before June 1. She hadn't asked the manager, but she assumed she would be moving into Rick and Eli's apartment. After she moved out of the dorm on Sunday, she would need to find someplace to stay until the apartment was available. Todd and Christy's living room was an option. Going to a hotel was an option.

What if I took a vacation for a few days? That would be fun. Who would go with me? Where would I go?

She smiled to herself. *I'm fully immunized. I could even take one of those sketchy old people's cruises through the Panama Canal. Or I could lounge around at a resort in the Bahamas. That would be a nice graduation present to myself.*

Glancing down at the caged dove, she heard Jon's words about how she would be okay if she were released into the wild.

Or I could go to Africa.

Her heart beat a little faster. The pull to that corner of the world wouldn't go away.

I could go to Africa except Eli's going there, and even though it's a big continent, I don't want to look as if I'm following him to the ends of the earth.

Then, in an attempt to spiritualize her small epiphany about her draw to Africa, Katie said aloud, "But I do want to follow you to the ends of the earth, Lord. Where do you want me to go? Say the word, and I'm there."

"Coo," the dove sounded.

"The Land of Coo, you say. Exactly where is that, my little dove?" Katie had stopped at a light. She realized the man in the car beside her was looking at her. She pushed the button that rolled up her window.

Turning her attention back to the traffic light, she said, "Don't mind me, Mr. Nosey. This is what college graduates do. We drive around and talk to birds that you can't see just so you think we're talking to ourselves."

Heading up the hill for the university, Katie thought aloud. "I would have to sell my car if I went to the Land of Coo, wouldn't I? You know, I could sell it to Christy. For a dollar. I've heard of people doing that. That way she and Todd would have a second car and you, little Clover, would have a new family."

"Coo. Coo."

"I know. You're right. I am cuckoo for even thinking about this. I'll take Rick and Eli's old apartment, and I'll find a job somewhere doing something important and life-changing. You'll see. You can fly over and visit anytime you want. I'll put bird seed out for you the way Christy used to put cat food out for Mr. Jitters."

Katie held the birdcage behind her garment bag when she returned to Crown Hall. She knew the rules. No animals. This was different, though. This little dove was going to play an important part in Julia's wedding in three days. Certainly in this case an exception should be made.

She couldn't do it.

Katie turned around and walked back to her car. She drove back down the hill to where Christy worked and left the bird in the car. Entering the bookstore, Katie found Christy stocking shelves in the Bible section.

"I need to ask a favor. Can you keep a secret and a bird?"

It didn't take much to convince Christy to agree to birdie-sit for Katie for the next three days. The only part of Katie's explanation that upset Christy was when Katie told Christy she had driven all the way to the pet store in Escondido and not taken her along.

"Jon wants you to go in sometime and say hi. And when you do, I think you should take him one of these Bibles. An easy-to-understand version. He needs some hope, light, and truth in his life."

With the dove and bird food handed off to Christy, Katie returned to campus and found Julia in her room. Julia had prepared a list of small wedding tasks and was grateful that Katie offered to take care of them for her. Katie accomplished half the list while she was on-duty at the front desk that evening. She called the campus grounds supervisor to verify the number of chairs they would need to set up. She called the events rental company and left a message asking them to call back and verify that they had the right length white runner for the center aisle and that it would be delivered along with the garden arch before ten o'clock Saturday morning. The final call Katie made for Julia was to the tux rental shop. They were still open, and Katie asked if the groom and the best man had picked up their tuxes. The answer was yes.

The rest of the items on the list Katie attacked one-by-one on Thursday in between packing up her room. Her greatest organizational tip from Nicole that semester had been, "Only keep what you consider to be beautiful or useful." That motto helped her to decide on a whole lot of miscellaneous items that had served their purpose.

She went from simple living to bare essential living after two trips to the Dumpster and loading three boxes of giveaways in the Salvation Army trailer that parked on campus every year during the last week of school.

Katie's worldly possessions could fit in the backseat of her car. She felt like a gypsy. She even parted with the stand of a table lamp that had burned out at the beginning of her sophomore year, but she had kept, saying she would have it repaired. The lamp was toasted and needed to be tossed. Her next task was to take down what was left of the decorations of their hall's Peculiar Treasures theme from that year.

Carrying the lamp stand and her final trash bag through the lobby and out the front door, Katie nearly ran into Rick.

"Hey!"

"Hey, yourself."

"Hey, it's Thursday," Katie said.

"Yes, Thursday."

He looked great. A little nervous, but his true, suave self.

"So Nicole told me you guys are going to hit an art show and then have dinner someplace tall."

"Someplace tall," Rick repeated.

"You know, some place high. A tall restaurant."

He nodded. "You're sure you're okay with this, Katie?"

She laughed at her own gibberish. "Yes, really, I am. I didn't expect to see you here. Not like this." She was in her oldest T-shirt, which she planned to throw away at the end of the day. Squaring her shoulders, Katie gave Rick a smile. "Have a great time. I hope you guys have fun."

"I hope so too."

Katie turned to head to the Dumpster when Rick said, "Oh, hey, Katie, did you get the email about the café opening? It's set for Saturday."

"This Saturday?"

"Yes. We got the pizza oven installed and cleared the electrical inspection. Everything is a go."

"I have a wedding this Saturday. Julia's. I don't think I'll be able to do both."

"Right, the wedding. Well, I hope that goes well too."

"Thanks. Congratulations, though, on the café and on reaching your goal and everything." Katie lifted the stem of the broken lamp she held in her hand. "Here's to you, Rick. A job well done."

He laughed. "I don't think I've ever been toasted with a lamp before."

"Well, it's a toasted lamp, so there you go."

Katie made a point not to return immediately to her floor after dumping the trash. She didn't want to go past Nicole's room and see her in her perfectly gorgeous, dressed-up state of happiness. The two of them were going to work together on the wedding flowers the next day. Katie imagined she would receive enough of a report then to fill in for any visual glimpses of Nicole on her way to meet Rick.

Quite a few students were packed up and ready to check out during Katie's shift Thursday night. In past years, the exodus hadn't started until Friday and ran at uncharted intervals all weekend. Katie stayed busy her whole shift and remained on duty for another two hours to help Jordan once he came to work. When she headed for her basically empty room at 11:10, she realized that was the last time she would ever have front desk duty in her life. She was done. Her official hours as a resident assistant were over.

Katie didn't expect to feel such emptiness as she walked down the hall with its bare walls and partially vacated dorm rooms. She paused in the quiet space. "Thank you. Thank you for all of this. This whole year. All these women. Everything that happened. Thank you."

She found it hard to sleep that night. Her appetite had never quite returned since ... Katie tried to think of when she lost interest in eating at her usual capacity. She realized it started the morning of the sunrise trip to the mountains. When she bought the warm donuts, and she and Eli tapped them together and she said, "To us," he had looked at her and said, "To us." That's when she felt the buffalo stampede.

Eli's African quote came back to her about going fast alone but going far together. Putting her pillow over her head, Katie turned in her bed and let out a muffled wail. "No!"

A tap sounded at her door. "Katie?"

It was Nicole. The doorknob turned, and she pushed the door open a few inches. "Katie, are you all right?"

"Yeah, I'm fine." She bucked up her courage. "How was your big date?"

"Amazing! Do you mind if I come in? If I don't talk to someone, I'll burst."

Katie was experiencing the same feeling but on the opposite side of the love teeter-totter. "Yeah, sure. Come in. Just don't turn on the light. And don't worry about bumping into anything in the dark. My room is empty." She sat up in bed and made room for Nicole at the end.

The light from the hallway shone in as Nicole entered. She left the door open a few inches to provide enough light for her to reach the foot of Katie's bed. Nicole sat down in her elegant red dress. Katie remembered how Rick used to tell Christy he liked her in red, a color Katie couldn't pull off with much success because of her red hair. Nicole looked great in red.

"We had such an amazing time, Katie. The art exhibit was world class. They had original pieces from museums in Russia, Vienna, and Paris. I saw an original Monet. Original! It was breathtaking. Rick knew so much about the paintings of the Italian artists. I didn't know he had relatives in Italy. He's been there. And the restaurant had the most amazing view of the harbor and the lights. We talked nonstop. Katie, I'm so happy. So happy."

Katie's eyes had adjusted to the light. She could see the soft glow on Nicole's face.

Katie knew she could snipe Nicole's experience with Rick to pieces with resentment and jealousy and make Nicole a victim of Katie's self-pity. Or she could extend to Nicole the same love and inclusion God offers and make Nicole a victim of grace.

Reaching over, Katie gave Nicole's hand a squeeze.

This was going to work out nicely between the two of them. Katie wondered how long it would be before Rick and Nicole realized they were going to end up married.

Maybe they knew already.

28

The morning of Julia's wedding, Katie headed over early to Todd and Christy's apartment. It had rained sometime during the night. Clouds hid the sun, hinting at the possibility of another sprinkle.

She went through her to-do list for the day, starting with turning in her check to the apartment manager and picking up the dove from Todd and Christy. The previous afternoon Katie had gone to the apartment complex with her rental papers and her cashier's check. However, the manager was out. She left a note on his door saying she would be back this morning.

Since it was only 7:35 when Katie arrived, she decided to go to Christy and Todd's apartment first. They were expecting her, and that way she wouldn't run the risk of waking the apartment manager on a Saturday morning and making him even grumpier than usual.

Christy answered the door with the birdcage in her hand.

Katie laughed. "You wouldn't be overeager to get rid of the little darlin', would you?"

"No, the bird was a perfect houseguest. I'm in a hurry to get going. Todd has to drop me off at work early because he has an outing with some of the high school guys. Hey, did you turn in your rental papers yet? We're so excited about you living here."

"I'm on my way to the office now. Thanks for watching this little dove." Katie held up the cage.

Todd appeared behind Christy. "Did you decide yet where you're going to stay for the next week or so?"

"Not exactly. I've been kinda' caught up with the wedding stuff."

"Stay with us," Christy said.

Katie looked at Todd.

"Yeah, just stay here, Katie. We were serious when we invited you."

"Are you sure?"

Todd and Christy said, "Yes," in unison.

"Okay, if you're sure. It'll only be for a few days. You can kick me out anytime if I snore or make too big a mess or blow up your microwave again."

"Those sound like reasonable terms," Todd said with a half-grin.

Christy made a don't-listen-to-him face. "We'll be eager to hear how the wedding goes today."

"I'll tell you all about it tomorrow when I move in with my two bags and two boxes — the extent of my worldly possessions."

"We'll have the air mattress ready for you."

Katie thanked them again and headed for the office with the birdcage in hand. She turned the corner of the path that circled the apartment complex and saw the manager heading in her direction.

"'Morning! I was just on my way to your place."

"Is that a bird?"

"Yes. You know what they say. One of these in the hand is worth two of these in the bush."

The apartment manager didn't look amused. "Is it your bird?"

"Yes, but it's not moving in with me. Christy was watching it for me for a few days."

"How many days?"

"Three. Why?"

"She'll need to pay extra this month."

"Are you serious? Here." Katie pulled from her jeans pocket all the cash she had on her. "Will that cover it? Three days of bird security fees."

He looked satisfied and stuck the cash in his pocket.

"I have all the rental papers and my check with me." Katie put down the cage. She pulled the envelope from her shoulder bag and handed it to him.

He took it from her and looked even more disgruntled than usual.

"You saw the note I left yesterday, right? I said I would bring everything over this morning."

"I saw the note. But the apartment's not available."

"What? What do you mean?"

"Someone else put down money yesterday morning. I'm waiting for clearance on their paperwork."

"But you knew I wanted the apartment. I —"

"That's the way these things work. You're first on the waiting list. I'll call you next week." He moved past Katie and kept on walking.

She stood there in shock for several moments before the cooing dove nudged her to get going. Striding back to her car, Katie picked up her pace and tried to think of what to do next. The only sane choice was to put this unexpected turn of events aside and worry about it tomorrow. Today, she had a few other pressing matters to focus on.

When she arrived back on campus, Katie couldn't believe how the front of Crown Hall had turned into a circus of boxes, trucks, and aggravated students trying to force their overstuffed car trunks to close. It had been this way for the past two days. The congestion this morning was double what it had been the previous days. Once again, Katie was grateful she had put in all her front desk hours before the moving frenzy broke loose.

She showered in an eerily quiet dorm bathroom and was met with a stream of open-dorm visitors roaming the halls as she scurried to her room with her robe pulled tight. Closing her door, Katie put on some music and turned it up to drown the noise of the moving traffic in the hallway. Katie's new dress fit. Her hair dried just right, even though she knew she needed to have the ends trimmed soon.

A little makeup, a little spritz of something fresh and fruity she had tucked in her makeup bag. She had tossed all the used-up lotion and fragrance bottles Thursday. She was ready. More than that, she was early.

Katie regretted that she couldn't trot down to Nicole's door as she had so many other times that year, give a big ta-dah, and hear Nicole exclaim how impressed she was that Katie was early and that she looked gorgeous.

Nicole wanted to get to Rick's new café in Redlands as soon as she could, so she had left early that morning to work with the campus grounds people to place all the flowers as they set up the chairs and put down the runner. The plan was for Nicole to leave the bouquets and boutonnieres in the chapel on upper campus, and Katie would take it from there.

Since this wedding was small and simple, Julia had cut back on a lot of traditional extras such as a rehearsal and rehearsal dinner. That made Katie feel even more confident her small gift of the dove would be a special touch.

Katie went upstairs and tapped on Julia's door.

"If you're Katie, come in. If you're not Katie, then I'm not here."

"It's me." She entered and then asked, "So how's it going? Do you need me to fasten any hooks or snaps on your dress or jewelry or anything?"

"No, but come on back. We're in my room."

Katie stepped into Julia's bedroom and was introduced to Julia's mom and dad. Then Katie let out a long, low, appreciative, "Ooh, Julia, you look absolutely stunning. What a perfect wedding dress for you."

The dress had classic lines and followed all of Julia's best curves. Katie loved the way the skirt flowed with a timeless sort of elegance.

"Thank you." Julia was radiant.

"I'm so happy for you." Katie leaned in and gave Julia a light-touch sort of hug that wouldn't ruffle her gown or veil.

"Thanks, Katie. Did Nicole work out everything with you on the flowers? I know she drove out to Redlands this morning."

"Yes, I'm leaving now for upper campus. I'll let you know if there are any glitches. But you know it will be fine. Nicole did this. It'll be flawless."

"When you get up there, if the minister arrives, could you tell him we changed the song for when I come down the aisle? It's Handel's "Water Music" now. That won't affect anything he does, but I don't want him to be caught off guard."

"Got it. Do you need anything else?"

Julia grinned. "No. We'll see you in about half an hour."

Katie went out to her car and retrieved the bird. Instead of driving through the mess of cars and trucks left everywhere they shouldn't be, she walked to upper campus, gently swinging the cage.

Small tremors of uncertainty over the now-unavailable apartment came back, but she tried to ignore those thoughts. This was Julia's wedding day.

God will work everything out. He always does.

It was quiet when she arrived on upper campus. The late morning air had warmed up nicely, and a pleasant breeze rustled through the palm trees. Katie smiled at them all lined up, shaking their shaggy manes like a bunch of surfer boys returned from the blue and awaiting the next promising set.

Katie remembered how, at the reception for Christy and Todd's wedding, Julia had approached her about being an RA. That provision for her senior year had been an out-of-the-blue surprise from God.

God will work everything out. He always does.

The chapel was open, and the flowers were exactly as Nicole had promised. Katie's woman of honor bouquet was propped up with the door of the hidden cage open. She placed the dove's current home right next to it, opened the door, and tilted the cage. Gravity was her friend and helped persuade the little dove to slide on into the new digs.

"Cozy and fragrant. What do you think of that?"

The dove protested with some wild wing flapping and not-so-content cooing.

"Hey, it's okay. You'll be fine. Relax. It's only for a short time. Then you'll be free. Free as a bird. There, that's not so bad, is it?"

Katie put the bird in the bouquet to the side and let the dove settle down. Then she went outside to check on the setup. The cake was in place under the yellow canopy. A woman with a baby in a stroller beside her was leaning over the cake with a pastry tube, adding final touches.

All hints of another shower had passed. The sun was doing what it did best. The air felt light and cool. It was a perfect day for a wedding.

Katie spotted the pastor standing near the arch that Nicole had laced with flowers and greenery. Katie walked over, introduced herself, and gave him Julia's message about the music.

"And one more thing," Katie added, as the violinist tuned up. "I'm going to release a dove from a cage hidden in my bouquet at the very end, before they go back down the aisle. Julia doesn't know about this."

"Does John know?"

"No, Dr. Ambrose doesn't know either."

The minister looked skeptical. "How do we know the dove will exit on cue?"

Katie shrugged. "Are you a praying man, by any chance?"

"As a matter of fact, I am," he said with an amused look.

"And so am I," said a voice behind Katie.

She felt the return of the buffalos even before she turned around and looked at a version of Eli she had never seen before. Dressed in a black tux, standing tall and resolved only a few feet away, Eli looked like the most handsome and daring man Katie had ever seen.

His wavy hair was combed back. His goatee was shaved off, and on his lips was that irresistible grin that made Katie nearly forget where she was and what she had just said.

"I'm a praying man," Eli repeated. "Was there something you needed to pray about? Any big life decisions? Future plans? Relationships you're considering?"

His boldness surprised the response right out of Katie's mouth. "No! Don't pray any more. Not for me. Don't pray for anything." She felt her face blush in a fluster and quickly trounced through the grassy field back to the chapel. Scenes from the past year flashed through her mind with each step.

In this same meadow a year ago Katie had chased Todd and Christy's getaway limo. She lost a shoe and her floral head wreath in the mad dash. Eli approached her that day with the lost "halo," and she nonchalantly told him to toss it.

Instead, Eli hung the wreath from the rearview mirror of his car. Months later, when Katie asked him about why he kept the dried-out wreath, he told her it reminded him to pray. For her. Eli had been praying for her for a year.

So what? That doesn't change anything.

Katie fought the urge to glance at him over her shoulder.

Why didn't anyone tell me he was going to be the best man? Why does he have to look so ... so ... good? What's wrong with me? Come on, Katie, breathe. This doesn't change anything. Couple more days, and he will be gone. And you'll be ...

She yanked open the chapel's door and saw Julia standing there, holding her bouquet and posing for a photo by the stained-glass window.

Katie blinked away the piercing revelation that she didn't know where she would be in a few more days. *Don't think about that now. This is Julia's day. This is her moment. You are the woman of honor. Time to do the honorable thing and put your full attention on the bride.*

Julia's parents stood to the side. Inhaling fresh courage, Katie went to them and whispered, "Did you see your corsage there in the box? And your boutonniere? Let me get them for you."

From that moment on, all was movement, photos, smiles, and guests arriving and filling the seats.

The violinist played her solo, and Katie took steady steps down the runner, holding her birdie bouquet in front of her as unswayingly as possible so the dove wouldn't flap about.

She glanced at Dr. Ambrose. He looked happy and confident, standing there under the arch, waiting for his bride. Katie gave him a quick grin and kept her focus straight. She didn't dare let her eyes venture over to Eli where he stood next to the groom.

Katie made the turn at the front gracefully and heard the distinctive coo of her stowaway.

It's okay. It's an outdoor wedding. No one will think it's unusual to hear a bird out here.

Julia's mother rose from her chair, and the other guests rose with her. The violinist changed to what Katie now knew must be Handel's "Water Music," and down the white runner floated Julia.

All brides are beautiful, of that Katie was sure. Julia was no exception. She came forward serene and radiant. As Julia took her place beside her husband-to-be, she let go of her father's arm and handed off her bouquet to Katie.

Katie had forgotten about that woman of honor duty. She had been doing fine with the swaying bouquet as long as she had both hands to hold it secure. Now she had Julia's bouquet in one hand and hers in the other.

You can do this. Relax. And whatever you do, don't look at Eli!

The ceremony was traditional and lovely in its simplicity. During all of it, Katie could feel Eli's persistent gaze on her. She looked at him only once, when he handed his uncle the rings. Katie thought Eli would be looking at Dr. Ambrose when he did the hand off, but no, Eli met her gaze, and her poor stomach was a mess. She looked down and noticed a white splurt freshly deposited on the front of her black dress from the nervous dove.

Great! I know you're a bit rattled in there, little dove, but could you try to hold it just a little longer?

Katie focused back on Julia. Vows exchanged, Dr. Ambrose was invited to "kiss your bride." He gave Julia a short kiss followed by a second and then a third. The guests rustled with warm murmurs the way guests do at weddings whenever the kiss between the bride and groom is especially tender.

Julia and Dr. Ambrose turned to face their guests, all smiles and rosiness. Katie handed Julia her bouquet.

Okay, this is it, little dove.

Katie reached for the latch on the backside of her bouquet.

The pastor said, "It is now my privilege to introduce to you for the very first time ..." He glanced at Katie, waiting for her to release the dove.

Katie gave the cage a little wiggle. *Come on, baby, spread your wings. You can do it!*

" ... these two people whom all of us have come to know and love ..."

Clearly, the pastor was stalling for Katie's benefit. She tipped the cage. Gravity had been her helpful assistant earlier. Why not now?

Katie shook the bouquet, and the dove tumbled to the grass and lay there, unmoving.

Oh, no! It's dead!

Before Katie could panic, the pastor raised his voice saying, " ... the newly married, Dr. and Mrs. Jonathan Ambrose."

At that moment, the strong-hearted dove raised her head, stretched her wings, and up she flew. Everyone gasped. It was as if the dove's wedding flutter had been choreographed. She flew in a half-circle above Katie's head, then over the pastor, then over Eli, and then, with lovely, slow-flapping white wings, the dove seemed to rest midair over Julia and Dr. Ambrose just as they walked down the aisle.

Katie's mouth opened in amazement, as the gentle dove followed the bride and groom to the end of the runner and then, in a magnificent show of strength and bravery, soared into the heavens.

Everyone saw it. Their faces expressed astonishment and delight. Especially Dr. Ambrose. When Katie saw his expression, she knew the gift of the dove was more than just her idea of a fun little surprise. It was a God-thing. It was God's idea of a special wedding gift all along. He simply had nudged Katie to help him pull it off.

Katie's face felt like a pink sunrise of heavenly glee. She stood in place, grinning wildly and forgot the next and final step in the ceremony. She was supposed to meet Eli halfway, at the altar, take his arm, and exit down the aisle with him.

The pastor cleared his throat. Katie glanced at him out of the corner of her eye. He dipped his head and raised his eyebrows above the top rim of his glasses as a signal that Katie was up to bat.

"Oh!"

Katie looked over at Eli. She took her three steps toward the middle. He did the same. Only, with each step Eli took, his hand was over his heart, and his eyes were fixed on Katie. Just as she had seen him do before, Eli thumped his chest with the flat of his palm. One ... two ... three times.

In a deep and resonating place inside, Katie heard the unspoken words that attached themselves to those three beats. They came over her unforced, like a wave.

I ... love ... you.

29

Y ou should try to eat something." Christy gave Katie a concerned
look. "I have English muffins. Do you want me to toast one for
you?"

"No, I don't think my stomach could take it." Katie flopped
back on the air mattress where she had set up camp in the corner of
Christy and Todd's living room. "Man, when did you ever hear me say
I couldn't eat? Like, never, right?"

"And you said you don't have any other symptoms? No more
sweats or aches or anything?"

"No, I just can't eat." Katie looked up at the clock. "You don't
have to stay up any longer, watching me melt away to nothingness."

"Not to destroy my bedside manner, or should I say, air-mattress-
side manner, but I was waiting up for Todd. He's usually home by this
time on Sunday nights. He's probably talking to someone. That seems
to be half his job lately, just listening to teens and counseling them.
At least the Elder Board recognized the uncharted hours he spends
doing the counseling, and they agreed to keep him on staff through
the summer."

"Then what?"

"We don't know."

Katie untangled her legs from her blanket cocoon. "I guess God
is keeping both of us in suspense about what's next."

Christy smiled softly. "He's kept us in suspense before. But he's never abandoned us."

Katie picked up her pillow in its Little Mermaid pillowcase and hugged it to her chest. "Well, there could be a first time for everything. Especially if your charming manager doesn't call me this week and say that the other renter backed out so I can have the apartment."

"Katie, you know God is going to do one of his God-things. He always does. How many times over the years have you been the one to tell me that?"

"I think it's easier to believe goodness and hope for your friends than it is for yourself."

"Then it's a good thing I'm your best friend, Katie, because I believe. I believe God has his hand on your life. He has from the moment you were conceived. God has plans for you, surprising plans. Your life was his idea. This isn't a dead end but a beginning of new adventures."

Just then the front door opened. Todd gave his wife a big smile. His gaze fell on Katie, and he frowned.

"What's wrong?" he asked.

Katie wiped away a tear. "Nothing. Your wife was just trying to cheer me up."

"If I had known the two of you were here cheering each other up, I would have had you come help us." Todd headed for the kitchen and opened the refrigerator.

"Help who?" Christy asked.

Todd pulled out some apple juice and drank the last of it directly from the bottle. "Eli. Some guy bought Eli's furniture. I was helping them to dismantle and load the stuff into the guy's truck. There wasn't a lot, but it took awhile. Eli's leaving in the morning. You knew that, right, Katie?"

Katie felt as if Todd had punched her in the stomach. "No, I didn't know when he was leaving."

"That's right." Todd stepped back into the living room and gazed at Katie with his silver- blue eyes. "You probably didn't know when he was leaving because you haven't been talking to him. He said you avoided him at the wedding yesterday. Are you okay with his leaving without you saying good-bye?"

Katie shook her head slowly. "No, I guess I'm not okay with it. I thought I would be, but I'm really not. I need to go up there and say good-bye. I mean, he's going far away. I may never see him again." Katie's eyes filled with tears.

Christy said, "You should go, Katie. Go talk to him."

"He's not there," Todd said.

"Where is he?"

"He went to his uncle's to stay overnight since he sold his bed and had nowhere to sleep. Julia and Dr. Ambrose are on their honeymoon, so their house is empty."

Katie felt her hands clench and unclench inside her sweatshirt's front pocket. "Do you know where Dr. Ambrose lives?"

"No."

"Well, maybe I'll just call Eli." Katie strode across the room and scrounged in her purse for her phone. "Have you seen my phone, Christy? Did I plug it in somewhere?"

Todd sat down on the couch. "So what are you going to tell Eli when you call him?"

"I don't know. I'll wish him a safe trip. Where is my phone? Maybe I left it in my car."

"And after you wish him a safe trip, what are you going to tell him?"

Christy now had taken a seat next to Todd. Both of them focused on Katie.

"I don't know. I'll tell him I hope he has a nice life in Africa."

"Is that all?"

"Probably." Katie faced her friends with both hands on her hips. "What is this? Some sort of intervention?"

Todd and Christy looked at each other and exchanged expressions Katie couldn't categorize. "Now there's an option we never thought of," Todd said.

"Listen." Katie tried to calm down by sitting in a chair across from the board of examiners. "You guys think Eli is wonderful. I get it. No argument there. But as far as he and I or him and me or however you say it ... no."

"No?" Christy's blue-green gaze was burning a hole in Katie.

"Why?" Todd's voice came across demanding and authoritative, which wasn't his usual style.

"He's ... I'm ... we're ... no!"

"Why?" Todd asked again, this time with less verve.

"He's going to live in Africa," Katie blurted out. "Probably for the rest of his life. That's the home of his heart, Africa."

"You said you always wanted to go to Africa," Christy reminded her.

"I did. I do! But I was thinking more like for a visit. Go do some good and come back."

"Come back to what?" Todd asked.

Katie felt the bottom drop out. She couldn't answer him.

"What do you have here that you couldn't leave behind?"

She didn't answer.

Todd asked again. "Really, what do you have that would permanently tie you to this place?"

"Nothing!" Katie shouted the answer true and clear. "You know that. All my belongings fit in the back of my car. I don't have anything that's keeping me here."

"Now we're getting somewhere." Todd leaned forward. "So what would you have to lose if you let go of what you have here — and letting go does seem to be a key to what's going on here — and what if you bought a one-way ticket to Kenya? What would you have to lose, Katie?"

She wished she had some sassy sort of answer, but all she had was truth floating openly on the top of her spirit. She scooped it up and handed Todd that answer. "Nothing."

Todd scratched the side of his square jaw. "I see such a picture in all this. A picture of Christ and his bride, the church."

Christy gave Todd a questioning glance, as if she couldn't believe that was what popped out of his mouth.

"It's like this, Katie." Todd sat back on the couch. "You have been given every reason to believe Eli wants to be with you and share life with you. But you resist even though you have nothing to lose. It's a matter of the heart, really. Free will and all that. You get to choose. You know he wants you. You know it. The question has been, and still is, do you want him?"

Katie couldn't move. Her stomach was a mess. Swallowing the tears she refused to let out, she lifted her chin. "So what do you think would happen if I said yes?"

Todd folded his hands behind his neck. "You tell me."

Christy grinned. "For one thing, I'm pretty sure your appetite would come back."

"And you're saying Eli and I would go live with the giraffes and lions and end up happily ever after." Katie could hear the quiver in her voice.

Todd and Christy looked at each other with soft smiles.

"It can happen," Todd said.

Katie felt like a hundred kernels of popcorn were going off inside her head. "I can't believe you guys are telling me it's okay to just pack my bags—"

"Your bags already are packed," Christy interrupted.

"—and buy a one-way ticket for Kenya tomorrow."

"Why not?" Todd asked. "Wonders of the modern world. You can buy a plane ticket to anywhere right from the comfort of our apartment. And if you don't have enough to cover the cost of the ticket, Christy and I will help you out, won't we?"

"I think she has enough." Christy kept her blue green laser beam fixed on Katie. "She has enough of everything she needs to make this decision, including all her immunizations and malaria pills. As a matter of fact, I think you made this decision awhile ago, Katie. You've just been waiting for someone like us to give you a little kick out the door."

The room went still. Katie didn't look away from Todd and Christy.

Todd's calm voice rode across the silence. "Katie, what are you afraid of?"

A little covey of tears clouded her vision. "I invested so much in Rick. So many years. So many emotions. So much of myself. It seems I should wait longer. Not be vulnerable again so soon. It would be safer to wait, don't you think? It's better if I hold off and not get emotionally connected to anyone. Especially not to someone on the other side of the world. It's too much, too soon, too far."

"It hurts when you fall off a cloud," Todd said. "Even if you jumped off. We all understand that. So does that mean you're going to lie on the ground and play dead?"

Katie thought about the dove tumbling from its floral cage yesterday and lying without moving on the grass.

"No." Katie's voice was barely a whisper. Then again, with more certainty, as if her soul was starting to flutter upward, she emphatically said, "No!"

"Then do it, Katie." Christy's eyes sparkled. "Get on that plane tomorrow and see what God has for you and Eli together in Africa. You can always come home. We'll be here for you. But if you don't take this chance now, you might miss the next surprising God-thing he has waiting for you."

Katie and Christy exchanged a deep-hearted expression of understanding.

"Okay."

As soon as Katie spoke the golden word, Todd stood up. "Okay," he repeated matter-of-factly. He opened the laptop sitting on the kitchen table. "Eli's flight goes out of San Diego at 6:30 tomorrow morning."

"How do you know that? Are you giving him a ride?"

"No. Eli gave his car to Joseph. I heard them talking about what time Joseph needed to pick him up. I also heard Eli say he had a layover in London. All we have to do is find a 6:30 flight to Nairobi out of San Diego that connects in London and see if God saved you a seat."

"Start sorting out your things," Christy said. "We'll keep what you don't need here in our storage closet. If you want any extra toothpaste or shampoo, you can take whatever I have."

Katie set to work packing once again, this time simplifying her life down to what she could fit in one large duffle bag and a carry-on tote. Todd found the flight that matched the criteria and booked Katie a window seat.

"Or would you prefer aisle?"

"I don't care. I can't believe we're doing this. The two of you are accomplices, you know. If this whole thing blows up, you'll have to admit your involvement. Could get messy."

"Love tends to be messy," Todd said.

"And inconvenient," Katie added, remembering what Eli had said at Strawberry Peak Lookout. "Do you guys really think this is love? Do you think I'm in love with Eli, and I just haven't admitted it to myself?"

"Whatever it is, you'll have lots of time to figure it out on your way there. Your flight is twenty-seven hours," Todd responded.

"With a four-hour layover in London," Christy added. "Do you want to take a shower?"

"In London?"

"No, now. It's 1:45 in the morning. If you're supposed to be at the airport two hours before departure for international flights and if it takes us an hour to drive to the airport, that means we should leave in an hour."

Katie dashed through a shower. She put on her most comfortable traveling clothes and snagged a bar of soap from under the sink. Pulling together some important papers from her portable file, Katie called out, "Chris, do you have a dollar?"

"I think so. Aren't you going to need more cash than that?" Christy opened her wallet and pulled out a twenty-dollar bill and some ones.

"All I need is a dollar. Now, can you sign this and mail it for me?"

"What is it?"

"The pink slip on Clover."

"Clover?"

"My car. I just sold her to you for a dollar. Sign here, and she's yours."

"Katie!"

"Don't make a scene, Mrs. Spencer. What am I going to do with a car? You need one, I don't. You just bought it."

Christy and Todd thanked Katie way more than was necessary.

"If this blows up on me, I may buy it back from you for a dollar. Oh, and tell your landlord I withdraw my rental application. Shred the check for me too, will you?"

After pulling together a few more loose ends, the three of them rolled down the freeway at three o'clock in the morning. The hazy half-moon slipped behind a rolled-up fist of clouds, and Katie bit her lower lip.

"Tell me again why this is a good idea?"

Christy said. "As soon as Eli sees you, you'll know."

Todd and Christy went into the airport with her and escorted her as far as they could through check-in. Eli wasn't anywhere to be seen.

"I'm not boarding the plane if he's not on it," Katie said.

"He could be running late," Todd suggested.

"Or he could already be through security and at the gate," Christy said. "You should go on through security, Katie. You have your phone; mine is on. We'll wait out here, and if he's not there by the time the plane boards, then don't get on. Call us, and we'll figure something out."

"Okay. Well, 'bye." The lump in Katie's throat was too big to swallow as she realized she was saying good-bye to her friends for a very long time.

Christy's eyes brimmed with tears, but her confident grin was still in place as she hugged Katie. Todd placed his large hand on Katie's perspiring forehead and blessed her. "Katie, may the Lord bless you and keep you. May the Lord make his face to shine upon you and give you his peace. And may you always love Jesus first, above all else."

With a barely whispered, "Thank you," Katie entered the security line. As soon as she was through security, she hurried to the gate, watching for Eli. She had no idea what she was going to say to him when she did see him. If she did see him.

This is crazy.

Arriving at the gate out of breath, Katie checked every passenger seated in the waiting area. No Eli. She walked over to the adjoining waiting area. No Eli.

What if Todd had the wrong day? Or the wrong airport? What if the flight is really at 6:30 tonight? This has to be the most on-a-whim thing I've ever done during my entire career as a peculiar treasure. So what happens to my luggage if I don't board the plane? Does it go to Nairobi without me?

The stampeding buffalos were demolishing what she had left of her empty digestive track.

Just then her cell rang. She scrambled to answer.

"He's here," Christy whispered. "We just saw him get dropped off at the curb. We're hiding behind a pillar so he can't see us. He's checking his luggage right now with a skycap. He's wearing a brown jacket and a baseball cap."

Katie didn't know if she should stay there and wait or retrace her steps back toward security to meet him there. "What should I do: Stay or go back to security?"

Todd's voice came on the line. "Meet him halfway, Isaac and Rebekah style. Every working relationship is between two people who are willing to meet each other halfway. Go!"

Katie snatched up her bag, picked up her pace, and ran back toward security. She felt like the woman in Song of Solomon who ran through the streets trying to find her beloved.

Her stomach hurt. She couldn't breathe. Slowing her pace, she drew in a breath, and then she saw him. He was picking up his carry-on from the security scanner and wiggling his right foot into his shoe.

Eli!

She stopped right where she was and waited, her heart pounding like an African drum.

Eli looped his backpack over one arm and lifted his carry-on with the other. He held his boarding pass in his right hand and stopped at the electronic schedule board, checking his pass and then checking the board once again.

He was only ten feet away. Katie waited for him to see her.

Turning away from the board, Eli walked three steps before looking up. That's when he saw Katie right there in front of him. He blinked as if she were a dream. Then he dropped his luggage.

"You're here!"

"I'm here."

"Why?"

"I'm ..."

"You're coming to Nairobi, aren't you?" Eli's face lit up.

"That's what my ticket says."

"When? When did you ..."

"Last night. This morning. A few hours ago. I don't know. Todd and Christy made me."

Eli's stunned expression relaxed into a grin. "Did you tell my parents you're coming?"

"No. I should have emailed your dad, but everything happened so fast."

Eli reached over and smoothed the back of his fingers across Katie's cheek. "It's okay. It doesn't matter. I think they know."

"How?"

"My mother told me you might be coming."

"Your mom? How did she know?"

Eli dipped his chin and looked at Katie with one of his rich, mesmerizing looks. "My mother is a praying woman."

Katie felt her eyes tear up. Everything inside told her this was right. This was true. A place had been prepared for her even before she realized it. Even while she was being obstinate and fearful. All the hesitancy was gone. Katie knew she was right where she was supposed to be, doing what she was supposed to be doing.

Her stomach rumbled, and she knew her appetite was back. So was her deep and humble amazement of God and his intricate design for her life. Love had come to her on its own schedule, and it had been inconvenient and organic. She had every reason to believe this was very real.

Releasing her breath, Katie took one step back. She lifted her arm and opened her hand. With her gaze fixed on Eli, she tapped the palm of her open hand against her heart three times.

Eli's expression made it clear he had received the message. He reached for her, took her face in his strong hands, and looked into her eyes.

"Are you sure?"

"Yes, I'm sure."

"Then I'm going to kiss you."

And he did.

Eli kissed Katie with all the astonished tenderness of a man whose prayers have just been answered.

Katie received his kiss, feeling as if a magnificent dawn were rising inside her as vivid and transforming as the mountain sunrise they had experienced together. The darkness was gone. She could see wide-open possibilities ahead of them.

This man was a warrior. A prayer warrior.

He pressed his forehead against hers and then pulled back far enough to look her in the eye. What Katie read in his gaze was deep and mysterious, like a midnight meteor shower, shining with tiny shivers of light.

Eli took her hand in his and led the way to the departure gate.

Katie knew right then and there that the Author and Finisher of her life story was about to start a new chapter in the book of her days. This chapter would be filled with everything she had dreamed of—adventure, mystery, hope, and love. Yes, most definitely love.

She gave Eli's hand a squeeze. "I guess this means we're going together."

Eli grinned. "Yes, we are. We're going together. And you know what that means, don't you?"

Katie remembered the African saying Eli had spoken to her in the cafeteria. "It means we'll go far."

As soon as she spoke the words, Katie was aware of the sweet sense of peace that had been weaving back and forth between them. And that's when she knew. God's Spirit was doing his work. He was knitting their hearts together.

At last.

Dear Peculiar Treasure,

Okay, so I know Katie isn't a real person.

But I felt so close to her as I was writing this story that I woke up several mornings realizing I'd been dreaming about her. When I wrote the last few pages, I cried because I felt so happy for her. At last the door of opportunity she had been waiting for ever since she first appeared at the sleepover in the second Christy Miller book had swung wide open.

What will happen to Katie now? I don't know. To be honest, I never know what will happen when I start a book. That's one of the ways I've always felt connected to Katie and the rest of the gang. The possibilities are endless. The next step is always a surprise. God keeps us wondering about what the next "coming attraction" will be. And that's one of the many reasons I love him so much. What an adventure!

With each of the Katie books a portion of the sales has gone to ministries. This time the ministry is Media Associates International (www.littworld.org). MAI is committed to training writers and publishers in difficult places in the world. As you might guess, one of the locations for MAI training is in, yes, Nairobi, Kenya. Lord willing, I'll be at the next training session, and you can be sure I'll catch myself looking around for Katie and Eli.

What are the "coming attractions" God has just around the corner for you? Be assured that you have been set free to soar. I love the way this thought is expressed in Isaiah 44:21b–22 "I, the Lord, made you, and I will not forget to help you. I have swept away your sins like the morning mists. I have scattered your offenses like the clouds. Oh, return to me, for I have paid the price to set you free" (NLT).

So, fly, be free, dear Peculiar Treasure! Keep on trusting the Lord no matter what happens. He has his hand on your life.

With a joyful heart,
Robin Jones Gunn

I love keeping in touch! I hope you'll stop by www.robingunn.com and sign up for the Robin's Nest e-newsletters.

KATIE WELDON SERIES

Peculiar Treasures

Robin Jones Gunn,
Bestselling Author
of the Christy Miller Series

Katie Weldon catches more than just the bouquet at the wedding of her best friend, Christy Miller. She also snags a job offer that launches her into an adventure she never imagined.

Katie eagerly accepts the job as resident assistant at Rancho Corona University only to find herself in a community of conflict. She thought this was where God wanted her, but how can God use her—love her—when everything is falling apart? Especially with her boyfriend, Rick.

Katie turns to the women in her life for solace. In the safety of their love and encouragement she finally allows herself to spill her heart about her relationship with Rick. But even their advice can't postpone the decision Katie must face, a decision that will define who she is and the woman she's becoming.

The first book in the Katie Weldon Series, *Peculiar Treasures* follows Katie as she struggles to believe that God can love her, faults and all.

Softcover: 978-0-310-27657-9

Pick up a copy today at your favorite bookstore!

Read the first chapter of *Peculiar Treasures*, Book 1 in the Katie Weldon Series!

1

Katie picked up the skirt of her bridesmaid dress and playfully elbowed her way through the gathering circle of female wedding guests. "Pardon me. Coming through. Woman on a mission, here! Make room."

Most of the guests knew Katie and responded with equally high-spirited comments. Katie planted herself front and center and took her softball outfielder's stance as demurely as she could before flipping her swishy red hair behind her ears and calling out, "Right here, Christy! I'm ready for ya' now."

The other young women crowded closer and called their own directions to the bride.

"No playing favorites, Christy!"

"Over here. On your left. Throw it to me on your left!"

"No! Throw it to me, Christy! Me! Here!"

The bride kept her back to all of them as her ever-efficient aunt bustled into the moment. Aunt Marti adjusted Christy's position so her profile was just right for the photographer's lens.

"Keep your shoulders back, Christy-darling," Aunt Marti directed. "Turn your chin slightly to the right. No, not so far. Back ... there. Just like that."

The camera flash captured the pose before the bride could breathe or blink. Another flash came, aimed this time at Katie and the other restless women. Katie was a little taller than many of the high school girls bunched beside her. So far the competition didn't look too challenging.

"Maid of honor, right here!" Katie called out. "Follow the sound of my voice, Christy!"

From the sidelines, someone called out, "Throw it high!"

Katie knew that voice. It belonged to Rick Doyle, her "almost" boyfriend. Rick had joined the rest of the groomsmen on the edge of the crowd of women. The other guys, all surfers at heart, had removed their ties long before the toasts were offered an hour ago. They were ready to more comfortably enjoy the warm southern California afternoon. Rick was the only one who had remained "camera ready," as Aunt Marti called it. She indicated she was pleased with Rick but exasperated with the others, including the groom, Todd, who had peeled off his tux coat right after he and Christy had cut the cake.

Tall, good-looking, brown-eyed Rick cupped his hand to his mouth and called out again, "Throw it high, Christy!"

Why is he saying that? I'm right up front. Katie turned her head to see who Rick was looking at in the back row of the eager bouquet catchers. Before she could spot anyone in particular, something smushy and fragrant hit the left side of her head.

All the women around her screamed.

Katie's quick reflexes prompted her to pull the flying object close to her side. A young woman bumped against Katie in her attempt to make her own crazy, off-balance lurch for the flowers.

"Hey!" Katie felt herself topple and knew the bouquet was about to be snatched from her haphazard grasp.

Just then, Sierra, a friend of Katie's, swung her arm forward without making clear trajectory calculations and unwittingly launched the bundle into the air. The bouquet was back in play!

From the sidelines the guys yelled. From inside the huddle of surprised women a chorus of squeals rose. All arms were up in the air.

The runaway bouquet seemed to enjoy its moment of flight and tagged the fingers of one eager-reaching wedding guest, who batted at it like a badminton birdie. With a hop and a skip the white ball of mischief released a single white rose to the woman with the longest arm before Katie regained her balance, leaped forward, and seized the bouquet. *Carpe bouquetum!*

The tall girl beside Katie blinked at the single rose in her hand. Katie raised her arm and let her cheer be heard across the meadow. "I caught it!"

"I almost had it," muttered Sierra.

Christy, who had turned around to watch the momentary circus act, broke into a wide grin when she saw where the bouquet had landed.

Katie echoed her best friend's delighted expression, beaming back at her. The two of them had speculated about this moment for years. Many years. Both of them seemed to know that Christy would be the first to marry. Katie always maintained that Christy's groom would be Todd, even during those seasons when Christy had her doubts. To boost her friend's confidence during those dreamy-yet-doubting moments, Katie's best cheer-up line for Christy had been, "Just promise you'll throw the bouquet to me."

That line always caused the two of them to smile at each other the same way they were smiling at this moment.

Mission accomplished.

Spinning around once in a twirl of triumph, Katie caught Rick's gaze. Whomever or whatever his "throw it high" comment referred to no longer mattered. Rick was watching her with his chocolate brown eyes, and she felt herself melting a little inside, just as she had ever since her first, puppy-dog crush on him in junior high.

"Look over this way, please," the photographer said.

Katie tilted her head and gave him her widest smile.

"One more. This time a bit more subdued."

Drawing the fragrant, gardenia-and-white-rose bouquet up to her nose, Katie dipped her chin and took a lingering breath of the pure white sweetness.

So this is what getting married smells like.

The photographer captured the shot, readjusted the camera's angle, and took another. "Great. Thanks."

Katie glanced up, ready to twinkle one of her bright, green-eyed looks of alluring charm at Rick, but her smile fell. Rick was no longer watching her. He had turned his attention to the single guys, who were lining up to catch the garter. She ambled over to join the group, brushing her hair off her forehead.

Being so dressed up and having her picture taken felt strange. Yet it was a nice sort of strange. An improvement over how she usually ran around. Katie's clothing selections had long been in the realm of jeans and a T-shirt or sweatshirt. During the past year, however, she had done what she called a "Katie-version" of a makeover. It started with a haircut that gave her swishy, red mane a more sophisticated, yet easy, wash-and-go style. She added some fun skirts to her wardrobe and went in search of comfortable but feminine tops. This bridesmaid outfit was way beyond anything she would normally wear, but Katie liked how sophisticated she felt in it.

A casually dressed guy with a trim goatee and distinctive, rectangular sunglasses leaned toward Katie as she stood to the side of the group of guys. Without turning to look at her, he said in a low voice, "Your halo is slipping."

She squinted into the late afternoon sun and blinked at him, not sure if his comment had been aimed at her. The guy kept his face forward. He didn't repeat his comment or return her glance. Behind his left ear she noticed a thin, white scar in the shape of a backward "L."

Ignoring him, Katie turned her attention back to the group of guys that was now heckling Todd, the easygoing groom. Todd had positioned Christy's garter between his two thumbs in a slingshot position and impishly aimed backwards. If he let go, the garter undoubtedly would land somewhere in the palm trees that bent over the wedding party like gentle giraffes sheltering their young.

One of the guys called out, "Hey, wrong way, dude."

Doug, a groomsman and the only married guy in the group, stood beside Todd to direct him in the garter launch. Doug turned Todd back around to face the pack. "Just aim it this general direction. It'll fly off crazy, so you don't need to have your back to them the way Christy did."

Todd looked as if he was enjoying this as much as he had clearly enjoyed the wedding and the leisurely paced reception. For all the arguments that erupted among Todd, Christy, her parents, and her eager-to-be-involved Aunt Marti during the planning of the wedding, it had turned into Todd and Christy's special day. The wedding and reception had only a few touches of Marti's influence here and there — most of the day had been quintessential Todd and Christy. Katie couldn't be happier for her friends.

The guys stood back with nonchalant postures, indicating by their expressions they were too cool to go after the garter. But Katie knew this group well enough to realize that the competitive streak in them would spring into action the second Todd launched the ball of lace.

True enough. Todd jutted his determined chin forward. On Doug's command, he launched the lacy white elastic band into the cluster of too-cool guys.

Mayhem broke out.

Katie noticed that Rick was one of only a few guys who didn't spring into action. The garter seemed to make a beeline for the guy with the goatee next to her. But before he could secure his grasp on the flimsy, fluttering piece of lace, another hand reached out and snatched the prize.

Katie's shoulders involuntarily slumped when she saw who caught the garter.

David, the little twerp.

Christy's fifteen-year-old brother broke into a spontaneous victory dance. Sadly, the dance was too clever for his large feet to maneuver and too painful for Katie to watch. She lowered her head and made her way to the other side of the crowd where Rick had ended up. He was talking to Todd's dad.

"Great save on the bouquet catch, there, Katie." Todd's dad tipped his plastic punch cup her direction and added, "Way to go after what you want."

"Thanks." Turning to Rick she said, "I didn't notice your making any heroic efforts to catch the garter there, Doyle."

Rick gave her a grin and a shrug. "It wasn't coming my direction."

That is such a Rick-Doyle-philosophy-of-life statement!

In the past six months Katie had watched Rick roll through several challenging situations without lurching forward with the sort of aggression he had displayed during their high school years. He had mellowed. Maybe too much.

She gave him a long look. This was her friend. Her "almost" boyfriend, according to their last "DTR"—Define the Relationship—conversation. They had been around each other nearly every day for the past seven months, and yet she felt she didn't really know who he was or what he was thinking at any given moment.

Of one thing she was sure. She was glad she had "come his direction" on the night Todd had proposed to Christy at the Dove's Nest Café. Rick was the manager of the Dove's Nest, and although they had known each other since junior high, their paths hadn't crossed for several years.

After they reconnected that night, Katie and Rick fell into a steady, side-by-side rhythm of being together. She even took a job at the Dove's Nest. The past half-year had been the most stable stretch of her life, and she didn't want anything to change. All she wanted was a label for their relationship. She wanted to be established once and for all as boyfriend and girlfriend.

"Katie!" Christy's aunt motioned sharply from her staging position next to the wedding trellis. David already was posed, holding up the garter. The photographer was checking the fading light with his meter.

"You're being summoned," Todd's dad said.

"So I am. You want to come with me?" She reached for Rick's arm.

"You go ahead. I told Doug I'd help him with a little, ah ... project."

"You guys aren't going to mess with Todd and Christy's car, are you?"

Rick only smiled.

Todd's dad stepped away. "I didn't hear that. I'm not in on whatever you guys are planning."

"Rick, Christy doesn't want you guys to do anything to their car. You and Doug know that, right?"

"Katie!" David's voice interrupted them. "Aunt Marti says to hurry up!"

"Promise me you won't do anything to their car, Rick. I'm the maid of honor. I'm supposed to protect Christy. Help me out here. Please don't—"

"You'd better go." Rick pointed her toward Aunt Marti and the photographer. "Your flowers are crooked, by the way."

She took off for the trellis, glancing at the bouquet in her hands. What did he mean the flowers were crooked? They didn't look out of balance to her. A little fluffed up and missing a rosebud, maybe.

"For goodness sake, Katie, bend your head down." Aunt Marti reached up and repositioned the headband of white baby's breath Katie wore as the crowning touch of the bridesmaid's outfit.

Suddenly Goatee Guy's comment made sense, as did Rick's. Her halo had slipped. Katie made her own adjustments with the two remaining bobby pins after Marti finished her attack. Smoothing back her silky red hair, Katie asked, "Better?"

"It will do." Marti stepped aside and gave an irritated snap of her fingers, as if she were in charge of giving directions to the photographer.

David moved closer to Katie and put his arm around her shoulders.

"What are you doing?" Katie asked.

"Posing for the picture."

Katie wiggled out from under his lumbering arm. "Just smile, David. That's all you have to do. Smile. Like this." Katie gave the photographer her best, cheesy-faced grin.

The perturbed photographer looked up from behind the lens. "A little less exuberance, if you don't mind." He took another shot. "Now give me a casual pose."

David stretched his arm in Katie's direction. The scent of his adolescent sweat was strong enough to wilt the flowers in the bouquet—and the trellis that surrounded them. "I'm warning you, David. Keep your paws off me." Katie's words leaked out through her closed-mouth smile. David lowered his arm.

"That's it." The photographer gave them a nod and walked away with his camera.

Katie tossed out a "thank you" and noticed Goatee Guy standing at the end of the aisle next to Tracy, the other bridesmaid. Tracy was married to Doug, and the two of them were expecting their first baby in a little more than a month.

"Are Christy and Todd preparing to leave?" Katie called to Tracy across the rows of empty chairs.

Tracy nodded, her hands folded on top of her round belly. "I came to find you. They're in the chapel signing the marriage license, and they need you to sign as a witness."

Katie scurried across the grass toward the small prayer chapel located on the corner of the university property. The chapel was one of Katie's favorite hidden treasures on the Rancho Corona campus. This grassy meadow on the high mesa that encompassed the university campus usually was used for long strolls along the trail. Having an outdoor wedding in this gorgeous space had been Todd's idea, and it was a great one. No doubt the meadow now would become a frequently requested wedding location for other Rancho Corona students.

Taking a shortcut past the palm trees, Katie caught a glimpse in the distance of the flaming sun making its nightly trek into the hazy blue field of the Pacific Ocean. The air was cooling already. Thick, atmospheric layers of peach and primrose hinted at a touch of glory soon to be viewed in the sunset.

Katie smiled. She found it easy to believe that God, in his not-so-subtle way, was adding his celebration touch to the end of Todd and Christy's perfect day. In a whisper, Katie said, "Will you bless them,

Father God? Bless all their years to come. You have been so good to them."

With a catch in her throat, she added, "I don't know exactly what you have in mind for me, but would you bless me too? If Rick isn't the right guy for me, would you make that clear pretty soon? I don't want to convince myself that becoming Rick's girlfriend is one of your God things if it's really only a Katie thing."

Arriving at the chapel, Katie paused before she opened the door and added a P.S. to her prayer. "If you don't want Rick and me to go any further in our relationship, then will you break us up? This unsettled thing of being his 'almost' girlfriend is killing me. Especially today."

KATIE WELDON SERIES

On a Whim

Robin Jones Gunn,
Bestselling Author of
the Christy Miller Series

Ever since high school, Katie Weldon has
wondered what it would be like to be Rick
Doyle's girlfriend. As a college senior she's
about to find out.

In the swirl of Katie's upgraded dating
life, she receives an unexplained bouquet, an unexpected call
from her mother, an unprecedented girls' night out with Christy,
and an unhappy moment when her beloved car, Baby Hummer,
takes its last wheeze. Rick's new roommate, Eli, complicates things
by inviting Katie on a midnight jaunt to see a meteor shower. Under
a canopy of stars Katie grasps a new view of the universe — out
there as well as up close. As if she had nothing else to do, on a
whim, she singlehandedly starts a fund-raising campaign for clean
water for Africa.

With Rick caught up in making plans for the future, how will
Katie navigate her way through the remainder of her college career with no money, no transportation, no spare time and no idea
what God is up to?

On a Whim is the second book in the Katie Weldon Series.

Softcover: 978-0-310-27657-9

Pick up a copy today at your favorite bookstore!

More Fun

with Christy, Todd, & Katie

As Christy, Katie, and Todd head into the tumultuous years of college, each must make life-changing decisions about life, love, and God. From a whirlwind trip abroad to an engagement surprise to a beautiful wedding, the path ahead for these three friends will see both happy and hard times.

With important decisions on the line and fun memories to be made, you won't want to miss a single adventure with your favorite friends.

CHRISTY AND TODD:
THE COLLEGE YEARS
Until Tomorrow, As You Wish, I Promise

ROBIN
JONES
GUNN

Christy & Todd

The COLLEGE
YEARS

DON'T FORGET WHERE IT ALL STARTED...

Christy Miller Collection, Volume 1 (Books 1-3)
Christy Miller Collection, Volume 2 (Books 4-6)
Christy Miller Collection, Volume 3 (Books 7-9)
Christy Miller Collection, Volume 4 (Books 10-12)

Sierra Jensen Collection, Volume 1 (Books 1-3)
Sierra Jensen Collection, Volume 2 (Books 4-6)
Sierra Jensen Collection, Volume 3 (Books 7-9)
Sierra Jensen Collection, Volume 4 (Books 10-12)

 MULTNOMAH BOOKS